LEGENDS

OF THE ANCIENT SPRING

Into The Light

Charity Nichole Brandsma

First published by Charity Nichole Brandsma 2021

Copyright © 2021 by Charity Nichole Brandsma

This novel is entirely a work of fiction. The names, characters and incidents portrayed in it are the work of the author's imagination. Any resemblance to actual persons, living or dead, events or localities is entirely coincidental.

First edition

ISBN: 978-1-0879-5667-1

Editing by Nikki Facey Editing by Nico Russo
Cover art by Sara Oliver Designs Illustration by Rudolf Van Schalkwyk

This book was professionally typeset on Reedsy.
Find out more at reedsy.com

PRONUNCIATION

Michale'thia: Mee-cal-ay-thee-uh

Michale: Mee-cal-ay

Syra: Sigh-ruh

Dagen: Day-gen

Luik: Loo-ick

Enith: Ee-nith

Ilytha: ill-ith-uh

Cirren: Seer-ehn

Aleth: Ah-leth

Broyane: Bro-aen

Lohan: Loe-hon

Jyren: Jai-ren

Jyres: Jai-ers

Syllrics: Sill- rics

Anaratha: Ann-uh-rath-uh

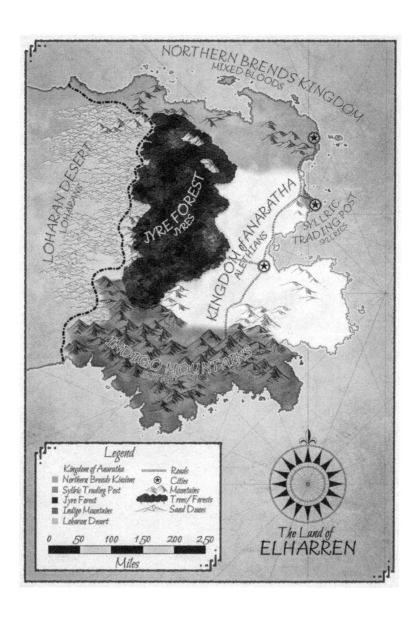

The Land of
ELHARREN

PROLOGUE

The worm inched its way toward the deep green leaf, avoiding the leaves around painted with bright blues and purples. It was painstaking to watch, the effort and time it took just to gain the leaf it knew to be safe, yet said so much of the world around. The man lifted the glass from his eye and slowly picked up his notebook, writing careful notes as he continued to study the worm. His long black beard came to a point near his chest, swaying gently. He shut his notebook and straightened his back, picking up his staff with wrinkled hands and looking out over the land.

People milled about as always. Preparing, building, readying for the time to come. He shook his head.

Who knew the time of the Ancient Magic?

He turned toward his small hut, the only one on his secluded island by his own choice. He licked his dry lips against the wind and began the slow walk toward the center of the island where a small spring lay hidden among trees.

He knelt, his heavy robes gathering dirt, and peered into the water. It was a normal spring, not the One. But he often came and peered in, imaging he was back at the Spring that fatal day and could have changed his own choice. He shook his head, closing his eyes with a knowing sigh. After a thousand years alone, he knew one thing more fully than most: it was the inner man, not the circumstance which fueled the desire to be great. Mighty. Powerful. Able to do anything without the help of another.

He winced, his slanted eyes sad as he remembered his own mind that day. Scooping up a bucket full of water, he grunted and lifted it onto his staff before heaving it over his shoulder for the short trek back.

The wind picked up around him, swirling leaves and sand through the air. The man lifted a weathered but strong arm to cover his eyes, puzzled at the sudden gust rippling through the trees.

Then he felt it.

The bucket crashed to the sandy floor and he turned sharply south, eyes suddenly alert with energy he hadn't had since his youth.

There, he felt it again. The pulse from far away he had been waiting a thousand years to feel in his soul. He picked up his staff and broke into a sprint toward his hut, fear and joy exploding in his chest as he grabbed a small sack of food and pushed his small fishing boat out onto the water. He rowed tirelessly until he reached the hidden beach, and quickly set out once again. He kept to the shadows of the kingdom, not wanting his face to cause a stir. This was between him and the Ancient Magic alone.

Hours flew by and he came to the place he had been shown those years ago by the Magic Itself. The sacred beginning and end to all. He removed his sandals silently, bringing hands to his head as he bowed in respect.

When he left his brothers after drinking the Spring, he had been overcome with guilt and determined to find the Ancient One to beg for help. He calculated too many horrible scenarios and knew even then none could fix what they were breaking. After years wandering alone in the Unmade, barely surviving, the Ancient Magic came *to him*.

He winced at the memory. No matter the love, it was never enjoyable to be in the presence of a justly angry father.

But instead of punishment, the Ancient Magic quieted and drew near, speaking as they once had when he was a child with a mind full of questions. He was to set aside the power he betrayed the Ancient Magic to gain, and then wait. When the time came, he would use the magic coursing through his veins to aid in a plan greater than he could ever imagined.

Now was the time. He raised the staff in his hands, inscribed with the ancient tongue of old, and drove it into the hard dirt beneath him with every ounce of strength he had. The land burst open, ripping dirt away from dirt and creating an endless cavern, then shooting east in a rippling line. The unmade became made only to be turned into miles of dirt sunken into the ground. It continued to spread, ferociously creating dirt foundations that formed into a conduit for what was to come. It snaked up and down, the precise length he had been instructed to make it before shooting out toward the mountain, shaking the peaks and quietly making its way toward what was hidden in the heart of the mountains. With a final cry, he brought his staff down again and felt the far off mountain crack under the weight of the magic opening a gushing hole.

And he felt it. The first drop burst from the larger mass and began to make the long journey to its final dwelling place in the cavern he had created in front of him.

Tears welled in his eyes and he fell back, heaving. He still didn't fully understand the plan–who could? Yet he felt a rightness in what was done. A slow shift back toward what beauty the lands once held.

He finally regained his strength and looked out toward the east. They would soon feel the change.

A thousand years of waiting, and now it was done. Lohan sighed and began rowing back to his small island. He had finally done it. He had fulfilled the promise to both his brothers to find the Ancient Magic's help and to the Ancient Magic to be a part of that help. Now he would go back home and wait again until the return of all that was lost.

CHAPTER 1

DAGEN

Dagen sat in the rickety chair by the fire, wrapping his bleeding hands in cloth for the fifth time that week. He winced as he attempted to scrub dirt from the wounds. The fire crackled quietly in the dimly lit room musty in its long abandoned state. He gingerly placed the last bandage around his palm and sat back, resting his sore neck against the wood of the chair.

The waiting was an eternity, and he couldn't understand why everything was constantly taking twice as long as he wanted it to. Was it his expectations that were wrong? No. He couldn't expect anything less than urgency. Every moment they wasted was a moment she was down there.

His eyes snapped shut at the thought of her and he forced his mind elsewhere. He drummed his fingers on the chair for a moment, staring into the flames. It had been nine months. Dagen shook his head and stood up, leaving his place by the fire as though *it* were the cause of his haunted thoughts. He strode over to the small table piled with letters and books, rifling through the ones on top.

When was she going to come?

He picked up an older text and opened to a page he had marked the night before. The book described architecture common in the time the castle was first built, and through it he had been able to send his contacts in the castle ideas on where hidden hallways and rooms may be. The wealth of information had saved them thus far.

He traced the text as he read further, a dry and detailed account of handrails and their Loharan roots. He paused, making a mental note of the Loharan relations back then.

The first knock on the door startled Dagen, but by the fifth knock he was eagerly unlatching hooks and hurrying in Ilytha's slender form. He stepped outside to glance around, ensuring no one passing in the distance had seen her arrival.

He turned back to her, rubbing his hands together against the chill. "You're late."

Her dark eyes narrowed dangerously, piercing him with a glare.

"We found a girl beaten nearly to death by her father and left in a canal. It was a worthy detour."

Dagen hated himself for his own frustration. *She was still down there.*

He nodded instead, warring against his own maddening mind.

"Did you bring it?" She kept her eyes locked on his as she pulled a rolled piece of paper out from her coat.

"It will not be easy. Finding the exact building will be nearly impossible from the outside, but the inside is still patrolled regularly to keep mixbloods in line."

Dagen read the instructions, grimacing at the too-few words on the page. He had spent the past nine months digging the tunnel from the cabin to the castle and now needed a place it could connect to. It had to be close enough to the dungeons for them to sneak Michale out and disappear, but couldn't be too far from the wall, otherwise he may run into other rooms or systems built beneath the kingdom. There was only one place that fit, and it was a sewing shop owned by mixbloods particularly loyal to both Enith and Michale. But the directions to find it were sparse and he would be digging blind.

He folded his arms, determination taking the place of hopelessness. He would do what he had to.

Ilytha continued watching him carefully, concerned as always.

"I wish there was an easier way."

He sighed and sat down again by the fire.

"Me too. Or a faster way. This is just hard and slow. I can't even imagine what she is going through."

Ilytha sat cross legged in front of him and tried to look disinterested.

"Have you heard from her brother?"

Dagen rolled his eyes, amused at her attempt to hide her own interest in the man she married.

"He nearly died coming off the drug two months ago, but since then he is nearly off it. Enith now plays a dangerous game in the castle, but he lives. It would seem his life as a royal prepared him for *something*."

Ilytha smiled and raised a brow at him.

"*You* are a royal."

Dagen scoffed, poking the fire with a stick.

"Yes, but I didn't grow up in the castle *or* with the pressure of a Testing Day they did. Their entire lives were built on the attempt to be perfect, and when any of them failed, they were left with a broken bitterness I can't fully understand." He smiled hollowly.

"*I* was raised as a farm hand, free to rampage around and make whatever silly face I wanted." They laughed then, an empty sound with little real emotion in it.

But Syra understood. They were alike in a way few others would ever truly comprehend. Both had married, not for love, but married nonetheless and felt more deeply then they imagined the loss of their spouse. It was ridiculous, yet true.

Ilytha's voice cut through his thoughts.

"So what is next. The next step. What else do we need to do?"

Dagen looked at the ceiling, dread filling him at the thought.

"I have one last trip through the forest, and then the last of the tunnel to dig. Other than that, we need everyone completely ready."

Ilytha shuddered and wrapped her arms around herself.

"You should not go into the forest. It is too dangerous... there is something... wrong about it."

His fist clenched involuntarily and he groaned at the pain. If only she knew how wrong it really was. It wasn't just that the Jyre's were inhuman, it was even the trees and the air that felt corrupted, as if the darkness could seep into your soul. Every step through was an agonizing battle against giving in to the many temptations the fog brought. The first time he made it through, he found himself passed out just outside the forest. The next time he stumbled out conscious, but barely able to walk. After that it became easier and he supposed they had given up on him.

Good.

Ilytha took her leave and Dagen once again sat alone in his cabin, dreading the morning to come and dreading that it was not yet there. He laid down on his cot and closed his eyes, hoping to dream of something better than reality.

Dagen kept his shoulders hunched and hood up as he walked through the small farm town just outside the castle walls. It was one of the few lucky enough to survive the onslaught. Those working the fields were dangerously thin, looking aged when they should still hold the wild and free spirit of those just joining adulthood.

They looked up briefly as he passed, leading large beasts through their field while women and children worked in groupings nearby, picking and organizing crops to be sent through the castle gates. Soldiers stood by, watching carefully with bored expressions. Dagen frowned. It was never safe for workers if their overseers were bored.

He ducked unto a sorting shack with a dusty blue scarf hanging from a window-their signal of news, and stood in a corner, waiting. He shook off his hood and watched as a man digging a trench looked around cautiously before wiping his forehead and casually shuffling over.

His thin frame blocked the sun, flaunting gaunt cheeks and hard green eyes. He pretended to inspect fruit at their stem and spoke quietly.

"Three months and they will arrange another showing, like they did before."

Dagen's heart began to race and his words tumbled out before he could think.

"Just as before? This is our chance!"

The man nodded gravely, squatting down and making a show of being disgusted with a few of the long green squash.

"Three months, all will be ready." He paused then and looked at Dagen, pleading silently.

"Do you think it will work for us. Will we really also go free?"

His breath caught in his throat and he berated himself for not thinking of this sooner. His mind had been so consumed with saving Michale'thia, he had failed to keep up with the plan to rescue the mixbloods closest to the kingdom.

Dagen the man in the eye with all the confidence he could muster.

"We will get you out. I promise."

The man nodded once, not looking convinced but not looking disheartened either. He ducked his head and withdrew back to his trench as though he had never spoken to Dagen at all.

CHAPTER 2

❖————•————❖

ENITH

Gray clouds floated in the sky outside his window, peeking through the tattered curtains and dirty windows. Enith watched the clock and counted the seconds as they passed, fighting the urge to take back his arm from the sleeping woman curled around it. Her straight, auburn hair hung limply around her face and Enith found himself disdaining the color, even though it matched his own. He found black hair far more attractive.

He clenched his jaw against the echo of yearning for *jintii* still in his system, a new battle every day. Time moved slowly and he allowed his thoughts to drift toward another woman, one he had no right to think about yet filled his mind with her dark eyes and raven black hair.

The clock finally stuck its first hour of the morning and Enith sat up with a sleepy smile, careful even in the confines of his shared room not to break character. He gazed at Gianne with a small smile and brushed a piece of hair from her cheek, like he did *every morning* for the past nine months. She opened her eyes and stared back at him in a haze. Her grin was more akin to silly than anything else and it was all Enith could do not to push her away from him. He'd come to despise her incessant lovesick remarks, clearly drugged and in a fantasy of her own.

He rose, dodging a kiss and began to pull a wrinkled shirt onto his chest. The same shirt he had worn every other day. When he was still under the influence of *jintii,* he saw this shirt as impeccable and his bride as everything. The shabby holes in the curtain never showed and the muck they were fed looked like a feast. Now he had to live with the truth acting as if he believed the lie.

"Ohhh," Gianne sighed breathlessly, "Can't we just stay in today, my strong delvior." Enith withheld a groan at the name. It took an extra level of naivety to believe calling someone a delvior would ever be a compliment. All he could picture was Syra's back torn open and bleeding…

He shook his head and smiled at his "bride", touching her nose with a figure.

"You know we can't! What would everyone say? Besides, I have a council meeting today." Enith moved around her and opened the lid to the breakfast dish on their table. Gianne gasped and brought her hands to her mouth, *as she did every bloody morning*, gaping at the feast she saw before her.

"Oh, they have outdone themselves!"

Enith rolled his eyes and handed her a plate. She filled it to the brim and continued chattering on about latest court gossip and the rich flavor of each food.

He pushed the bland porridge around on his plate, noting obscure black objects inside he suspected could be worms. A knock rattled the door and Enith shoved a bite into his mouth, relaxing his eyes into a daze and plastering a goofy smile on his face.

A pale Jyre entered, clothed in dark robes of a scholar. He glanced around the room with disdain and pinched his nose as if to ward of a smell.

"Your Highness, your meeting has been moved to the War Room for privacy."

Enith stood tall, swaying for good measure, and saluted. Beaming down at Gianne when she clapped with delight.

"Right, I will be there. They couldn't possibly run the kingdom without *my* help."

The Jyre scholar narrowed his eyes and sniffed, turning on his heel and allowing the door to thud back into place.

Enith slid back into his chair, rubbing his temples. How much longer would he have to endure this?

Three months. Three more months.

It was an eternity and a small breath of time with too much to endure and too much to do. He patted Gianne's arm kindly and gave her a palacating smile.

"Now dear, I must retire to my study to prepare for the meeting. Be a good girl and visit with Lord Thilan's wife, would you?"

Gianne gasped and began racing about the room, searching through cloths for the perfect dress and giggling on about the latest couple in court falling in love.

Enith strode through the joined door and into the room he had made his study, firmly locking it behind him. He opened a curtain to the courtyard and made a show of standing on the balcony overlooking his people. He beamed with pride, playing the starstruck prince, but watched every movement of the servants below.

They were waning. Wasting away from too much work and too little food. The hope they once held in their frames when they realized the prophecies could be wrong, was long gone.

The Jyres had done a cruel job of beating down those with mixed lineage. At first, they were rounded up and set to harder labor than before, but as hints of rebellion spread, the Jyre's violently forced the mixbloods into submission. Families were separated, children were ripped from their mothers and sent to work in the fields under a quick whip. When that didn't stop the rebellions, the hangings began. Any whisper or sight of anything contrary to the "Perfect Age" brought death. Eventually, entire families had been hung in the middle of the town square, random ones, displayed to show the danger of allowing *any* in the community to plot against the Royals.

He turned back to his room with tears pooling in his eyes. *Nothing* was fair right now and all he wanted was to watch the royals burn. But he was helpless. Any move too early could ruin the only chance they had.

Enith would never fully understand the strength of a people who could bear such a heavy load and still fight for freedom. The Jyres didn't know who they were dealing with.

He shut the curtains and pulled out a few arbitrary books on leadership, opening one on his desk before moving toward a wall across the room. The fireplace sank deeply into the stained stone, and the hearth was etched with quotes from past kings in gold. He counted five stones down and wrestled a large smooth one from it's place. Reaching inside, he pulled out a small piece of paper before quickly returning the stone and hurrying back to his desk. He laid the paper just under the book, ready to appear as if he had been reading if anyone decided to stop by.

A Southern Sky brings sunrays
Five stars to sing of how they stay
The Queen sings but will someday quit
To Home to Home to Home

Enith memorized the numbers silently, adding them to his note small page full of notes he kept hidden in his pocket.

The first line would always describe the gate least often guarded that day. The second line would describe the number of minutes between guard changes when gates were unmatched, something that hadn't started until *after* he was no longer commanding the army, he noted. The third line sometimes didn't come, but when it did it described if Michale was alive, and the fourth line was their rallying cry.

He tallied the numbers alongside others from the past three weeks, taking note of the Southern gate appearing to be the least guarded most, and the time between watch changes being anywhere from 4-7 minutes.

He sat back in his plush chair and raked a hand through his hair. If the next three months brought similar figures, they could make this work. He crumpled the paper and lit it on fire with a candle, listening closely for any footsteps near the door.

Springs, he was tired of this. He would take any life over this one.

He settled in to reading war tactics as he waited for his meeting, searching for any glimmer of truth he could use against both the Jyres and his father. He couldn't tell if his parents were awake or asleep. Outwardly they resumed life as normal, but their eyes held the dazed, far off look *jintii* gave those under its spell. Could they be faking too?

Enith shook his head and squeezed his eyes shut, wondering if he was going insane.

The knock came two hours later, announcing the meeting and Enith followed his guard to the War Room.

The dimly lit office had been stripped of its sparse decor and now held an eerie air about it. As if inhabited by ghosts rather than humans. Men shook hands through glazed eyes and lopsided smiles before being hushed by Enith's father.

Thilan whispered something in his fathers ruddy ear and the king nodded, clearing his throat.

"We will make this meeting brief, since I know there is much merriment to be had on this special day."

Heads nodded and jovial fists raised in agreement. Enith followed suit, wondering what holiday he was missing.

"There has been a slight drought this year, and our food shortage is beginning to affect our poor farmers." He pointed a lazy hand in the direction of a stout man to his left. "Neal, what are our options. We need crop that can withstand less sun than normal and less care."

Neal chuckled and drew a circle on the table with his finger while speaking.

"There is a variation of seaweed that can be planted on land as long as it is grown in at least an inch of water. It won't taste the best, but it is packed with nutrition and can be dried for storehouses."

Thilan tapped Enith's father and they shared a look, signaling to a servant behind them to take notes.

"Good, good. Enith, my boy." He smiled with beaming pride, making Enith sick.

"Our armies have been busy cleansing the land, but we have been one step behind the rebels who are warning villages to flee. As if they can outrun the Ancient Magic's will. It's their own fault for dirtying their own bloodline." He scoffed, grunts of approval echoing back. "Eventually we will want to make our last push toward the Botani Mountains to weed them out. How would you suggest we prepare?"

Enith smiled easily, sliding into his roll of perfect prince. He opened his hands and shrugged.

"The Botani kingdom is an iced over graveyard, let them die where they will, it ought not matter to us. At least they are gone." He huffed the last words, gaining support from those around him.

His father bent his head in agreement, but pressed further.

"Yes, yes, that is true. But it is wise to have a plan in place should we ever decide to pursue. What would you suggest?"

Enith leaned toward the table, lowering his brows as he met his father's stair.

"We would want to ensure our men had the strength to climb, so arranging a fitness regimen to fit the journey would be necessary. It may also benefit us to create weapons that can be easily used with one arm, in case we are attacked while climbing!" He rounded his eyes slightly like a madman and fought to suppress a laugh. The bloody things he could get away with while people thought he was drugged.

Thilan rolled his eyes and waved his father on, moving the meeting passed Enith's self-proclaimed brilliance.

The discussion continued for another half hour, discussing methods to keep servants in line and trade agreements with the Syllric kingdom, who *still* refused to take a stand on anything other than their own gain.

Enith waited tersely for the meeting's end. If he knew Thilan well, this meeting was to address the food shortage and test Enith's knowledge of the Botani Mountains. His father ended the meeting and hands were shaken all around as they went back to their false lives.

Enith checked the clock as he trailed behind the councilmen out of the War Room, wishing it was time to retire. Instead he had dinner with Gianne's parents to attend. The evening would be full of her incessant flitting around and fixing his jacket as he groveled in front of her parents and tried to avoid her sister's flirtations. Springs, even in their drugged state the family was wretched. They were probably dreaming *they* ruled the kingdom. Well they could have it.

He pulled his lips into a smirk and sauntered down the hall carelessly, all too conscious that every step he took trampled his sister beneath the kingdom.

Three months. He had to make it three more months. He could do this for her sake.

CHAPTER 3

DAGEN THREE MONTHS LATER

The night was cold as wind whipped across the dreary hills, relentless against the weak and weary travelers who held their threadbare coats tightly around their waist, laboring forward down the dirt path.

Down into the shadows of the valley below the dusty boots and narrow road, was a tree with vine-like branches brushing against the earth, battered by the wind yet silently refusing to break. With the moon hidden, no one would notice the lone form suddenly joined by another dark silhouette, and then another. A man stood tall before the ten warriors on horses, their number growing quickly as more arrived. Swords hung proudly at their sides, and their thick leather armor was sparsely placed on the most necessary vitals. They ran fast and light.

"Did you memorize the map?" Dagen's hushed voice whispered.

"We are not fools. We are ready."

Dagen gave a nod and motioned the outliers to gather around, watching as they slid gracefully off their horses and moved toward him without a sound. They had improved incredibly since he last saw them.

Springs… how had the days passed so horribly fast and slow at the same time?

"Are *you* ready?" Ilytha peered at him, a hard compassion etched on her face, ready to be either the toughened warrior or the gentle friend, but usually not the one he wanted in the moment.

He shook his head, tamping down desperation as he did often of late. "I am more than ready." Dagen's eyes traced the kingdom's outline as if searching long enough would bring Michale'thia to the gate. "I've been ready since the moment she was captured."

Ilytha pressed further, folding her arms across her chest and ignoring the harsh wind as it whipped loose tendrils out of her braid.

"You are afraid you might be hurt?"

Dagen scowled and faced her, biting back a growl of anger at the subtle accusation.

"*I would have given my life for her a year ago if it would have set her free.* I am not afraid of pain or death for my sake. I'm afraid of *her* pain continuing. They have had that entire cavern guarded so tightly it's taken Enith every waking moment to get back in their good graces again just to gain us this single opportunity." He ran a hand over his face and breathed deeply, trying to calm his nerves.

He grimaced and looked back at Ilytha. "I'm afraid it won't work. I'm afraid I will leave my kind, fiery wife who I barely had a chance to know, in a cage just so this bloody kingdom can have their sick utopia."

Ilytha's eyes softened and she climbed on her horse, waiting for him to do the same.

"Well, we will not fail. Someone else has come to ensure that."

Before he could ask further, she gave a nod to her group and took off, the stomping of their horses lost in the wind.

Dagen kicked his own horse into motion and set off toward the northern walls.

They came to a halt a hundred yards off and tied the horses outside of a small, familiar farm cabin before entering into the dimly-lit home. The wind's howl and the moonless sky was the greatest gift the Ancient Magic could have given for this night.

A small candle lit the cabin, and Dagen's eyes flew to a white contrast in the dark. Syra.

He smiled broadly, seeing Belick there too, at her side as he had been since he had bonded together with her. Dagen crossed the small distance to clasp forearms with him, thumping their chests in the traditional Botani greeting. He pulled Syra into a hug and let her go, looking at her for a moment.

"You look.. Different."

She smiled and lifted her own forearms, now lined with white markings.

"That's what happens when you don't see someone for nearly a year." She smiled softly. "I have been practicing with Belick. We have been getting close to something, and I think I can help."

Belick nodded, his low rumble filling the room, "For some reason, the Ancient Magic favors her. She can do much more than I."

He looked down, a dry chuckle directed at the ground. "But she also didn't steal from the Ancient Magic's spring, so…"

Syra laid a hand on his arm and gave him a reassuring look.

Dagen nodded toward the small clock in the corner and then back to the small band of people around the room.

"Tonight, we free the Heir to the Kingdom of Anaratha. Ilytha, you and your warriors will go in first, dispersing throughout and finding your posts. Make sure to remain unseen. My hope is we barely need you tonight."

Jassah, one of Ilytha's more... forward warriors, rolled her eyes and smirked, raising a brow.

"We have been trained since birth to remain unseen. You don't need to worry about us." She smiled knowingly at the women around her.

The Syllric trading port was large with a rich and beautiful culture, offering every kind of food, silk, and new technology. But their focus on the material bled into their view of women too, who were considered property and oftentimes beaten into submission. Over a year ago, Enith's quick thinking saved the life of a woman, but resulted in an accidental marriage to her.

These women found much freedom in the band Ilytha made, which modeled the first women's purpose in Elharren. They trained their units to be both wise and fierce, reminding mankind of what it means to rule justly and pursue mercy.

Dagen continued with a shaky chuckle.

"Right. I- and I guess Belick and Syra, will follow the southern path toward the city's center, keeping to the shadows as much as possible. Enith said the rotation happens right at midnight, so that will be when we will creep down and take out the first guard. Another guard shouldn't check in for an hour, so we will have a tight window of time. The minute Michale'thia crosses the cage, the city will know she is gone. We move fast at that point, get to the tunnels, and disappear as far away as possible."

Syra's face turned to him with solemn concern.

"We will not be able to ride with you when you are through. Once we get her out, Belik and I will ride to the south, while the Ilytha and her warriors spread out. There will be too many tracks to trace, leaving your tracks toward the forest as the least likely to follow."

Dagen responded with a nod. He wasn't sure it would work, but he was throwing everything he had into the plan anyway. Even the smallest chance made it worth it.

They had all waited too long, agonizing and keeping each other from rushing in to try to rescue Micahle'thia by force, knowing it would only end in their own bloodshed. But this week was the week citizens lined up to see her, as they did a year ago, reminding the kingdom of what it took to gain their utopia. Tonight, even though people were sleeping by this hour, the guards would have keys to the room. Keys usually only held by Kallaren or Thilan, who kept themselves diligently out of the public.

Dagen threw the dingy rug covering the trap door aside and opened it, revealing a small hole with a rope ladder, leading downward into a bigger opening that then had a hole big enough to crawl through comfortably.

The tunnel leading under the castle walls was risky to say the least. He didn't know if it would cave in or if they could even get Michale through it, but he had spent the last year working to get it ready for tonight and he was willing to take the risk.

He lowered himself down and lit a small, hand size torch they had created for this purpose, giving it a long handle to keep it far enough away, and a small flame to light the path before them while they crawled through.

One hundred and fifty feet of crawling. Then back. Dagen breathed, focussing on what he was doing instead of the confined space around him. He pulled the scarf around his neck over his nose and picked up his pace.

All that could be heard was the sound of heavy breathing as each pushed their bodies through the cold, dirt hole. A mental task as much as physical one.

It wasn't long before Dagen saw where the tunnel met a cavern opening upward to their contact's small sewing store in the square. He climbed the ladder and cracked the wood door open slightly, looking up at a woman with dark curls bouncing as she hurried over to open it the rest of the way.

She was a part of the few left in the rebellion, but had a personal connection with Enith and Michale'thia that made her even more eager to see them free.

The Anaratha officials had first meant to kill off mixbloods within the kingdom, but thankfully realized full-blooded Anarathans would not stoop so low as to become servants or farmers, even when drugged. The mixbloods had then become his greatest allies.

Dagen helped the others out of the hole, only getting a glare from a few of Ilytha's warriors still intent on proving their own strength. Each person disappeared quickly out the door, soundless as they melded into the night to go take up their posts.

Dagen watched Ilytha disappear, giving him a nod before creeping through the kingdom walls to pave a way to the dungeon. He waited stopped Belick from leaving with a hand, allowing five full minutes to pass before inching the door open and signaling to leave. Syra, whose hair was covered by a scarf, grasped the woman's hands in thanks and left behind them all, following silently as they used the dark corners of the kingdom to their advantage. He had never been thankful for stone floors until now, praising the Ancient Magic for yet another gift as their feet moved so easily without sound.

Heart pounding, Dagen slid around a corner toward the prison entrance below the castle. Why did he feel like he couldn't breath?

A guard lay propped up against the wall as if sleeping and Dagen assumed the man had a large welt on his head.

Moving carefully, he removed the key ring from the inside of the guard's coat and too the final step to the prison door.

He fumbled, shoving a random key in the door and yanking it out when it didn't work, doing the same thing four times before he finally heard the telltale *click* he was hoping for. Dagen pushed open the door and tried to calm his shaking hands, not knowing what he would find.

He had never gone down to the cage. He couldn't. He couldn't look her in the eye and leave. So he had dug, and dug, and dug, until his hands bled.

They crept down the stairs lined with torches, surprised to find no more guards inside. Enith had mentioned guards not being able to stomach the sight, but he hadn't believed they would stop coming altogether.

The small cage was in the middle of the room, hooked to wires and vials behind it. And there inside the cage was a creature from childhood nightmares. Head up and mouth frozen mid-scream, with no noise coming out. Her skin was a grayish hue and deep lines covered her face where her freckles used to be. Sunken cheeks and a bone-thin form was all that was left. Dagen bent over and emptied his stomach on the floor, clenching his fists as he fought for control of his emotions.

He straightened, holding his stomach and beckoned to a frozen Syra and Belik, signaling for them to watch the door. Dagen pulled out the keys again and stabbed one into the lock on the cage.

"Michale'thia." He whispered, not gaining a response.

"Michale'thia, it's Dagen. We are going to get you out."

He threw the iron door open and took a hasty step inside, halted by an agonizing pain unlike anything he had ever felt before. His insides twisted over and over again and his bones ground up against themselves violently, ripping apart anything and everything he was made of. He screamed and jumped back, eyes wide in terror as tears streamed down his face from both from the pain and the understanding that *this* was what Michale had lived for a full year now. His knees buckled and he caught himself on one knee, looking up at Syra and Belik who had rushed to his side, wide eyes now looking over the cage with renewed concern. They hadn't planned for this.

Belick could barely be heard through his own clenched teeth, anger showing like fire in his dark eyes. "This system… I can feel it. There is something dark and twisted in it."

Syra nodded, tears streaming down her cheeks and her voice shaking with struggle. "It… It is not a different entity than the Ancient Magic, like an enemy. It is more like the absence of it. A void it is creating within the cage." She shuddered, holding her own stomach in her arms, as if struggling not to vomit.

She glanced up at Belick before whispering to Dagen again. "Dagen, it is somehow sucking out and emptying whoever is in there of any Ancient Magic in them.

The Ancient Spring the brothers took from so long ago is what made new creation possible. It is from the Ancient Magic's Spring that anything new is made. A new child, or leaf, or even new skin. We have it infused in every small part of us. But if it were to be taken… it would be as if every small part that makes up our bodies was being ripped out over and over again, then brought back together by the Ancient Spring regenerating inside of us. That would happen hundreds of times a minute."

She paused, biting her lip and looking up to the ceiling while she blinked away tears.

"If someone with the Ancient Magic were to go inside, I think the extraction would cause an explosion. And from past experience, a big one."

Dagen shook his head, lost now, and feeling the urgency of the time. He studied the cage again, looking for any other way.

"Why an explosion?"

Syra nodded, knowing the question would come.

"The Ancient Magic inside isn't the same as the Ancient Spring. The Ancient Spring *comes* from the Ancient Magic, and is One with it, but it is given to all and can be taken in death. But the Ancient Magic chooses people. It cannot be taken or rejected, even if one wanted to. And when threatened, I have seen it do incredible things, like explode. If I or Belick were to enter that cage, and It felt the pull of someone trying to manipulate it, I think it would bring this entire Kingdom down to the ground."

"Well maybe that's exactly what we should do..." Dagen muttered, knowing it was wrong.

He tensed as he stared at the cage, trying to think as quickly as he could. Every lever, every cord, was all protected behind more locks with keyholes that looked nothing like any he had on his ring. Thilan had thought this through well. He took a breath and clenched his fist, knowing there was no other way yet agonizing at the thought of *ever* feeling that pain again. But she was worth it.

One step was all it took to knock the breath out of his chest, every muscle clenching together as his body filled with sickening pain. His bones were melting and his head was being hit continuously with bricks with each passing heartbeat.

Desperation kicked in and he fell to a knee, forgetting why he had come. It was excruciating to exist and Dagen dreaded the next breath he took in. How did Mich–

Michale'thia.

Dagen roared, no longer thinking of guards or anyone else, and rose, taking a step forward. And another, and another, until he was there before her, barely able to grab hold of her small body before digging in to find the last reserve he had and backing out. The fire burned everything in him, and his head hurt so much he could no longer see or hear. All he knew was crippling pain.

His foot hit something on the floor and he fell backwards out of the cage, Michale'thia still in his arms.

Coming out of the cage was like jumping into a cool lake on the hottest summer days as a child, every part immersed in the reprieve from the sun. It was disorienting, to have the agony gone in a second but the memory still there.

He could feel Belik taking her from his arms, and he found himself on his hands and knees, bent over as sobs overtook his body.

He sobbed for the minutes of pain he just endured. For the year and a half of torture Michale had gone through. For the evil, twisted minds in the world.

Syra knelt beside him and laid her head on his shoulder, allowing her own tears to fall with his. His body trembled weakly and he knew he had exhausted his strength. Dagen fought to rise but fell back to his knees.

He felt a cool hand on his arm and heard Syra whisper a few words to Belick. Then it was like that lake he jumped into flowed through his body and soothed every muscle and bruise. His mind sharpened again and he rose, shooting a questioning, but thankful, look Syra's way.

She shrugged with a small smile.

"I have learned the Ancient Magic in my veins is less of a power and more of a…Thing. It is Its own Self, with anger and compassion. I know now when I can ask it for something."

Dagen blinked, deciding to tuck that away and think on it later.

"Right. Thank you… can you do it to her." Syra nodded slowly, putting the most careful hand on Micahlethia's unconscious body.

Tears came afresh as she closed her eyes and sat there, silently healing what the cage had broken. Dagen thought he could see the slightest bit of color return, and a small stirring, but nothing else.

Syra stood and shook her head.

"The rest will take time." She bit her lip, looking back at Belik, whose own eyes were hard.

Belick glanced at the door, categorizing his emotions better than Dagen and Dyra had been able to.

"We need to go. We have little time now."

Dagen gathered Michale'thia up in his arms again and Belik cracked open the door, peering into the dark.

They opened it and crept out, trying to stay as silent as possible while sticking to the same shadows they used to get there. As they moved he just make out Ilytha's warriors leaving their positions to meet him back at the sewing shop.

Dagen held his breath as they crossed the square, halfway to their destination. Sudden shouts pierced the air and bells began to clang violently, lamps turning on in houses as doors began to open and confused people poured onto the streets.

Pulling his cloak over Michale'thia, they walked faster, trying to blend in with the crowds and avoiding eyes as they maneuvered their way through the chaos.

Suddenly someone bumped Dagen on the shoulder and soldiers began pouring through the courtyard. Dagen tried to keep going but the tall, thin man peered at him with suspicion, his eye gray brows shooting up when he saw the thin, dirty leg dangling over his arm.

Belik had disappeared, making his way to the sewing house on his own to keep from drawing more attention, Syra looked back just in time to see the situation unfold. Dagen prepared to run as he heard the clanging of swords now in combat, but a firm hand clamped down on his shoulder.

"Stay calm, friend." Dagen's eyes shot up in surprise, finding piercing brown eyes staring back above light, barely noticeable freckles and gaunt cheeks. The part Alethian and likely part Syllric man motioned with his head, pointing behind him. There, in between him and the doorway to freedom, was a crowd of mixbloods, all of them thinner than he remembered and looking straight ahead, intentionally not toward him. Then a few of them shifted slightly and a clear path was made, hidden by their bodies all the way to the door.

The man glanced at him again, "Thela warned the community that a rescue might be happening soon from her shop. We are with you." The man brought a fist to his chest subtly. "To home."

Dagen didn't understand but gave a breathless nod and plunged through the crowd, stooping so he would be hidden behind those standing. His chest filled with gratitude as he passed by person after person, gently touching his shoulder or encouraging him with a smile, allowing him to walk through the sewing shop's doorway with his beaten bride.

He entered the shop and looked around, taking note of who was missing.

"Where are Belik and Ilytha?"

Syra looked around, her eyes fastening to the east.

"Belick is coming."

Dagen turned to the warriors for an answer. A woman with half a shaved head Hiva he believed, responded curtly, worry in her own eyes.

"Ilytha and Jassah will be here. They went around back, pushing over barrels to distract the guard."

Dagen nodded and nodded toward the hidden door on the ground.

"Then let's start. We don't want a back up when anyone else comes in." He started toward the opening and paused, realizing he hadn't planned for Michale being unconscious.

Thela gave a quiet "oh" and left the room, returning with a stretchy cloth.

"It isn't much, but it will secure her to your back."

He gave a quick nod and turned around, allowing the women in the room to help set her gently in place while they wrapped her frame in the cloth and then tied it firmly to his. Belik slipped in as they were doing so, motioning to a few women to get down into the tunnel and go while they prepared.

Finally, after too much time had passed, he climbed down the rope, trying to be as careful as possible. He couldn't safely crawl on his hands and knees with Michale'thia on his back, so he lowered to his belly and began the crawl.

He trudged on, going as fast as he could and fighting against burning arms as he did so. It took longer, but he finally made it to the cavern of the old cabin and started the climb up, meeting the warriors at the top and taking their helping hands gratefully.

He waited until Belik and Syra were up, stopping for only a moment to say goodbye.

"If you hadn't come…" He shook his head, knowing what the outcome would have been.

"We wouldn't have missed it. It's taken everything inside not to try this too soon." Syra's large eyes looked over at her best friend's limp form.

Her next words came out in a small whisper, and she looked at him with such pleading he almost reconsidered.

"Be careful in there."

Belik nodded and pulled a pack onto his back. "You need to go, and so do we. We will see you again, brother."

His low Botani voice resounded as he carefully untied the cloth holding Michale to Dagen's back and lifted her fragile body down to the ground on his own jacket.

Dagen had just settled onto his horse when they all heard a sharp intake of breath, and turned to find Michale awake, laying on her back, blinking her eyes in confusion.

He slid down from his horse and knelt beside her, eager and terrified. Her sunken eyes took in the sight before her, each movement animal-like and sharp.

She sat up and looked out from under her eyebrows, staring at the dirt floor as she spoke.

"Is this real?"

Dagen moved to lay a comforting hand on her arm, but she slid away quickly, gasping for air in terror and looking about wildly as she did so.

He didn't think his heart could break any more, but it did then. Any piece left standing was crushed beneath the weight of guilt and shame he felt from leaving her *this* long.

Running a hand over his face to wipe the hot tears springing up, he drew in a breath. She had been hurt more deeply than he could understand this past year. It would take time. And he would give all he had to her.

Speaking carefully, and not moving toward her this time, he answered, "It's real, Michale'thia. It took too long, but we were able to get you outside of the kingdom and we need to go now before all we have worked for is lost."

She kept her distance still, searching each face in the dark night. Syra finally stepped forward and knelt down beside her, quietly staring at her for a moment. Then in a quick move she threw her arms around Michale, who jolted and gasped, struggling to get away. After moments passed and no pain came, her bone-thing arms stopped fighting and she hung her head. Syra let go and gently took her hands.

"When I escaped the Forest, you took me in. And you sat with me when I cried, and you slowly showed me that there were people different than my father. Now it is your turn to learn."

Michale'thia searched her eyes, memories flooding back as she gave Syra's hand a squeeze, neither smiling, nor responding other than that.

"We have to go, now. The guards are likely to be finished searching the kingdom in a short hour, and we need to put as much distance as possible between us and them." Dagen jumped back on his horse, and beckoned to Michale, who stared at him for a moment before silently attempting to climb on but falling in a heap of trembling bones.

Syra and Belik helped her mount, settling her in front of Dagen. He gave them both one more look before giving his horse a kick and taking off in a full gallop toward the Dark Forest.

CHAPTER 4

MICHALE'THIA

Reality was a blur. Her hair didn't fly about her face like it used to, there was too much dirt.

Her body was stiff, tense with the fear of reality shifting again into a grotesque nightmare, or even worse, a caged reality.

She closed her eyes, at war with the rising panic inside. She had too little space. *His arms were trapping her...*

No. No. She opened her eyes again.

This was real. It was.

She looked at the forest growing larger before her eyes as they neared. Once, long ago, she had been terrified of entering this forest, where every Royal eventually journeyed to test if they could withstand every temptation it brought. She had passed, and had been named the Heir of the Prophecies, the one they had waited centuries for.

And then they all turned against her, and used her up. All for the sake of their precious Age of Perfection.

She should feel anger. Or hurt. *Something.* But she couldn't feel at all. Had the cage taken that away too? Michale wasn't sure she cared.

Dagen slowed the horse as they drew near to the forest, sliding off and lifting Michale down. She stared at her hands for a moment. Thin, layered with dirt and round ulcers. Faint memories came of water splashing over her and the pain stopping for a few small moments. Once every two days they would even give her stale food and water. The water must not have been enough to wash the dirt away.

Rustling snapped her attention back to the present and she watched as Dagen shirked off his coat and put it around her shoulders, hesitating when she flinched, but not stopping. Her shivering stopped without her ever realizing it had been there in the first place.

She glanced up at him, her matted hair barely leaving an opening for her face and she-

It was black. Why was her hair black?

Panic set in again and her breath came quickly in shallow patches. This wasn't the way she used to be. Her hair was a brown. With red. A brown-red, not black. She sucked in air and fell to her knees, rocking back and forth as she heaved, pulling at her dirt infested hair and covering her head in a sob, knowing the blows and pain that were about to come, like every other time she had dreamt of escape. Why couldn't it have been real?

Her lungs restricted and she gasped for more air, feeling the world begin to swim.

"...ale'thia..."

"Michale'thia!"

Dagen's voice cut through her thoughts and jolted her back into reality. Her forehead was covered in sweat and she could feel Dagen's hands grasp a hold of her face, bringing her head up to meet his eyes.

"You are ok, I'm here. I am real." He grabbed her hand and placed it on his cheek, his own calm beginning to flow into her lungs and bring peace to her racing heart. He tapped the side of her face lightly and guided her hand over his face.

She could feel every stubble, every crevasse. Lines she didn't know where there. And somewhere in the distraction of feeling, her breathing slowed too. This was real. It was real.

"My hair isn't Alethian." She said simply, distrust filling her with suspicion again. He would never understand, but she had dreamt of escape almost every night for the first six months. Every time she would be saved, only to find some small detail about reality wrong; the only indicator that it was a dream. Then she would wake again to the agony of the cage.

Dagen nodded, and spoke gently to her.

"There is too much dirt in it. I don't think it's been washed in a long time. It will return to the color you remember soon." He held a hand out to her. "When we stop we will get you cleaned up."

She nodded, looking down as shame filled her and letting his hand drop away.

He smiled anyway. "We have to keep going now, no matter what." He nodded toward the trees and slapped the horse, sending it north of them.

She obeyed, not understanding but also not caring like she knew she ought. Dagen looked up at the trees and around the entrance, walking south before stopping again and peering inside.

He held a hand out to her and she gave it to him, already feeling her strength waning.

They entered into the Jyre Forest, keeping far away from the path the Royals used to take on their Testing Day, in case it brought on the hallucinatory temptations the Royals were tested with.

It was darker than the moonless night inside, and eerily quiet, as if this section of the forest had been abandoned. Creeks and echoing whispers would say otherwise.

Michale looked up at the web of trees before them shuddering. Their arms were jagged and pointing, and their trunks bent this way and that as if they too were in endless torture.

She crept through the thick foliage behind Dagen, trying to keep as quiet as he was, not noticing when scratches and thorns pierced her.

They had only been walking an hour when her headache began, a low pulse that slowly grew into a deafening pound, but she trudged on, thankful the only pain she felt was this. By the time an hour had passed, her vision began to blur as the pounding seemed to encroach upon all of her senses, making it hard to move.

With arms out to find the next branch to move under, her foot collided with a log on the ground, and she went tumbling down, hitting her head along the way. Dagen was at her side in a moment, kneeling down and offering water which she gladly partook of, disciplining herself not to drink the whole thing.

She moved her legs so she could sit, vaguely registering Dagen lowering himself to do the same. He rummaged around in his bag, pulling out some soft bread and tearing it in half before handing her a piece.

They ate to the creaking and groaning of the trees, both looking about anxiously as they did. Each bite of bread seemed to melt in her mouth, filling her stomach to the brim within moments she savored. She had forgotten what warm, fresh food tasted like.

Feeling Dagen's eyes on her, she shifted slightly, letting her hair fall over the side of her face to feel as though she had some semblance of privacy. She could see her pointy shoulders jutting out painfully and knew her face looked grotesque, like a monster from a children's story. She didn't want to be seen right now. Especially not by her... husband.

She finally looked up at him, frustrated by his staring, but found him instead reading a small, creased piece of parchment in his hands. Michale looked up at the trees, her hair standing on end as she *felt* eyes watching, but saw nothing in the dark forest beyond where Dagen's torch could reach.

Before Michale'thia could ask what he was reading, whispers began to rise, like a wind passing through, easing and growing as if all around them. Dagen stood with his sword drawn, waiting quietly for movement. He took a step toward Michale protectively, eyes guarded.

In a swift movement, something dropped from the trees, landing in a crouch before them, more catlike than human.

She was beautiful, with large eyes and full lips, her white hair thrown over one side of her head in soft waves cascading down a tall, perfect figure accentuated by skin tight clothing. And she didn't look evil, or hardened, or anything like Michale'thia had imagined. She looked innocent. Calculating, but innocent.

The Jyre woman studied them, looking back and forth between the two with parted lips and a slightly tilted head, not worried in the least about Dagen's pointed sword.

Michale rose. She had been through this forest before and withstood everything they threw at her, and she would not bow now.

The woman watched her slow rise with interest, looking back at Dagen to see his reaction, studying her prey.

"You are the Perfect One." She spoke in a measured voice watching them both closely.

Michale'thia flinched, the name now a curse in her mind more than anything else.

She shook her head, anger rising in her throat, "I am not-"

"Not you." The woman's voice remained neutral as she kept her eyes on Dagen, pointing.

"Him."

Michale'thia looked at Dagen with questions in her eyes, but Dagen stayed silent, watching the woman warily.

The woman chuckled, looking back toward Syra.

"He is famous in these parts. A legend, if you would. He has walked through the Testing Path two times, and through the path once, never taking any of the gifts we offer him."

She began to walk toward him slowly, a pout forming on her lips.

"He doesn't like us very much… we don't have the right kind of blood for him."

Before she could get within arms reach he lifted his sword, the tip barely touching her chest.

"It's not your blood that I don't like, but you already know that. However, it would be nice if you all just let me take my strolls through the woods in peace."

Micahle watched them, her mind swirling as she worked through all she had learned in the last two minutes. How had he gone through the test twice? And why? Had he seen a chance to take the throne and seized it? Her heart squeezed as she felt the pang of betrayal settle in, hardening anything that had begun to soften.

The woman peered over at Michale'thia, a smile forming on her lips again as she saw something on her face worth pursuing.

"Or maybe he just came to us because he wants me." The whispers in the trees began to grow again and Michale'thia tensed, remembering the game the Jyres played so well.

Jyren, the Ancient Brother who betrayed the world to gain more power, bore these people. They lived to twist and pervert creation, as well as any human who ventured in. But then there was Syra… the gentle soul who had fled.

"It is ok, you know." The woman glanced at Dagen again.

"To want a beautiful woman is only natural." The woman ran a hand down her own arm, looking back to Michale'thia.

"Any man would want soft skin and a beautiful form."

Michale strained against her desire to fidget under the woman's bold look, self-conscious of her own appearance yet not wanting to let it show.

Her white hair seeming to shine, even in the night. The Jyre pulled a mirror from her pocket and before Michale could look away, snapped it open in front of her face.

Michale'thia saw her reflection only briefly before squeezing her eyes shut against the image, unable to bear the image staring back.

She was a monster. And *they* had made her that way.

The woman bent down to her, a look of compassion on her

face as she reached out to take Michale's hand but found herself at the end of a sword's tip again.

"My name is Raishara." She bent her head down to intentionally catch Michale's eye.

"I am a powerful Lord in the Jyre Kingdom. I can help you

get them all back for what they've done to you, Princess. I can make sure they each have a cage of their own."

Michale'thia hated herself for how much she wanted to give in. For the hatred upon hatred compacting inside her soul. For the jealousy she now had for a Jyre woman, living in a dark forest and knowing nothing of the sun.

The tip of the sword pushed further into Raisharas neck, causing a trickle of blood to drip down her collarbone. She smiled at Dagen, a smile that looked too familiar, like she knew him too well. *Had* something happened between them?

"Leave us, Raishara. We will make no trades with you."

Her look darkened as whispers above rose again and she glanced toward the treetops as if she was listening for something specific.

Then, without warning she spun around the sword and was pressed up against Dagen's chest, a hand forcefully on the back of his head as she spoke to him.

"You will not make it out of this forest alive if you don't make a deal this time." She hissed. "Your cargo is too precious. You must make a deal. We will let you out peacefully, but you must promise something in return."

She hadn't even finished when Dagen's head began shaking in a determined "no", trying to peel her off of him.

She looked up suddenly and could hear something, fear beginning to grow in her eyes. Then from *somewhere,* Michale'thia couldn't fathom where she was storing these things, she had a knife at his throat.

"Listen to me." Her pale skin seemed to pale more, desperation bringing a guttural sound to each word.

"You will not get out of here alive, Dagen Thorn. Even now our king comes for you. *She* will not make it out alive. *Make a deal with me* and by our law I will have license to get you out."

Michale could see something on Dagen's face change as he weighed her words, and even Michale'thia couldn't tell anymore what was true and what was lie.

"What would you require." His words came out in a whisper now, realizing the danger she was facing from above.

She glanced at Michale'thia, her eyes wide with hope for a second before looking back to Dagen and rushing on.

"When the time comes, bring my family and I to the Botani Mountains with you."

Dagen blinked in disbelief. Michale's own thoughts raced as all the consequences of that deal came to her. It could be a trap. They could be sending people in to infiltrate Belick's Kingdom. Or they could be working with her parents.

Or she could be like Syra and want to escape this life.

The whispers above quieted, and Micahle could hear their audience above waiting anxiously for a reply.

He closed his eyes then, taking only a second to think before snapping them back open.

"I promise to allow you to come. That is my deal." Her own eyes widened in what Michale thought was hope, quickly replaced by urgency again.

"Now hurry, you must perform the binding-"

"We will not bind our souls to the dark. It is not an option."

The whispers silenced and the forest was still.

Raishara stood there, her eyes glued to Dagen as she whispered the next word.

"Run."

Dagen jumped up and grabbed Michale'thia, quickly lifting her into his arms and taking off through the forest at a speed she didn't know he could run. The whispers overhead turned into sharp, angry cries that seemed to be following them from tree to tree.

Dagen ran with his sword drawn, looking at the trees that loomed upward and blocking out any bit of the sun. His eyes strained as he started to slow looking about wildly now for *something*. Micahle could hear the screams above getting louder as their number grew, and her own panic began to grow.

Seeing what he was looking for, Dagen suddenly laid her down on the ground, and slung his pack in front of him, taking out a large axe.

Michale's brows shot up as she watched him, trying to understand what he could possibly do with an axe that he couldn't do with a sword.

But then, as she looked at the tree, she could see a third of it already hacked inward and she gasped. He was going to try to bring the tree down.

In the blink of an eye he was throwing the axe blade against the tree with apt skill, sending chunks flying through the air. He worked with surprising efficiency, and somewhere in the back of her mind Michale remembered hearing Dagen's father talk about the importance of having Dagen work alongside the servants for chores.

The screams were too close and Michale could hear the thump of *something* dropping to the ground. The form began crawling near to them, hissing as it did. She struggled to back away as she took in the grotesque site before her. It was like the delvior, but smaller, with sharp teeth threatening from a face that looked as if someone had physically twisted it into a circle. Whatever this creature had been, it shared little resemblance to it now.

She looked up and saw three creatures drop from the treetops, salivating as they slowly crept toward her.

Dagen looked about but didn't stop his hacking away at the tree, now getting close to felling it. Then all at once, one of the twisted creatures attacked, teeth bared as it flew through the air. Michale covered her head anticipating pain, only to find Dagen now before her with his sword in the middle of the mangled creature. Another came and another, not missing a beat but jumping toward Dagen as he fought desperately to keep them off.

Michale looked around wildly, searching for any way out. With no other option than to blindly trust Dagen, she jumped up and grabbed the axe, using all her strength to bring it down over the large gap in the tree trunk. She heaved at the energy it took, but lifted it again and used everything she had to bring it down again. And again. And again. Dagen now was barely keeping himself alive, as more of the dark creatures dropped from the tree tops, shrieking as they slid toward Michale, their faces contorted and movements spastic.

Michale brought the axe down again, and again, glancing at the nightmarish animals that were almost upon her. She had no strength left, and the tree still stood. Dagen could barely be seen and Michale'thia looked helplessly back and forth between the tree and the creatures. Then, with every ounce of strength she had left, sh lifted the axe once last time and sank it into the trunk.

When nothing happened Michale spun back toward their attackers, dropping ot the ground just as one pounced, missing her by mere inches and crashing into the tree.

But that was all it took. The tree groaned and creaked and then rumbled, began its descent. As it began to fall, light from the morning sky peaked through the top of the Jyre forest, bringing shrieks and cries from the creatures around them.

The large tree shook the earth with its collision, knocking Michale down and breaking a few trees on the way, moving more treetops aside and exposing more light.

Dagen stood heaving, his sword still pointed out as his head swiveled, looking for more danger.

Michale froze, realizing what had happened. They stood there, in the only light that Jyre Forest had seen for possibly hundreds of years. Protected by the thing that scared Jyres and their creation alike, but fueled the hearts of so many on the outside of the Forest.

The dark canines yipped and snapped, but refused to enter the light patched on the ground, fear dancing in their eyes as they stared at it. The whispering was gone too then, as if even the Jryes no longer thought they were worth chasing. Not if light was the consequence.

Michale watched as Dagen dropped to the ground and laid back for a moment, closing his eyes and slowing his breathing again.

Took stock of her own body, not quite believing they had survived.

Shuffling over, she lowered herself onto her knees, sitting beside Dagen in exhausted silence. Eventually, he rose and helped her up, looking back toward their own path through the forest.

He picked up his pack, weary and slower than before. Small gashes littered his legs and arms from the attack, but he didn't seem to notice, his eyes were studying her for signs injury.

He spoke quietly, relief settling into his features. "We have about two miles left to go, and we need to move fast. Can I carry you while I jog the rest of the way?"

"Won't they just attack the moment we move?"

He shook his head, more comfortable with the forest than she could fathom.

"Their eyes can't take the light. For one to come out of the forest takes months of training, but for any who were here and saw the sky through the gap, their eyes are likely in shock, making the rest of the forest look darker and hard to navigate. They won't be able to do much for the next half hour, except warn others. We have a good chance."

She squinted at the open sky, barely blue with the morning's twilight and yet already too bright for her malnourished eyes. If she was being honest, she didn't think she could walk much more anyway, so she gave a curt nod of compliance.

Dagen adjusted his pack, took a sip of water from his canteen before hooking it back on his belt, and scooped her up into his arms, setting out at a pace Michale could hardly call a jog. It was more like a sprint. Or maybe she had just never been carried by someone while they ran. Either way, his pace was fast, and they had only just begun to hear shrieks in the distance when they saw the end of the forest and burst into the shining light now coming up over the Indigo Mountains.

Michale clutched her own face, wanting desperately to take in everything before her but agonizing from the pain of seeing so much light for the first time in a year. Dagen didn't seem to notice as he slowed his pace, glancing behind them at the forest and laughing in relief as he gloried in the end of the chase.

Glancing down at her his smile faded and he fished something out of his pocket, seeming to remember something and producing a thin cloth from his pocket. He unwrapped a long rag and held it out to her.

"You can see through it, but it will add a shade between you and the sunlight. Once you feel comfortable, you can take it off, but until then this should help you see."

He tied it gently around her sunken eyes, somehow managing to fit it over her caked hair. To Micahlethia's surprise, it worked. It was still hard to keep her eyes open beneath the cloth, but she could just manage it.

How had he anticipated that? She wondered.

They walked up the small hill before them toward the Loharan desert and came to a place at the foothills where a pile of rocks lay, and Dagen immediately set to work moving aside the large stones on top to reveal a pack inside, sitting beside five canteens of water.

She arched a brow, impressed.

"You've certainly thought of everything." She muttered, unsure herself why she was so disgruntled.

He paused then and gazed at her, eyes suddenly ablaze and hands still. She could feel the weight of his eyes even beneath the rag.

"I most certainly have." Dagen picked up the pack, opening his own, and began transferring contents over. He finished and stood, sighing.

"This will be enough for a week if we are careful. We'll have to find the Loharans by then."

She nodded, enjoying the warmth the sun brought, and moving Dagen's jacket closer to her body as a gust of wind blew through.

Carefully, hesitantly even, he took her hand, barely touching it at all and looked at her, his eyes full of understanding. She slid her hand out and took a step back.

He closed his eyes and Michale'thia stared ready to brave his anger. She did not owe him anything.

Dagen opened his eyes and winced, groanin and bringing a hand to his eyes again.

"Michale, I'm sorry. I'm doing this all wrong, I know." He sighed and looked to the sky before continuing.

"Keep teaching me what you need. I'll do my best."

She stood there like a fool ready for a fight and only gaining surrender, which was more confusing.

Dagen continued with his hands firmly behind his back.

"I know you are tired, hungry, and probably sore. But we need to put in a few hours before we can stop. This wind is a gift and will blow over our tracks, but it won't always be here. If Anarathan guards decide to plow through the Jyre forest to find you. I assume they will end up here eventually, but my hope is they'll go around the forest after a few days of searching locally. That would give us over a week's time to put as much distance as we can between us and them."

When she didn't reply, he nodded uncertainly, gesturing forward and beginning their journey again, west, into the sands of the Loharan desert.

CHAPTER 5

LUIK

Four hundred sixty-two. He had searched day after day through piles of stone and rubble, pulling children out from under the bodies of parents, and looking into the eyes of too many lifeless bodies with crushed bones and charred skin. He had rescued countless malnourished babies who survived only because their cribs, made by the hands of their fathers, stopped the rubbage from crushing their tiny bodies to death like their families. Then he watched those same babies die from lack of milk. In the end, four hundred and sixty-two had survived and made it to the Botani Mountains.

Luik sat on his throne and gazed out over his leveled kingdom as he did most days. He clenched his fists. All because *they* deemed the very blood of his kingdom unworthy of life.

He could still see the explosion boulders crashing through walls and hear the screams of his people as they died on the one night hope had been born.

Michale'thia left with her brother, riding off with claims of sacrificing herself to save his kingdom. A kingdom of mix-bloods, wars, and drugs. But hope was rising- the clans who had set the kingdom into civil war after the death of his father signed a peace treaty Dagen had created. The treaty would bring a unified trade between the clans and in doing so bringing peace, the first peace in 20 years.

But Michale'thia was welcomed back into her Anaratha as the Heir of the Prophecies. He watched as his childhood friend then turned around, pointed to his kingdom, and unleashing death.

The army behind her came in full force, first sending fiery catapults, then ensuring they finished his people off with the sword. Women. Children. Elderly.

Belick and Aleth had raced Syra out through a tunnel and Fain had pulled him away in hopes of saving his life. In his shocked state, he did what Fain asked and ran. Into the tunnel, away from the nightmare. He came back two days later, when the army had begun to retreat, to find the sight that would plague sleep for the rest of his life.

Luik glared out over the land, his fury burning beneath the surface. It festered there, growing into something dark and heavy on his soul.

Syra had begged him to stay in with his people when he got them to the Botani villages, but he couldn't.

He couldn't sleep or eat without seeing Michalethia's arm raise up with sword in hand and the cheer from the army resound as they readied their weapons. Following their Heir to battle. The beautiful, bloody perfect, Michale'thia.

Slowly, Syra stopped checking on him and Belick and Aleth let him be. Sitting on his throne day in and day out.

She deserved the cage ten bloody times over.

His shaggy hair had grown out, now pulled back into a bun atop his head, and his face was covered beneath a thick layer of beard. He no longer cared. Let him look like the bloody beast he was inside.

Luik rose from his brooding throne high above the crumbled kingdom and pulled his fur jacket tighter against the cold winds, looking up toward the morning sun just peaking through the mountains. Where his small remnant lived safely. Wounded and scarred for life. All four hundred and sixty-two.

He turned on his heel and climbed down the pile of stone that had once been a towering wall, treading carefully until he jumped to the green grass below where his horse was waiting.

Luik took one more dark look at what used to be his home, and nudged his horse, beginning the half day's journey southwest, into the Jyre Forest.

The light of the day nearly bounced off the entrance of the forest, as if the darkness rejected it entirely, blowing it away with the wind or shutting some unseen door. Yet as Luik stepped inside, his eyes adjusted quickly, the dark seeming lighter when the light was not longer there to contrast it. His boots crushed dead branches beneath them, and he carefully passed beneath tree after tree, moving south through the middle of the forest without trepidation. He knew why he was there.

Only half of an hour had passed in quiet before he heard a light thud *thud* behind him, and smiled as he stopped, waiting for the Jyre to speak.

"You are not shy, that much I can see." The woman before him was tall and slender, hair stopping just at her bare shoulders and her full lips parted below large, breathtaking eyes.

"*Shy* isn't exactly something I value." He looked at her, tossing his pack to the ground.

"Mmm." She eyed him, merriment dancing in her eyes as they roamed his body brazenly. She glided over to him with a dancelike grace.

Her smile was full, suggestions dripping from the corners of her mouth. "And why is it you are here, Lost King?"

Luik flinched at the title which had somehow spread around the lands, painting him as the broken ghost of a soul rather than the strong man he prided himself to be.

He smiled back, the motion not meeting his eyes as he touched her cheek, playing the game.

He took a step back and spread out his hands, winking jovially. "What else? I'm here to make a deal."

Her mouth parted in surprise and her lips pulled back into a dark smiled. She placed a palm on his chest, stepping only a breath away as she all but purred.

"And what is it that you want from us?"

Luik stepped closer, bending down to whisper in her ear. "Take me to Jyren."

The beautiful creature wrenched out of his arms, a knife suddenly out and at his gut, her sharp eyes piercing his own.

"Who told you?"

Luik chuckled, enjoying the reaction and the end of the facade. They weren't used to being played.

"Who told me what? That your leader is really Jyren back from the bloody dead?" He flicked the knife, rolling his eyes. "Oh. Just a rumor." He glared back at her as he picked up his pack.

"Take me to him."

From everywhere and nowhere, whispers began to flood the treetops, a symphony of hushed voices spoke, and the woman's head snapped up, listening. Then without a word, she jumped and disappeared into the trees.

Luik waited silently, listening to the ever so slight rustling above him impatiently.

When she didn't return, he lifted his pack up onto his back and continued on, southward. He knew where Jyren would be. He would live where any paranoid ruler would reside: in the center of his loyal people. .

He stepped around a root sticking up from the ground, settling into a fast pace, ready to be out of the despairing forest as soon as possible.

It was silent for a while, eerily so. The type of silence that says more than it omits. After he had walked what he guessed was two miles, the whispering began again, low at first, but rising with a steady hum until it grew to be so loud he could barely hear anything else. He shut his eyes against the sound and clutched his head before growling in anger and throwing his pack off, choosing a tree and beginning an upward climb.

The bloody Jyres wouldn't scare him. He would find Jyren, and he would make Anaratha pay.

He climbed higher and higher, seeing shadows begin to take form until they resembled people, thousands of them, all perched on branches and watching with blinkless stares. Somehow the further upward he climbed the darker it became.

Luik ducked under a branch and swung his weight up to the next, eyes adjusting to the dark just as he began to register red lights up ahead. Fire?

It couldn't be fire. The whispers had stopped again and he now lifted himself up onto larger branches, twisted and gnarled but wide enough to walk on. Hanging bridges connected each tree to small dwelling shacks built securely in every crook. The red lights were unlike anything he had ever seen, but allowed everything to be seen. He walked close to one, stepping carefully as he inspected a light. It was red inside, but surrounded by a thick crystal on the outside-

"One of our older inventions."

Luik tensed, straightening at the sound of the women who first met him in the forest. He turned raising his brows lazily with a smirk.

"Is it?"

She looked back at him blankly. "He will see you now."

Luik gave a curt nod and followed her up a branch and over a hanging bridge, her feet moving swiftly, as if walking on solid ground. She didn't look back at him to see if he followed, which irked him a little, knowing the powerplay at hand. Instead she led him on and on until finally they reached a large dwelling with a single bridge connecting it to the rest. It was probably the size of fifty of the small houses surrounding it, with gold and jewels covering the outside lavishly, as if trying with all its might to be grander than the stack of wood it was.

Luik could feel eyes on him as he carefully crossed the bridge, hair standing on end. The structure was lit with red lights, giving the jewels and gold an evil glint.

The woman stopped well before she reached the actual house and waited, watching him gruffly stop before her.

Her brows furrowed together slightly in what could have been mistaken as concern. "He is waiting for you."

Luik nodded, his own apprehension rising as he turned away toward the door. Before he could take a step she caught his arm in an iron grip.

"Watch what you say, Lost King. He isn't like anyone you are used to."

Luik looked at her with a half smile, saluting her with mock seriousness before striding to the door and giving a loud knock.

Minutes passed, and he knocked again, fighting the urge to look back at the woman for an answer. He stood, waiting longer than he knew was necessary until the door was opened by a tall, muscular man wearing only a shift skirt opened the door. His features would have made women swoon, but his eyes looked… distant.

Without a word he turned and walked away, leaving the door open for Luik to enter. He peered in before committing, finding the house adorned with more jewels on the inside, gold lining the floors and what may have been marble on the ceiling, with… uncomfortably intimate pictures etched along the sides. Even for him.

He followed the silent servant down a long hall, the lights brightening as they went until it almost seemed as if dim sunlight lit up the room. Luik looked around confused. It was a bloody palace in the trees. How did they hold all of this?

He kept his eyes on the servant, counting the passing servants as he went, not surprised at all when he entered the throne room to find women, some of the most beautiful he had seen, lounging on cushions and lining the walls, frozen in poses as if they were sculpture decoration.

Luik kept his eyes down, disgusted by the sight about him and growing increasingly aware of how many large servants there were about.

When the servant finally stopped him a few feet before large steps to a throne, Luik looked up, finding his eyes suddenly pinned by a dangerous, chiseled face. Jyren sat stone still, studying Luik openly.

A fierce looking woman sat beside him, her hair tied up in a high band on her head and two swords on her hip. She gripped the arms of the chair so tightly her pale knuckles were nearly translucent.

Jyren finally rose, smiling as he strode to meet Luik.

Luik found his arm grasped by the Ancient brother in a familial way and was surprised to find himself grasping it back. Jyren's smooth voice filled the room.

"Luik, King of the Brends. I have been waiting." He released Luik's arm and motioned to his servants, who came running with a table and chairs. Within seconds they had produced a table filled with steaming foods and smooth wine.

Jyren motioned toward one of the chairs and sat down himself, filling his plate with a few items and topping off his cup.

"Tell me, what brings you to my forest, Luik." Charm oozed from every word Jyren said and he picked up a piece of bread, tearing the corner before tossing it in his mouth.

Luik sat silently, not touching the wine or the food on the table, but staring at it as an excuse to gather his thoughts. He looked up at Jyren, his old rage returning and making it hard to speak with civility.

"I want Anaratha dead."

Jyren paused, raising his brows in surprise, though Luik doubted he was really surprised at all. He took a thoughtful taste of the wine before smiling at him again.

"That is no easy task, my boy. Why would you want such a thing?"

Luik's eyes clouded over, memories of walls crumbling on children readily filling mind.

"The lands would be better without them." He gave Jyren a smile of his own through tight lips. He was already tired of this game.

Jyren studied him as he leaned back in his chair, lifting a piece of cut melon into his mouth. He paused mid-chew and spit it out, sighing sadly before lifting his hand.

Two servants came running to the table, eyes wide with terror. They had to be no older than fourteen.

Jyren spoke softly, gently even, like a loving father to his children.

"Which one of you brought me my plate of food."

The reaction was so swift Luik knew these boys had been trained for years. One pushed the other in front while taking a step back, eyes trained on the floor.

Jyren sighed, standing before the boy and taking his head gently in his hands, bringing his eyes up to meet his own.

"It is a shame." He brushed his knuckles across the boy's lips, sending visible shivers down Jyren's spine. The touch neither looked fatherly nor kind this time.

"My melon had a seed. You should have caught that."

And with one more hand raised, the woman on the throne came down, not running yet swift, and in one quick movement, ripped the child's back and jerked left. The body crumpled to the floor.

The snap and thud shook Luik, and he swallowed down bile rising up, working hard to keep his face neutral as Jyren studied him. This was a show. A flaunting of power. And he was being tested.

The child's body was dragged out of the room and everything continued as normal, the woman returning to her seat and placing her long hair over one shoulder, stroking it as if it were a pet.

Luik clenched his stomach against the waves of nausea hitting him, almost thankful he felt anything at all when it came to death. At least he wasn't that bloody far gone.

Jyren waited for his plate to be cleared and took a sip of his wine, giving a signal with his left hand that brought to life music with skimpily clad men and women dancing around them. He grinned and sighed with contentment cocking his head to the side while eyeing Luik.

CHAPTER 6

SYRA

Syra clenched her knees and straightened her back, straining to see the land behind them. They had ridden their horses hard the first few miles before slowing to a fast trot. She could sense the horses' fatigue and knew they couldn't go on much longer without a break.

There were no soldiers in sight, but both Syra and Belick knew they would be coming. It was only a matter of time before they sent out every soldier possible to scour the lands for their lost utopia.

Syra and Belik had spent weeks working to coordinate their roots so they could rescue Michale'thia without dooming villages to death in their escape, and they now felt the relief of that decision.

"What do you think?" she asked Belick, looking out over the hills ahead of them.

His deep voice cut through the wind, thoughtful and careful as ever.

"It is time. We should have seven miles before we reach the first of the southern villages, and we can rest there."

She nodded, wondering if he would keep a slower pace for her sake but knowing there wasn't a chance.

Syra slid off her horse and loaded her small pack onto her back, tying the extra rope around the front of her torso in an "X" to keep the pack tightly against her frame. An old trick Belick had taught from the Botani people..

Belick slapped their horses, sending them trotting to the east, and turned to give her a nod. South they went.

Despite the fast pace, Syra suspected he was *trying* to keep the jog slow for her sake, but no matter how slow he went, his extra foot of legs made it hard to keep up.

The land around them was greener than she had been used to. This past year had brought ravaging massacres, with entire towns burned down by the Anarathan army. Gray and black filled the hills now, re-placing the lush green that used to be.

"How many refugees now have made it to the Botani mountings? Have your people sent word?"

"Our people. Ours, Syra. You are my sister, and these are your people too."

Over a year ago now, Belik had taken her hand and performed an ancient ceremony, rarely practiced by the Botani people, and adopted her as his sister. Since then they had a bond she couldn't fully explain to those on the outside. She could almost feel echoes of his emotions or intentions, a part of him was etched into her soul. He had stayed by her side ever since, even preparing to interrogate a man she was infat-uated with.

Syra's mind strayed to Luik, a deep ache throbbing inside at the thought of him. She believed a year would be enough to move on, but she was wrong. Each day was another battle not to dwell on his brown dimples and browner eyes, and not just because she once thought herself to be falling for him, but because he was deeply broken inside, and alone in that brokenness. A thing no one should ever experience. But he shut her out, and she couldn't keep fighting for someone who wouldn't fight back.

"Stop, Syra."

"Stop what?" She huffed as she struggled to talk while keeping up.

"Keep your mind far from that mad man. He is lost and must pull himself out of the hole he has fallen into." Belick turned around, jogging backwards while grinning at her playfully.

"You know, there is a man in my kingdom named Mijono. He is tall, and so so handsome. His face is like beautiful chiseled stone, and his singing voice brings every girl to his door!" He winked, ignoring her rolling eyes as he laughed to himself, turning around again.

She padded softly along the rode, adjusting her pack so it no longer flopped against her back with each step.

"You never answered the original question. How many have made it? You have been sending letters to your elders through bird, yes?"

He nodded, waving his hand, "They have been counting, and they have received close to ten thousand refugees. Some of those being from the Brend's kingdom, but many being villages that left right after we warned them and made their way to safety."

Syra smiled as she kept pace with Belick. Those numbers meant everything they were doing this past year and a half hadn't been in vain.

After the Kingdom of Anaratha pledged to eliminate mix-bloods, or those not from a pure blood line reaching back to the Ancient brothers, Syra and Belick set off to bring both medical aid and warning to villages in the surrounding regions. They had soon been named the Free Elharren Warriors by those they aided, finding those same people much stronger than they had realized.

While most in the farming villages packed up and left, trusting the Jyre and Botani messengers before them, men and women began to follow them, training every morning and forming a type of defensive army of sorts. They all created a good routine, going into villages raided by Anaratha's army and bringing emergency aid, or sending scouts to learn the whereabouts of the army and evacuating villages to the Botani Mountains. The Free Elharren Warriors had become both a beacon of hope and a healthy rebellion formixbloods, and Syra couldn't be prouder.

Syra's heart swelled with pride as she thought of all the men and women who had given up everything for a life of hard training and hiding from the enemy. With more delviors loose in the land, they needed the extra help escorting villages to safety.

Syra shuttered at the memory of a delvior sinking its jaws into her back, shredding her flesh to pieces. She had healed quickly with the magic in her, but she would still never wish the pain on anyone.

They jogged in silence for a time before coming upon their first village, slowing to a walk as they came closer. The dirt streets of the small town were empty, and Syra mused many families would still be out farming at this time.

As they slowly made their way to the first shop of the village, they were greeted by a tall man, young in years and strong in build, his skin not quite the deep hue of the Botanis, yet still sharing much resemblance to them.

His long strides met them halfway and he pierced them with his pale gray eyes, reaching out a hand.

"Are you who they call the Elharren Warriors?"

Syra could feel Belick's chest tighten with pride as he reached out a hand in return.

"We are they. It would seem our news has traveled faster than we did."

The man gave a single nod, the shaved sides of his head accentuating the longer, dark hair pulled into a bun.

He folded his arms, looking at them with sober wisdom few held so young without seeing too much. "We have heard the news many times over. For most of this year we dismissed it, but too many have passed through our village with tales of death and loss for us to deny it any longer."

He beckoned them to follow, leading them down the dirt path between shops and to a larger meeting hall. The door opened as he neared and Syra caught a glimpse of men and women sitting around a large table inside.

The man paused. "I am Senji, of the Volrath family. Please, come." He gestured to the door wide wooden doors.

"We saw you coming from far off and have gathered the elders of our village."

Syra and Belick exchanged a look. This was one of the most southern villages in Elharren and would technically be part of the Anarathan Kingdom, yet they had elders as the Botani people did, and there was no mistaking Senji's Botani mixed blood.

They entered into the dimly lit room, candles and windows beckoning in the outside sun. Around the table were men and women of differing ages and skin colors sat in unity. Some had Alethian freckles with their dark hair, but most no longer sported any resemblance to the Anarathan kingdom, taking on a mix between the light brown Brends and the darker skinned Botani people.

The table quieted as they entered the room, being shown chairs with cups of water and bread set in place. They sat gratefully and nodded in thanks.

A older man sat across from them, his hunched back the only sign of his old age. He allowed them to eat before speaking.

"The land of Elharren owes you two a great deal." His crackled voice held an easy command Syra had began to understand came from a lifetime of leadership.

Belick gave a nod and turned to Syra, a small gesture he did every other town.

She took the unwanted que, groaning inwardly. She was no Michale'thia. All she wanted was to do the work that needed to be done, and rest in the shadows afterward. She hated speaking in front of crowds of any size.

"Thank you, sir. But we do not do anything less than what the Ancient Magic would ask."

The man raised a brow, giving her a pointed look.

"And yet the King and Queen of Anaratha say the same when they pursue this quest of murder. So which is it? Is the Ancient Magic a murderer or is it a savior?"

Syra nodded, understanding his meaning.

"It is true, they claim the prophecy has given them direction to do what they believe is the will of the Ancient Magic in this. But they base their claim on little more than a stretched interpretation of one single word, which does not follow the historic example of the Ancient Magic or It's commands elsewhere." She looked at Belick then, reminded of his own memories with mankind.

"We know mankind has not been perfect. We twist and mold things to our own gain, even at the cost of others. How easily can we then not look at a prophecy and interpret *that* to our own gain, missing the heart of the Ancient Magic completely? But does our mutilation of the prophecy *change* its original meaning? No. It only points toward our own ability to maim. We know the Ancient Magic delighted in the creations of the brothers, and Aleth created people of every kind and appearance. Every single one was created with dignity and honor, loved by both Aleth and the Ancient Magic. There is nothing but selfish ambition behind an interpretation of "lead the pure into the sun" to mean "kill all mix-bloods".

She looked into the eyes of the elders around the room who now nodded in agreement. Taking a breath, Syra prepared herself for her next argument.

"And if that is not enough, the Ancient Magic has called and marked me. I speak with the magic flowing through my veins."

She held up her arm to unwrap the cloth covering her forearms, exposing bright, light-filled markings now covering her skin.

Gasps rasped around the room, and the elders began to murmur to each other, sorting through the implications of her admission.

Belick rumbled then, settling all chatter.

"We come to do nothing more than to bring news and show you the way to the Botani Kingdom where you will be safe."

The old man across from them nodded thoughtfully, giving Belick the support to continue.

He leaned forward in his chair and moved his gaze across the room, meeting every pair of eyes at the table.

"We have freed the one Anaratha believes to be the Heir of the Prophecies, unleashing the anger of the king. Soldiers will be sent out in greater number and force." Gaps and murmuring began around the table as his message set in.

"You must leave today. My kingdom will give you each land and welcome you under our rule."

An older woman with graying hair squinted at them, folding her arms stubbornly. "We have prepared, and most families are ready to leave at your command. But our wagons may not make it up the mountain. Are we to leave behind all we own just to enter into a king-dom *you* say will welcome us?"

An argument they had received often, Syra opened her mouth to explain, surprised when a woman in the corner of the table cleared her throat instead.

She sat tall, her beauty almost regal with a touch of strength and gentleness in every word. Her auburn hair was braided down her back and her freckles proved Syra's first thought wrong. There was definitely an Alethian here.

"We will give up all that can be replaced, Mialdine. For the sake of our sons and daughters, we must go. The cost will be worth it."

Syra watched in awe as the woman's words seemed to inflate those around the table, raising bowed shoulders and trembling chins. She turned back toward the woman and was startled to find her eyes staring back with a burning intensity.

Unsure what to do, Syra nodded in agreement, playing with the fabric of her shirt under the table.

The older man stood then, looking around the room.

"Go, gather those under your care. We meet here with what we can carry and leave at once." He turned to Belick and Syra then. "If you will, Senji has a small group of men who will sit down with a map and mark out the way. We will follow where you tell us to go."

Belick nodded and followed Senji out the door, leaving Syra alone in the small crowd of elders now rushing to get home.

She stood quietly and lifted her pack again, deciding to find provisions for the next part of their journey while she waited. As she pushed the heavy chair out and turned toward the door, she came face to face with the Alethian woman.

"I'm sorry," the woman laughed softly, "I didn't mean to catch you unaware." She held out a hand. "I am Cirren."

Syra smiled, thankful for a friendly face in the town.

"I am Syra, it is nice to meet you, Cirren."

At her name, Cirren's eyes widened slightly, and she frowned, seeming to struggle to find the right words.

"And... you are part Jyre and Alethian?"

Syra nodded, now understanding the reaction. Ever so often someone would be brave enough to ask how she was created, their curiosity winning over their fear of the Jyre people.

She smiled gently, hoping to put her at ease. "Yes, my father is Jyre, and my mother was Alethian. I left the forest when I was very young."

The woman tilted her head to the side folding her hands in front of her brown dress.

"You said 'was'. Is your mother no longer alive?"

No one had asked this far into her own story yet, and she only nodded in response.

Cirren seemed to sense her hesitancy and strung an arm through Syra's, pointing toward a building a few doors down.

"My good friend owns the bakery right there, and she travels far to find spices I had never had before moving here. Would you like to join me? We could take our lunch to the pond while the men discuss routes?"

Syra studied the woman before her, unsure of what to make of her friendliness, yet determined to presume the good in people.

She gave a faint smile as a response and they made their way to the now deserted bakery.

They took a few leftover rolls and followed the dirt path to a small pond behind the town, filled with sunken logs and green moss.

Lowering herself down on the soft grass under a tree, Syra smiled at the beauty before her.

"It's amazing isn't it." Cirren commented, her own eyes trained on the view before them. "That the land of Elharren can hold such a vast array of beauty."

Syra nodded, having just thought the same thing. She had traveled the past year and found the land to be much more diverse than she once thought, growing different flowers and plants as they made their way south.

Syra turned to look at Cirren, her legs folded under her as if she could be home anywhere she sat.

"You speak as if you have seen much of the land too."

Cirren nodded, her smile fading as she lost herself to memories.

"I used to live in Anaratha, or at least in a small estate close, but have since journeyed here, where I lost my heart to a kind, hardworking man. Our son Benji just turned eight." Cirren tore a small piece of bread off and smiled at Syra, motioning toward her.

"And you, are you close with your family?"

Syra tried to stop her body from tensing, but the image of her father's looming figure and cruel hands over her vision, turning her stomach with it. How could she be so terrified of him after all this time?

She shook her head, relaxing her tight hold on her bread and looking back toward the pond.

"I am not. My... father was cruel, and my mother died shortly after I was born."

She shifted her weight under her own discomfort, suddenly feeling as though she were unclothed before this stranger. But Belick had taught her through this journey that a person's story, freely given even in discomfort, had the power to change the lives of those around. She would share, even if it did make her cringe.

Cirren sat still beside her, seeming to understand her inward battle. Her voice was soft when she did speak, daring to ask further.

"I am sorry. A daughter should be loved. How did your mother pass?"

Syra took a shaky breath in, wondering if this venture was worth it after all. She missed her mother. The woman she never knew.

"My father killed her."

The sharp intake of breath beside her confirmed Cirren had heard her soft response, and Syra sat there, wondering who she could have been had her mother been alive. It wasn't a desire for fame or greatness, but the yearning for a life without the pain and sorrow she had borne in the Jyre forest all those years.

She started when she felt an arm wrap around her shoulder, and Cirren mourned with her. They sat like that for minutes more before Syra finally gained the courage to ask the question on her own mind.

"Cirren, thank you for your kindness, but you have very little time before you leave to journey up the mountain. Why spend this time here, talking with a stranger?"

Cirren smiled at the question, a hint of sadness showing through her eyes.

"I know what it is like to be in a new place with few people who care. My family has been packed and ready without our wagon for some time now, so I am not worried." She turned her pale blue eyes toward Syra with new light in them. "Would you like to meet them? They are likely in the village by now, if elder Ceffris spread the word."

Syra warmed at the thought of being around children again, smiled. They rose and made their way back toward the village, still far off when a small figure came barreling toward them with strange flat board in his hand. Benji's hair was lighter than Cirren's own auburn head and his cheeks were sunkissed from hours outside. He wore no shoes and came to a halt before them with a large grin covering his face, his eyes bright and dancing as he rattled off his question to his mother so quickly neither could understand.

Cirren knelt down in front of her son and listened, bemused, shaking her head when he finished.

"I am sorry my dear one, but we will not have the space to carry it. You will just have to make another when we get there. What have you decided to name it though?"

He danced from foot to foot, unable to contain himself.

"It is my wave rider, and mother I can't leave it! I just finished sanding it! You said you would take me to the ocean soon so I could test this new one out!"

Cirren looked up and muttered something, sighing and turning to Syra.

"The ocean is only a half day's journey from here, and we try to go often. Benji loves it more than anyone I have ever known and has become quite *obsessed*," she paused to raise her brows at him, "with the waves. This past year he has spent every waking moment designing and shaping wood into these... wave riders as he calls them."

She smiled down at him then, taking in his giddy expression and hopeful pleas.

"And I must admit, it has been incredible to watch him on the ocean. He has even had a few friends learning too." She touched his chin with pride.

Syra smile at the scene and turned to Benji with a questioning look.

"How do you ride waves? I have been on a device that used the wind to move a board larger than that, but I have never heard of someone trying to use waves themselves. Isn't it scary?"

Benji's beamed as he rushed to explain, sounding much older than his eight year old self.

"No, well yes. It is scary, but it's the most magnificent feeling in the world! The waves push you, and as long as you swim fast enough when they come, you can stand on your board. Look, like this!"

He laid the board down before jumping up to stand on, balancing easily with his feet spread apart.

"And see, then the waves keep pushing you. It's like you are flying!"

Syra couldn't help but laugh at the young boy's passion, knowing it did not have to end because of their journey.

"Well Benji, I hear the Botani's have places to live right on the ocean's edge! And there are plenty of trees to make more of these wave riders. You may not be able to bring this one, but if what Belick has said about his people is true, then you will find yourself surrounded by many others who would love to try your board with you."

Benji's mouth hung open and he looked toward Cirren with round eyes and renewed excitement again.

"Ok, ok, I'll leave it, but I am going to make another once we get there!" He jumped and brought his hands to his head in awe. "We could live by the ocean, mother!"

He jumped a few steps and skipped over to surprise Syra with a quick hug, moving on to his mother next before bounding off again toward the village, presumably to leave his board somewhere safe.

The two women laughed as he ran and continued their own way back to the, where Cirren embraced Syra and went to greet her husband.

Syra stood there, watching a growing group of people form, all toting large packs and wide brimmed hats. She glanced up at the sky, thankful the weather was perfect for travel. The cold winds were gone, replaced by cool spring ones, ready to revive the weary traveler.

Syra found Belick's face on the other side of the crowd and made her way toward him, trying to give reassuring smiles to the anxious faces she met along the way.

Belick nodded in greeting. "They will be passing the last of the villages along their way, and will lead them forward." His precise pronunciation of each word showed his Botani roots, and his tired eyes closed for a moment. "It looks like our mission is finished."

The words settled in, hardly believable after what felt like an eternity of traveling and preparing villages to flee.

Mixed with relief was hope that she could soon see Michale again. "Then we leave for the desert next?"

She asked it as a question knowing it was their plan. Her heart ached to be near her dearest friend again, and seeing her so broken that day only amplified the loss already there. Syra had spent the past year twisting and turning at night, replaying images of walls crashing in around her as she lay invalid on a bed in Luik's kingdom. Then waking moments were spent thinking far too long on either Luik's hardened brokenness, or Michla'e constant torture.

After the attack, she had recovered and immediately tried to leave for Anaratha, physically fighting Belick and Aleth who held her back with more wisdom than she could understand at the time. She couldn't save Michale back then. It had been up to Dagen and Enith alone, and Syra's only help would be in the form of staying far from the palace to not raise suspicion.

Syra shook off the guilt creeping back in and began to jog after Belick toward the outer edge of town. The green hills were a soft respite from the burnt fields she was used to in the northern lands, and she tried to commit the beauty to memory. Green, bright, and inviting. That was how land was supposed to be.

She took one last look back at the town before they began their slow journey southwest to the Loharan Desert, where they would hopefully find Michale still alive.

CHAPTER 7

————•————

ENITH

Each footstep rang like thunder in his ears, exposing too much. Enith scanned the halls as he wove his way to his own room, his own desperate silence swallowed up by the sounds of royals retching all over the palace.

The high halls stretched before him, making his short walk a torturous mile under the eyes of painted rulers lining the walls. Enith had braved countless battles, but this was an entirely different level of fear.

You are caught.

The large door to his quarters was in sight and Enith hastily grabbed the handle just as the swishing of robes and low murmurs signaled Jyre scholars around the corner. He spun around with his back to the door and crumpled to the ground, barely holding himself up with an arm and letting his eyelids flutter shut as he pretended to retch.

"Water... I need something.. Give it to me, *please*." He moaned the phrases he was hearing all over the palace.

Two sets of polished black shoes stopped in front of him and he heard a "tsk" accompanied by a scoff before the men kept walking.

Enith strained to hear their next words.

"... they will find her. There are only so many places she can hide."

"... but how long until it wears off entirely?"

Thalem Ornto and Thilan disappeared around the corner, leaving Enith on the floor. He sat listening and waiting for a minute longer before scrambling up and into his study.

It wasn't until his large oak door was shut and fully locked that he breathed again, running a hand over his face as he slid down to the floor.

Dagen had gotten Michale out, and the royals were feeling keenly the loss of their "magic". Enith scoffed and his blood began to boil again at the wicked deal his kingdom had made.

When Michale'thia was locked under the kingdom to 'fuel the Age of Perfection', as his father had proclaimed, a change began to take place in the royals of the palace. Eyes became glazed over, and sleepy smiles covered blank faces. And he knew what they lived in for he had lived it too. For those first six months his mind had become entangled with a dark, slippery shadow. A shadow that painted a world where every dream he had ever wished was true. In those six months he believed he was married to the love of his wife. He held his daughter in his hands, tiny and precious, and lived as the respected captain of the army he always hoped to be.

But it was all little more than a dream. A facade of cruelty and myth. Dagen would have never known what was going on had his servants not began to ween him off the *jintii*. The first few days he had emptied everything and more into his bathroom, sprawled on the floor, convinced he would die. But slowly, through flashes of worried maids lifting his head and coaxing him to swallow water, he made it through.

Since then, his life had been a charade, played to the melody of the Jyres who no longer bothered to disguise themselves as scholars in their kingdom. He smiled like a fool, went where told and did what was commanded, keeping his ears and eyes open all the while. And the mixbloods had become his ally in every way. But he had no more daughter, and no more wife, something that ached inside more than he would like to admit.

He moved toward the fireplace and slid the stone out, scribbling down a quick note before thrusting it in the hole.

Southern skies are the only way
The stars have left to catch their prey
The Queen has quit her song
Rally to home to home to hom

Enith rushed to replace the stone, begging them to check it soon. He moved back to the door and opened it, swaying at the door frame and clutching his stomach.

"Can't anyone do anything around here! There are mice in these walls! Someone get a bloody cat in here!" He kicked a basket into the hall and a few passing maids scurried by, nodding and promising to check for mice. Jyres scholars strode by, smirks on their faces at the undignified scene.

Enith slammed his door back shut and sat back into a chair. There was nothing he could do now but wait.

Hours passed with only ceaseless pacing and hidden peaks out the window. His smooth hands, once rough from days filled with sword drills and fitness training, fidgeted as he sat. Waiting.

It had been an eternity. An endless eternity with no reprieve this past year. He heard the screams of his sister raging in his ears all night long, and fought the urge to rip apart everybody who stood in his way for the sake of her. But no.

He couldn't be the raging prince. He couldn't do this alone.

Enith sifted through his pack for the third time, ensuring he had the tools he needed. Tonight would land another blow against the pious kingdom of Anaratha, and he would lead it.

When the quiet knock came, he wasted no time in shooting up to answer, only remembering just in time to wait for the next two knocks as a signal. They came, and he opened his door silently, the dark of the night engulfing the halls. The man before him had too-light freckles and too-brown hair for Anarathan royals, but was a welcome sight to Enith.

One nod was all it took, and they were gone. The halls held an eerie silence. No fires lit the halls, and no servants bustled about in preparation for the next day. They were all leaving. Every single one of them.

They snaked their way through the halls, Enith's hand never leaving the sword at his side, until they finally slipped through the palace walls and down toward the main courtyard. By this time, guards would all be sick to their stomachs from the small dose of Embrog weed slipped into their wine vats that evening. They should be free to leave.

While most of the royals and "pure-blooded" had been doused with whatever poison filled the air, the guards had been carefully kept awake, given full authority to ravage the land and woman before them. Enith clutched his hilt tighter, swallowing the growl rising in his throat.

When the southern gate came into view, Enith felt tears spring to his eyes. It was up. Springs, the gate was up, and thousands of mixed-blood families silently crept out of it, heading south to the Botani mountains.

The man, Lain, slowed to a stop, turning to him to speak softly.

"These are the last of them. We have ten waves that have gone out as you instructed, each with leaders who have the map and will be waiting at the foot of the mountain for you."

Enith nodded his head slowly. "And were you able to train as many of them as you could? Did we get weapons to them if there is an ambush?"

As much as Enith had devised the plan, all orders had been carried out without him, with as little communication as possible to ensure no one found out.

Lain's lips thinned and he looked back toward the last families exiting the gate.

"Some. We were able to provide swords for about a hundred men per wave of people, but it wouldn't be enough. Those men at best are what a teenage boy's sword skill would be at in the guards barracks. They will slow a massacre, that is all."

Enith nodded and raised his brows, catching Lains eyes. "And provide confidence. Don't forget the importance of confidence."

Lain nodded in agreement, seeing the wisdom behind even rushed training now.

With one last look toward the palace, Enith adjusted his pack and took up the rear. If the Anarathan soldiers found them, he would bloody well send them to Jyren's grave. Even if it was now empty.

The dark sky glowed with anticipation and the cool breeze turned slightly frigid as they walked, tension in the crowd palpable. They would have at least a week's journey until they reached the mountain base, and then he wasn't sure how long it would take to climb it with all the children and pregnant women. He wasn't even sure if they would be welcomed, if he was being honest. But if they were welcome, and if what Belick said was true, these people would experience life for the first time. Real life. Where they could own a house, grow their food, laugh and play and be *real people* to the world around them. It was worth the gamble.

They walked in silence for hours. Enith made his way up and down the crowd, finding leaders and going over plans, as well as taking stock of food supplies. He couldn't promise what tomorrow would bring, but he could continue preparing them for anything.

Only years of military training set his ears on edge, the faint rumbling of hooves far in the distance causing every hair to stand alert.

They had been found.

Enith let out a shout of warning which soon passed from person to person as the waves of people surged forward, not realizing their running would all be in vain eventually.

Coming from the midwest was a group of what looked like hundreds guards on horseback, their silhouettes stark against the bright, moonlit horizon. Enith unsheathed his sword and dropped his pack, registering the sound of more swords behind him being drawn as men remembered their training. They would die letting their people get as far as they could if need be, but pray to the Ancient Magic they were able to stop them altogether.

The guards drew nearer, full of thundering hooves and dark forms. It wasn't until they were almost upon them that Enith's jaw dropped and he nearly let hold of his sword. Leading the large group was a smaller group, made up entirely of women.

Each woman had at least one sword at her waist with bodies toned from what had to be at least a year of conditioning. Some had their hair pulled tightly back into braids, while others wore it wild about their face. Then still others had shaved it right to their skull, bearing their beauty furiously.

And there in the front of them all, slowing to a halt, was his... wife. The woman he had fought not to dream about every single night, and whose eyes he had yearned to look into just one more time.

She gave him a quiet nod as she halted her group behind her. Her cocky voice rolled over the words smoothly.

"We heard you may need a new guard, Prince of Anaratha."

Reality came crashing back to Enith and scowled at the title, folding his arms across his chest.

"I am no longer a prince. I am a brother among brothers and sisters, seeking refuge in the mountains." He held her gaze for a moment longer, drinking her in. "And what are you, Ilytha? Gone to live with Rienah and back with a battalion?"

She stared at him, her mood visibly darkening. "Did you ask me to stay, Princling?" Ilytha slid off her horse, her hand securing itself on her hip. "No, no one did. I left to find the way of the first Women again. It would seem we were created with more strength than we once knew."

Enith eyed her, weighing the situation carefully. Springs, his mind was muddled. He finally sighed and bowed his head in respect.

"We would welcome the help if you would join us."

Ilytha turned her head to the women beside her and gave a signal, her eyes never leaving Enith's. He turned and watched as the women set off in groups, creating a barrier around the massive waves of people. As the women each found their position, men and women, villagers it looked like, now trained with anything from an ax to a bow, filed in behind them, creating *quite* the impressive guard.

No longer caring to keep the joy from his face, Enith turned back around to Ilytha, finding her nearly nose to nose with him, looking up from her dark eyelashes and dangerous eyes.

She smirked, her lips quirking upward as she kept her eyes fastened on his, not caring that every eye was on them. The leader of the mix-bloods and the leader of the new guard. Then without a hint of shame, she grabbed his face in her hands and brought his lips to her own, kissing him deeply.

When she let go, Enith's world spun and he tried to piece together the fragments of his mind, only able to stand dazed and watch her as she smiled knowingly and walked away, throwing another brazen grin over her shoulder as she declared all too loudly, "Your wife is home."

Enith rubbed his cheeks, even more thankful for the gift of the night hiding the red that covered them every time he looked toward his… wife. Though the darkness hid it, he knew her olive skin now sat upon toned muscle and a confident stride. She was different, and yet wholly the same. The woman who had only looked out at the world from the window of her eyes, now walked freely in her own skin, neither afraid nor yielding to the whims of men.

Enith swallowed, his mouth feeling dry. He remembered the day he first saw her, a small form shaking as she served her powerful brother.

One mistake was all it took for her beating to begin, and Enith had found himself mindlessly challenging the Chief of the Syllric people to a duel for her. Though he won, he never suspected the Chief's hidden plot to marry them together, and Enith left that evening in a daze, with a wife in tow.

But even then, those eyes made everything worth it. Brown and piercing beneath thick black hair framing her face, now a warrior trained by Rienah, the first of women created in Elharren.

Enith startled as Ilytha turned back toward him and waited for him to reach her, moving to walk by his side.

They journeyed in silence, and Enith clenched his jaw against the nerves now tittering in his body. He had faced delviors and been less scared! Springs, this woman would be the death of him.

He cleared his throat and glanced toward her. "So you are well then."

Stupid. Idiot.

Her lips turned up slightly and she kept scanning the area around them.

"Rienah gave me the training both physically and mentally to understand now what women were created to be. I am a woman, and I am proud of that. So, yes, I am well."

She turned her head to him then, her features softening in the moonlight.

"It is because of you. You saved me. All of us." She gestured to the women stationed on each side of the crowd. "Before you fought for me, I saw myself as nothing. As not even good at being nothing, but as scum on this earth. But you fought for me and gave me freedom. I needed someone to take that first step for me, and you did. I take that step for other women."

Enith shook his head, angry all over again at the life she once was forced to live.

"You shouldn't have needed to be a saved." He stared at her then as they walked, his brows knit together as he tried to understand the Syllric culture. "Is there anyone there at all who would change the laws?"

She quirked her brow then, studying him.

"Permission to be free and the means to be free are two vastly different things. Our laws changing would bring no change if those in power and influence do not pursue change, even when it hurts. You didn't just permit me to be free, you pursued my freedom at your own cost. That is what we need. More of men like you."

The wind ruffled her hair and Enith stopped his fingers from smoothing it down for her.

"I would do it a hundred times over, Ilytha."

He could see her smile before she turned to conveniently scan the land to their right. Enith's own confidence bolstered and he decided to plunge right in.

"So, we are still married?"

He watched as Ilytha's shoulders tensed ever so slightly, her eyes blanking as she stared ahead with disinterest.

Springs… what had he said?

Her response was cold and distant. "Only if you want to be."

Enith could feel danger lurking in every step now, Ilytha's shoulders taut as if her response had a thousand different meanings. He had somehow said the exact wrong thing and he wasn't sure what. Springs, one minute she wanted him, the next he was afraid she might stab him!

He opted for silence, watching her from the corner of his eye. Did she not want to continue the marriage? Did she feel trapped in something her brother forced her into? He cringed, feeling hope slithering away as it left grime in its wake.

They walked for hours in the night, knowing there would be no rest any time soon. His people would be ragged, but they would make it.

Enith paused, realizing his own train of thought. *His people.* These were no longer just mixbloods to him with the wrong lineage, they were *his*. The thought made his heart swell with pride as he realized for the first time he could call a people he loved his own.

Hours dragged on and he could hear the soft cries of tired children, no longer kept awake by the adrenaline of the move. They would need to rest soon.

Enith whispered into a young boy's ear and watched him scamper off ahead, spreading the news to a boy at the back of the grouping in front of them, who then ran to the front to share, and within a half hour all the groupings had stopped. They had about four hours until the sun rose, and they would sleep where they could for the time being. No tents, just their packs on their backs.

"I will set up shifts for my own to keep watch, tell your men to rest." Ilytha turned on her heel and walked away soundlessly, signaling her closest warriors to come.

She spoke to them in low voices, and Enith tried to pretend he didn't see them sending frowns of death in his direction. He focused instead on combing through the groupings to ensure everyone had what they needed.

The faint sound of pounding hooves came just before dawn as most were exhausted in sleep. Enith rose in an instant, the vibrations under him attesting to a sizable army heading his way.

Ilytha and her warriors were already up and standing, swords in hand and bows ready as those around began to wake with terrified shouts.

He drew his own sword, watching the army draw nearer.

"Please tell me you have another army of warriors heading this way." He threw over to her, but her steely eyes only watched the on-coming battalion as she gave a curt nod.

The designated group leaders were calling for the swordsmen, while the rest of the group began to run. Children were swept up by parents as the panic spread, giving swiftness to even the older in years.

They waited then, watching the band of horsemen grow and Enith's stomach turn as they neared. This would be a bloody battle indeed.

Enith's mind whirled as he realized the repercussions of his own wife fighting beside him. He may watch her die today. Or he may die today. Either way the battle before them could mean the end of a relationship he was never able to fully start.

His eyes flickered to Ilytha, then back to the guards coming straight toward them. With eyes still trained forward, he gathered his courage and called out to her.

"Ilytha!" She turned toward him for a mere half-second before looking forward again.

"Ilytha, you are a terrifying woman, and I want you to be my wife. I don't want anyone else, just you. But I also don't want you to stay if you don't feel the same, so just... do what you want."

The silence that followed was horrifying and Enith mentally slapped himself for saying it all out loud in front of their entire army- with another army nearly upon them. He would never distract a soldier before the battle! Springs, what a mess he was making of-

The hoots and hollers interrupted his thoughts and his head whipped toward the sounds, taking in the women with raised shields and swords cheering as they watched Ilytha's smile broader in response. She looked at him briefly before shifting a foot back, ready for the fight that was almost upon them.

"I will stay."

CHAPTER 8

MICHALE'THIA

H er back twisted violently and every muscle writhed in agony. She couldn't think, couldn't breath, and every second trickled by as if the Ancient Magic Itself had cruelty slowed reality. Every moment was an hellish eternity. Searing pain shot through her shoulder, then her ribs, ripping apart flesh from bone only to mend it together in an instant and start again a hundred times more. Faces came through the blur of pain and whispers and tears, and then she was alone again.

"Michale'thia... I'm here."

It had to be a nightmare, a false ruse of hope. His face began to twist inward, caving into bone and blood until Thalen's features dominated. He neared his teeth, his words coming out with a hiss.

"You thought you were free?" His mouth twitched dangerously. "You are barely human anymore, you belong in a cage."

She fastened her eyes to the hard floor. He was right.

No one could want her after what she had become, this perverted and twisted creature. And did she want anyone anyway? How could she ever go back to "normal" when everything was so twisted?

The cage bars around her morphed into claws covering her body and she squirmed, wrenching her body from side to side as she gasped for air-

Michale'thia jolted forward, clawing at the hands around her as she scrambled away. Her breaths came in short spurts, a cold sweat drenching her clothes. She paused with wide eyes, searching her surroundings for reality. All she found was Dagen, frozen hands held up in surrender and a putrid look of pity covering his shocked face.

Anger raged through her body and she gritted her teeth, swallowing down her own stomach as it rose up in sick heaves. She finally gave in and emptied her stomach.

Michale tensed as she heard Dagen approach, an animal ready to bolt. She heaved for the last time, regaining strength just as she felt his figures gingerly hold up her matted hair. Figures too close to her neck, throat- she couldn't breath.

"DON'T TOUCH ME!"

It was a nightmare. Or was this a dream, and that the reality? She couldn't know for sure. She would never know for sure.

When she had laid down to sleep that night, it hadn't been to the relief of her groaning bones, instead her muscles had rebelled and clenched painfully, making sleep long and hard to find. It seemed both her body and mind wouldn't soon forget the cage.

Dagen slowly moved back toward his own makeshift bed, but continued to watch her. She forced herself to turn around and move back toward her own. In that moment she hated him, even as she recognized the hate passing swiftly past his form and circling back to land on her own soul. She was wretched.

So she turned it off. Every emotion and care was thrown into the dark cavern she kept hidden inside, atrick she had learned early on to deal with the pressure outward perfection had once forced her to face daily. Now, she gave herself to it more fully, allowing her heart to become lost in the hole of unfeeling survival she once created to be her savior.

A few quiet minutes passed and she rolled over on her thin blanket, barely registering the frigid air as she studied the stars. Once in her life, they had represented something truly beautiful and perfect, a standard she longed to be for her own people. But now she saw the truth: even if she had been all they had hoped, she was destined to be picked apart and maligned by those in power. Humanity couldn't just leave beauty as an awe-inspiring art piece in their midst, they had to own it and use it. If her parents could, she didn't doubt they would ruthlessly enslave every star in the sky for their own use.

The thud of labored footsteps began to grow louder from the east, and Michale'thia jumped to her feet again, wishing she had something more hefty than a blanket to protect herself.

This is it. My freedom is over just like that.

Dagen stood between her and the oncoming intruder, his sword already drawn.

Out of the night the heavy footsteps crashed to the ground with a gasp for air, and a large form collapsed on before them. Dagen nudged his body onto its back and dragged him closer to the fire before a gasp escaped his own lips. The man's face was a sickly pale color and a layer of sweat coated his skin regardless of the cold wind blowing. But the man's state was not what caused their fear. It was his identity. Before them lay Luik, King of the Brends. The man whose kingdom she murdered.

Dagen jumped into action with a start, coming out of his own daze to check Luik's failing body for any clue as to the injury.

She scrambled over to him, her palms beginning to sweat in desperation as she checked for breath, then scanned his body, finding the telltale twin puncture wounds at his ankle. Her eyes widened and she could hear Dagen hiss as he saw it too. Luik would surely die.

But he couldn't die. She had too much to say.

Michale'thia felt her breathing become shallow and her chest began to tighten. She had to save him. There had to be a way. He had to live.

With swift movements, Dagen threw everything he had into his pack, quickly doing the same for her as she watched dumbfounded, still unable to move or produce a coherent thought.

He then stood and heaved Luik over his back, piercing her with a stare.

"We have to find the Loharans. He won't last long."

She just rose numbly, following behind his sure form as he began to trudge onward.

"Do you remember where they said they would be?"

Her eyes strayed to the night sky as memories flooded her: the old woman, the scrolls, the stars, all a lifetime away. She lifted her bony hand and pointed to the bright star in the north. Follow *that*, Ni had said.

Dagen gave one nod before adjusting course and starting their steady trek.

They walked through the rest of the night, stopping too often to allow Michale's frail body to collapse and regain energy. Something had shifted in Dagen, and she could feel it. His gentle prodding and stolen looks were now covered by his sense of duty, heavier than the pack he shouldered. He was still caring, but she no longer occupied his entire mind, and she liked that. He was the man that he is of his own accord, not for the approval of anyone else. She frowned at her own thread of thoughts. How had she so quickly moved from hate to admiration? She wasn't even supposed to feel emotion when she pushed them away. Michale shook her head, too tired to sort through any of it.

Michale'thia could feel warmth seeping from her feet as the hours passed, the blood the only indicator of pain her mind took note of anymore. Rigid wind cut against them but they fought on, Dagen looking more tense with every step and Michale'thia fighting the spinning world. Dagen couldn't carry the weight of all of them; she *must* keep going.

One more step. One more step. One more step.

The ground beneath her bare feet was smooth and frigid, growing harder with each step yet dulled by her heightened tolerance for pain. Her eyes flickered every so often toward Dagen, unsettled by his sudden change of attention. Before this, she could feel his eyes nearly every moment, even when he tried to hide it behind a turned head or sudden tightening of pack straps. Now however, his mouth was set in grim determination and his eyes were scanning the horizon, no longer distracted with her own brokenness state but undivided in attention on the task at hand.

He is a warrior.

The thought came with a start, sinking in slowly with a painful tinge. She studied him openly, taking advantage of his own diverted focus. His hair was freshly cut, sweeping to the side of his head and accentuating his strong jaw, now lined with scruff, and his arms carried Luik with a graceful ease only explained by the hardened muscle surrounding his arms. He was different now.

Dagen turned to look at her so suddenly she knew she had been caught staring, her cheeks warming and her eyes narrowing as she flicked them downward. Her anger surged again.

Dagen paused what he was about to say and frowned, studying her for a moment longer before continuing on.

"We are going to need to start moving faster. Luik's pulse is weakening and I fear he doesn't have much time left."

The night was still hours from being over when they heard the sound of heavy clomping, too heavy to be horses and yet too slow to be a delvior. They froze and waited in the night, hoping to catch sight of whatever was nearing them. Michalethia's stomach clenched in terror. Could it somehow be soldiers coming to take her back?

Dark forms began to take shape, large and wide creatures carrying human silhouettes on top of their bodies and dimly light lights interspersed throughout the caravan. The beasts had legs twice the width of old tree trunks and leathery skin gleaming against the light. Their long necks swayed, ending in narrow heads and large eyes.

Tied between the beasts were large blankets with ropes fastened in each corner then harnessed to the beast's front and back, creating a canvas for carrying goods between them.

They heard a soft click before the large animals slowly came to a halt almost in perfect time together. Dagen took a small step in front of her and addressed the strangers.

"Friends, we are in need of help. This man has venom coursing through his veins and will not last the night."

A dark form slid from the beast and met them with quickened steps, a torch in hand as they approached.

The man before them was shorter than Dagen, with an unassuming presence as if he did not want to disturb the air around them. His smooth olive skin and slanted eyes marked him as a Loharan, and Dagen allowed him to grab Luik's hand in his own, pressing areas with his thumb and moving up his arm to do the same.

His voice came out in a soft halted whisper, thick with an accent she immediately recognized as Loharan. "You are correct, he will not last the night, the venom has nearly reached every part of him. Come, we have herbs that will slow the process, but they will not help much. We will take you to our home where our healers have an antidote for desert snakes."

The man beckoned them to follow and Dagen quickly obeyed, lifting Luik up to a few men on the beasts and sliding him onto an empty blanket canopy. Michale'thia started, afraid for a moment he would fall, but instead the cloth surrounded his body gently, cradling him like a baby. She stood in awe, surprised at the efficiency of it all.

Dagen's hand reached out to pull her onto a beast, and she soon found herself sitting on a blanket with a few rolled blankets behind her tied down. Across from her sat a man beside a woman with layers of red and pink clothing and a larger scarf around her neck than Michale'thia had ever seen. The woman looked at Michale'thia and nodded, delight evident in her eyes as she pulled out a blanket and handed it to her. Michale'thia nodded back a thanks, snuggling into the warmth.

Dagen gave a faint smile as he looked at her, and Michale frowned. He could stop pretending. She wasn't so fragile that she couldn't take his disgust.

He sighed and looked away, studying their animal escorts.

"Can I ask, what do you call these creatures?"

The man smiled at the question, his full cheeks and passionate eyes seeming to light up at the opportunity to share knowledge.

"They are called riguls, and they are animals of the desert. Before we began caring for them, they died off quickly, unable to find food often enough. They are created perfectly for desert life physically, and breed up to twenty-five children in one year, but their minds are not the brightest. We care for them and feed them, and in turn use them in caravans to help resupply herbs for ourselves and the creatures." He grinned, "Riguls especially love *ongin* on their carrots, and would travel the world for that alone!" The woman laughed alongside him at the joke and Dagen chimed in with a chuckle.

He smiled again then, appreciation evident as he regarded the riguls again.

The woman stood with impressive balance, swaying with the animals as easily as walking on land, and beckoned Dagen to trade her places so he could talk more with her husband. Dagen gratefully conceded and to the man's delight, began asking every question on his scholarly mind.

She turned to Michale with a soft voice, "My name is Meili, and that is my husband Biln." Her warm eyes put Michale even more at ease and she found a small smile for the woman in return.

Leaning forward with the blanket around her, Michale'thia turned her head to the side and rested it on her knees. She was so tired.

"My name is Michale. Thank you for helping us."

The woman's dark short hair shone in the rising sun, as she tucked another blanket in around them.

"We would not allow our knowledge of healing to be wasted. You are lucky we came though. Your friend is very close to death."

Michale silently looked out at the horizon, her own emotions a flurry at the words.

When she didn't respond, Meili turned her own eyes to the skyline and continued gently.

"You have gone through much recently. Your bones, they need more food. And your hair will need much oil to untangle it all."

Her blunt honesty brought another smile to Michale's lips. There was no need to pretend here, and no need to wonder what she was thinking.

"I know."

"You will be brought into our home, a deep honor for outsiders. And when we get there I will give you some of our greatest tea. It will bring your body back to life. And my own Baba and I will fight every knot until every strand is smooth as honey."

Michale'thia responded with a tight-lipped smile, only causing Meili to wrap an arm through Michale'thia's.

In a quiet voice filled with compassion, Meili pressed further.

"You are her, aren't you?"

Michale stared ahead, unsure if she was this "her" spoken of, but hoping her silence would end the conversation.

"You are the one that found their prophecies wrong, and was locked beneath the kingdom for that knowledge."

Bile rose to her throat as the image of her small cage slid into her mind. If only she had just been locked away.

Michale turned a piercing stare toward her new friend and slid her arm out to hold herself under the blanket. Her voice was thick as she spoke.

"I passed my Testing Day only to find it was all a lie. For my hours of study and years living up to their impossible standards, I was drugged, made a murderer of thousands, and tortured. I am that girl."

To Michale's surprise, the woman's soft eyes gathered tears, but it wasn't pity etched on her face. It was grief. A deep, mournful grief that seemed to rip open Michalethia's own dark hole and offer her a hand out. To feel. To grieve. To face it for a moment without being alone.

Michale'thia clenched her jaw as her own emotions came flooding back. Saying it all out loud somehow made it real. And she wept.

Meili's arm circled around her hunched form, and her tears flowed freely in the arms of a stranger.

"So the drug, this *jinti,* in the Brend's kingdom...do you think this is somehow what the Jyre people use on your testing day?"

Michale's eyebrows lowered, and she tilted her head to the side, startled by the thought.

"What makes you ask that?"

Meili pondered for a moment before picking up a piece of her blanket and holding it up.

"This is a blanket, right?"

She nodded, and Meili picked a few pieces of fuzz off of the blanket, gingerly putting them in the palm of her hand.

"And these? Are they the blanket?"

Michale tilted her head to the side, studying the fuzz before her.

"I suppose, in a sense they are a part of the blanket, or were, but I would not call them a blanket anymore, since by definition they could not perform that function."

Meili nodded this time, satisfied with the answer.

"But they are of the same substance. Somehow this blanket and this piece of fuzz are of the same being, even though they are very different. *Jinti* then could also take different forms if mixed with different elements. Perhaps they condense it to an oil and rub it on trees lining the pathway?"

Michalethia's jaw dropped and she leaned forward, tucking a stray curl that wasn't there behind her ear, then grimacing as she wiped the grime off of her hand.

"There was a mist, or maybe a smoke? They must somehow be changing the *Jint* to be a hallucinogenic drug that they release in the air." She shuddered at the thought. That would mean they had a weapon that could make anyone who breathed it in see their worst temptations come to life. Or their worst nightmares. Was there a difference in the end?

She looked up to find Dagen watching her with a small smile, receiving a frown in return as she directed her gaze elsewhere. Why was he smiling? And he needed to move his ridiculous hair out of his eyes.

Yet for all her frustration her own eyes seemed to find their way back to his profile of their own accord and she eventually snapped them shut, determined to sleep. Michale couldn't afford to become lost in this false sense of perfection again. And Dagen was perfection.

They rode silently for the next hour, drinking a strange, cooled drink as the sun rose in the sky, and eventually slowed to a stop in front of a large grouping of boulders. The smooth marbled rock shot up from the ground into an impossibly large mass growing stubborn thorny plants in its crevices and radiating with the sun's early heat.

"We are here." Meili's whisper startled Michale as she searched for any sign of life within the boulders. Meili pulled out some pieces of cloth and held them up apologetically.

"I am sorry, but we cannot risk being found by those who would destroy our knowledge."

The Anarathans acquiesced, tying the cloth around their eyes. She could hear feet hitting the ground and padding over to the boulder, then with a small rumble, she could only presume *something* moved, and they once again began moving, the outside world turning notice-ably darker.

When they stopped, Meili helped Michale take off her blindfold and darkness turned to color again. She gasped.

Before her was an entirely different land.

Large shoots of crystals rose up in the center of the lush, green field, touching the ceiling and shining with the sun's light. Surrounding it were orchards and fields of food, all growing slightly toward the crys-tals, as if longing for them to draw nearer. Along the sides of the cavern were houses painted brightly with murals around large windows and spacious balconies where children played and parents read or worked. A small stream gushed from the boulder down through the village where larger, precisely etched structures could be seen, all playing with slanted designs of every sort. Then there in the center of all the build-ings was a gleaming palace made almost completely of glass, stretching taller than any other structure around. The five levels ended in a pointed tip of what she assumed was gold.

She motioned to Meili and pointed toward the building.

"What *is* that?"

Meili smiled knowingly, her own excitement shining on her face.

"*That* is what you who live above call a library."

CHAPTER 9

SYRA

Dry thicket pressed against Syra's skin as they crouched low, allowing a mass of soldiers to pass them by. Their footsteps pounded against the dirt road, mixing air with the refreshing hue of dirt. Their blue uniforms were ragged and torn, some still marked by the blood of those slain. Like Luik's people.

Her throat went dry and memories flickered of stone walls crashing down around and Belick throwing her over his shoulder as Aleth dragged Enith out of the window. The deafening roars of boulders striking and fire covering the city were all she could remember, the pain of her own wounds from the delvior attack reopening and causing her to lose consciousness.

What would it be like to love a people that were your own? This kinship and desire to protect that Luik held for the Brends was new, even in Anaratha. With Michale'thia and Enith, they had all shared their disdain for the Anarathan culture behind closed doors, longing to escape the confines of perfection the royals bore. But Luik felt something else for the Brends she couldn't fathom. An almost physical ache to see them well.

For all of his charading about like a drunken sailor, he worked years to mend what his father had broken during his reign and only moments before destruction saw a moment of peace and joy finally settle in. Right before Anaratha attacked and slaughtered those he loved.

She knew what he wanted. She could see it in his hardened glare, only sometimes breaking into the deepest of grief and longing for the atrocity to be undone. He wanted justice, and if not justice, revenge. And he wanted her to find it beside him.

Syra swallowed past her tightening throat, silently waiting for the last stragglers of the army to pass. She could not follow Luik where he was heading.

The dust settled back in new places, covering plants along the side of the road with a new shade of brown. Belick crept back onto the road and turned to Syra with a raised eyebrow.

He hefted his spear to his shoulder. "I can-"

"Yes, I know you can feel my thoughts right now. *You're* the one who bonded us though, so you must bear with my emotions too."

Belick sighed dramatically, a trait she found to be natural to him, as stoic as he may be. He began to walk backward, his deep brown eyes twinkling now as he fought a smile.

"You know, my friend Mijono- have I mentioned him? His arms are stronger than a *niroo,* and I am *sure* he would find you perfect."

He turned around to walk by her side, gesturing with his hands to paint the perfect picture.

"Ah yes, when we go hunting together, I make the kill and he *always* takes longer to pray the *dishi.*"

Syra held up a hand, her stare still scanning the horizon for any other troops.

"*Niroo* and *dishi.*" Over the past year she had learned much of the Botani language, yet the more Belick's excitement to return home grew, the more he reverted to using his home tongue, showing her how little she actually knew.

His smile brightened and he turned to her again, his own glee causing Syra to let a smile loose in return. If there is one thing the Botani people loved more than preserving their culture, it was sharing it.

"A *niroo* is a creature that hides in caves, they have small feet but large arms, twice the size of humans and much longer. They are covered in red feathers, and their mouths are made of bone on the outside to protect their food once they have it in their mouths. Like a cage, but a mouth. They are harmless creatures, unless you threaten their babies... and then you should run away very fast, because those arms can leave great bruises."

Syra looked up at him with a smirk, imagining the story he was reliving with his wide, arguably frightened eyes. He shuddered and came back to the moment, indignation covering his face at her mocking smile.

"Their arms are very, very big, Syra! I could barely move my leg for a week!"

"Why were you even that close to them?" She responded, not the least bit sympathetic.

He coughed into his hand and looked away, avoiding her gaze.

"I... was given a dare to try to arm wrestle one."

He said it with such seriousness that Syra could no longer hold back her laugh and she howled with delight. Belick's own grin turned to roaring laughter and they continued walking as they struggled to control themselves again.

Syra's laughter was cut off as she sucked in a quick breath and froze, feeling like she had been hit in the chest. It was as if what held her to the ground was no longer the only force holding her, something else pulled almost equally as strong.

She turned sharply left toward the west and her eyes roamed the far, dark, barren land they knew so little about, searching for something she couldn't even fathom.

Belick's low voice broke her trance.

"That is the land we did not create. It has nothing but gray, dull air and brittle pieces of land barely in existence."

Syra shook her head, her heart racing and body yearning to sprint toward *something* out there.

"No, there is not nothing. *Something* is there, Belick. And it's calling me."

A full day of walking and jogging turned to night and they unpacked their sleeping pads at the edge of the desert, quickly starting a fire to stave off the cool air. They lay down, thankful for a respite in their quick travels and ready for sleep.

Belick's breathing became heavy within seconds, but Syra continued turning under her blankets, unable to sleep with the sudden *thing* gently urging her toward it in the gray west. What could be out there, and how could she have anything to do with it? Yet there, as sure as her own heart, it called.

Syra stared up at the stars for the next two hours, working through her mind the vast possibilities until again and again, imaging every scenario she could. After hours of restlessness something became clear: she must go. And with that, she turned to face west and fell into a restful sleep.

Syra was up long before the sun rose, packing her bag and ignoring the disgruntled groans of Belick as he rolled to a sitting position, watching her with a blank face.

"You are changing our course."

It was a statement without a need for a question. Their bond was too deep, and time spent together long enough to know each other's mind.

She stopped her packing and sighed, lowering herself onto her knees.

"Belick, I cannot explain this to you. I do not know the workings of this, but it is as if my insides are missing something and they are pulling me toward it. *Something* is over there, and I must find it." She lowered her eyes, the pain of her next words already stinging her face.

"Even if it means going alone."

Belick's silent stare held for an uncomfortable moment, and she knew his own mind was working, even if his face remained impassive.

"How far do you think this thing is?"

"I don't know. Close enough to pull me?" She pulled her long white hair up and tied it high on her head, tired of it being flung about by gusts of wind.

"And how do you know this is not something of Jyren?"

Syra frowned at that, having wondered the same thing herself.

"I don't know. Maybe it is. I just… need to go anyway."

Belick sighed and rolled to his feet, beginning the packing process of his own blankets.

"Syra, out there... it isn't like anything you have seen. When the Ancient Magic set us free to create, we created and sat in our own spoils. We left the unformed to itself and lived in our own colorful worlds. It isn't like the desert, just dry and missing plants. The ground itself is barely made, unstable and without order. It is a wild wasteland there, and I do not know what we are to face."

She kicked dirt over their fire and heaved her own pack onto her back, leaving her dried meat and water canteen accessible for the journey ahead.

"I didn't know that, but thank you, Belick."

She raised a brow at him as he rose with his own pack, meat in hand.

"I'm hungry? Don't do that little eyebrow thing." He wriggled his finger at her. "This is what normal, non-obsessed-with-strange-far-off-objects people do. They eat before they travel."

A grin broke across Syra's tan face and she turned around to face the mysterious pull. She wouldn't have to go alone then.

They had both finished their breakfast before the sun completely rose, and broke out into the jogging portion of their trip. If she was correct, whatever it was could only be a few hours away at a fast pace. It grew stronger each minute, heavier and more solid inside of her as she moved. It wasn't stagnant somehow, she could now feel a sense of length and width forming, something grander than she had thought and certainly more powerful.

Time flew without notice, her own urgency building as this *thing* overtook her senses. She could see through a mist now, but her ears roared with power, and she hadn't realized she was sprinting until she suddenly stopped, and the pull eased. Her vision cleared and hearing settled, but her mind raced. Belick came to a halt beside her, dripping in sweat and panting to catch his breath.

He gasped, "I didn't.... know.. you could run... that fast for so long!" He turned around pacing, working to normalize his breathing to no avail.

Syra barely noticed him; she had found what was pulling her, it was a river, and she wasn't the only one.

The perfectly clear water rushed through its canal with powerful waves and white rapids, slowing at points downstream into peaceful runs. And on the other side? Gray. A fog too thick, and a ground too unstable.

The Unmade Land.

Syra's eyes fastened onto a form squatting before the water, dark brown hair to his shoulders and a loose tunic blowing slightly in the wind.

Luik?

Her heart began racing of its own accord, and she wasn't sure what to do with her hands. She took a step toward him, and he started, turning around to face his intruder.

But it wasn't him. This man's face was older, and his nose smaller. But the chocolate brown skin and eyes were enough to mark him a Brend. This was one of Luik's people.

His brows shot up seeing her, glancing over her hair before shifting to Belick, where his face split, showing white teeth and an easy laugh. He opened his arms wide and Syra heard Belick groan, turning around, away from the embrace.

"Brother! Why do you walk away? *How* can you walk away from all of this? I have become even *more* handsome in this second life!"

He jogged up and threw his arms around Belick's taller form, pressing his cheek against his back with a sly grin and a wink Syra's way.

Then, without the slightest chagrin, he smacked his lips, spittle flying out onto Belick's skin.

Belick jumped forward shoving the man off him with blatant disgust. He rubbed his hands over the area his mouth was closest to, visibly shuddering.

He pointed this time to the man, whose smile only seemed to grow.

"That has never been funny."

He flipped his hair out of his face and laughed, "Broyane, it has always been funny to anyone watching you squirm! Come on, give me a real hug!"

Belick rolled his eyes but smiled, opening his arms and laughing as they made their embrace.

Syra smiled, realizing she had been forgotten in their reunion, and did the only thing she ought to do when meeting a new Ancient Brother. She joined in. With loud, smacking lips she began to walk closer to Belick, whose neck seemed to arch to the side on its own as his eyes squinted as if they could be pained by a sound.

The man was doubled over with laughter, as was Syra, tears coming to their eyes as Belick continued to shudder and grimace over the noise. The man pointed to Syra, both still unable to control their laughter, and grabbed *her* into an unexpected hug, wiping tears from his eyes as he straightened.

Belick glowered at them both, jiggling his arms to rid himself of the sound. When they caught their breath, the man turned to Syra, only taller than her by a few inches, and stuck out his hand.

"Brendar. And you must be this new niece of mine!"

His contagious smile forgave the reminder that she was Jyren's daughter, and Brendar pulled her into a bear hug, spinning her around for a turn.

"So what brings you toward the Unmade land? And where did you wake up? Agh. There is so much to talk about!"

Belick shook his head, remembering the river before them and pushed passed his still talking brother to peer into the powerful entity. He crouched down as Brendar had been doing before and stayed there, frozen.

Syra stepped toward him, glancing at Brendar as she spoke.

"This is not a normal river, is it?"

Brendar's smile turned sad, confusion filling his eyes, and Belick responded without turning around.

"No. It is not a normal river at all." He rose to look at her, his eyes settling on his brother's smaller form.

"This is in fact a remnant of the Ancient Spring, and it wasn't here a year ago."

Brendar nodded, "I have been tracking its movements, and its flow comes from the mountains." He pointed toward the Indigo shadows to the south. "But it comes from inside the mountain, not some top frozen point. And if you follow it three miles up north, it curves into the Unmade land." He shuddered. "I haven't followed it there."

"It was calling me." She took her own turn to kneel before the raging river, longing to reach out and touch it, but afraid with her newfound knowledge.

"Does Jyren know about this?" Belick's low voice rumbled behind her, worry encircling every word.

"He can know all he wants, but this isn't a side of the Spring I've seen before. I tried to touch it and nearly lost my hand. We aren't welcome in it anymore."

"I felt the same thing, it's...wild. Or dangerous. It won't allow itself to be taken without its consent."

Syra studied the moving water, it's white shimmer more beautiful than anything she had seen before. She didn't feel danger. Instead she felt an invitation. To taste and see.

A thought occurred to her, and she reared back, turning on Belick.

"This river comes from your mountains."

Her accusation was met with a knowing nod, and Belick's eyes darted to Brendar.

He sighed and lowered himself down, looking suddenly tired.

They squatted down, settling in for what could be a longer explanation, but when it came it was simple.

"Yes. The Spring is in my mountains."

Brendar's head jerked back and he whistled a long note, leaning back on an arm.

"That is an age-long secret many would kill for, Bro."

Syra just sat, glaring at him as she waited for more. He looked content to nod and say nothing until he looked up and saw her face, tensing slightly and hurrying to explain.

"I do not know how the Ancient Magic decides where Its Spring goes! I did not create this! But It settled in my kingdom before we disappeared, and I swore to protect it! I was going to tell you when I brought you there, but you must understand, Syra, this is a secret my people would die to keep. Even uttering the words out loud of Its existence there is treasonous."

Stamping out her hurt, she pulled at the fabric on her dark grey shirt, welcoming the breeze her sweat-layered body craved. They were missing something important here. She shut her eyes, trying to put the pieces together.

"So the Ancient Magic can move the Spring-"

"*Its* Spring. They are connected, there is no separating the Ancient Magic and the Spring." Brendar spoke with a piece of grass sticking out of his mouth, not bothering to look at her as he broke pieces of foliage in his hands to pass the time.

Syra began to roll her eyes, but stopped short. She had never known that. The Spring was an extension of the Ancient Magic, rather than a source of objective power. If the Ancient Magic was all powerful, how could someone steal part of it? There had to be some intentionality to this all...

She shook her head, "The Ancient Magic can move Its Spring at will but you haven't ever known how. It has been in *your* mountains," She points to Belick with an open hand, "for the past thousand years? And now suddenly there is a river full of Magic neither of you have seen or created that runs from the Ancient Spring to the Unmade Land west."

Brendar gave another whistle and looked up from his growing grass-bracelet.

"She is smart, brother!"

Belick nodded in understanding, more perplexed now with answers than before without them.

"The Spring is moving, and It's going to the Unmade Land."

Syra nodded with shining eyes, getting up to go back to the river's edge.

"And it called me here. I think... I think we need to follow it."

Belick shot up to his feet. "Follow *that*? Into the Unmade? Both of those are horrible ideas separately! You are just putting two *very* dangerous things together! Let the Spring find a new home where no one can take it!"

Syra shook her head, her eyes following the rivers line out west. "There is a reason the Ancient Magic does things, yes?"

Brendar stuck his bottom lip out and shrugged an affirmation as Belick folded his arms.

"The Ancient Magic never does anything without wisdom. It knows everything." His face softened at the thought, an ache overcoming his features as memories brought him back to days when the Ancient Magic was his father.

"Belick, I think it is doing something even now. I know I felt pulled to this place, and the Spring is moving. I think the Ancient Magic is leading us somewhere, and I will go."

She turned to Brendar, tossing a rock his way to get his attention away from his now thick grass bracelet.

"You created water. Can you make me something that we could ride along this river?"

Brendar grinned ear to ear and raised a finger in the air, "Ah! No."

"What? What do you mean? Even your descendants ride waves smaller than these!"

Brendar just continued threading a blade of grass through another one, twisting it around to secure it in the weave.

"Yes, but *that* is just water. It deserves respect in its own right, but *this* river is the Ancient Magic Itself. Nothing I make could ever survive the Spring's power. Too risky."

Syra huffed, looking back at the river and seeing nothing so scary but realizing she had few other options but to turn to the Spring Itself for the answer.

She bent down to the water and thrust her hand in before either men could stop her, and the world exploded white.

CHAPTER 10

LUIK

Blurry images of dusty red and orange fluttered in and out of his vision as a man and woman's murmuring voices echoed from a distance. His head hurt, but he recognized them. Or did he? Bloody springs, his head hurt.

Luik groaned and attempted to sit up, waves of nausea pushing him back down. He closed his eyes again and drifted back off.

"... The term for..."

"How have we never.... histories are skewed.."

"Very skewed. That is the way of kingdoms, to present the past as they like it."

Luik opened his eyes slowly, placing voices with memories as he remembered this time to stay lying down.

He turned his head slightly to the speakers, his entire body tensing as his eyes landed on one who was nothing at all as he remembered. The sorry creature in front of him wore a simple dress that hung over her bone-thin body, and her hair no longer held a sheen of mysterious red and brown, instead looking a dull graying color with limp curls surrounding her sunken cheeks.

She spoke to a woman he could only presume to be Loharan at a makeshift table in a small room, lit by a multitude of lanterns.

"But how could Anaratha have missed so much? Why didn't you at least tell us?" Michale lowered her eyes and sunk into herself, obviously embarrassed by the outburst. *This* was not the bloody princess he knew.

His anger began to rise.

This… *thing* was not the strong hurricane of a woman he dreamed of seeing on her knees, sobbing over the loss of her own kingdom. This was a pitiful animal. Broken and tamed. Bloody springs.

The Loharan woman sighed, her full, attractive face turning downward.

"We have seen how Anarathans read the ancient text and would not give them more to twist to their own will."

Michale nodded solemnly, going back to her reading and picking up a glass of water with shaky bones.

What in bloody Jyren's grave happened underneath that kingdom?

His own thoughts were cut short as a soft gasp brought the Loharan woman quickly to his side, placing a hand on his forehead and feeling areas along his neck. She finally stopped, her calm demeanor giving way to relief.

"You barely lived. Use your life well." She looked at him pointedly and patted his hand. He squinted at her in return, unsure of what the appropriate response to that would be.

"I will get you some broth. You will be hungry for the next few days and need to double your fluids." She rose and hurried away.

Michale'thia sat on her seat, her wide eyes watching his every movement.

He scowled back at her and jerked his head away, regretting the forceful movement immediately. He could hear her chair scrape against the floor and knew she was fleeing. Not so bloody fast.

"What happened to you? You look like a street mutt without its gang." He kept his eyes fastened to the ceiling.

She didn't turn from the door, but he could still sense the slump of her shoulders. The room was silent as he waited.

"Nothing as bad as what I did to you." And with that she slipped out the door, leaving Luik confused and alone in his anger.

The broth brought to him did more than fill his stomach, it rejuvenated his body in a way he could only describe as miraculous. After two more rounds of sleeping, waking, drinking, and then sleeping again, he found himself able to rise without nausea and walk around his room, moving to the back of the room where a blanket covered an area for him to relieve himself. A mirror, bucket of water, and towel lay on the ground, and Luik pulled out his knife. It was time to be bloody charming. A half hour later his beard was gone and hair pulled back again. He searched his pack for a change of shirt, finding his own sticky with whatever mixture they had been putting on his skin.

By the time he walked out of his room, he felt like a new man. Or at least, he felt like he could act like a new man. He would never be as he once was.

No, instead he could feel something growing, something darker and crueler than he, and yet somehow now a part of himself. Well he would use it and make them all bloody pay.

Stepping out of the hallway, Luik prepared to wander around the desert settlement until he found Michale'thia, but found himself on a balcony instead, blinking back dizziness as he took in the sight.

"Springs... what is this?"

It was an entire world he had never seen, with large crystal-like objects glowing like the sun and farmers below tending to their fields. His eyes followed the walls upward and he realized with a start that they were *under* the world, not in a different one. He grinned to himself; the bloody Loharans had tricked them all.

"It's quite impressive, isn't it?" Luik tensed and turned toward the voice, finding Dagen sitting in a chair in the corner of the balcony, a book in his hands and a stack of six more beside him. He smiled wearily, new lines etched on his face since the last time they had seen each other. A year ago. A lifetime ago.

Luik took in his loose shirt and dark pants, studying his appearance as an excuse to gather his thoughts. This was his best friend. His greatest confidant and the man who brought peace to his kingdom through wisdom unheard of. The Anarathan who refused to be Anarathan.

Dagen scooted the chair next to him out and motioned leisurely for Luik to sit, but those eyes saw too much for comfort, holding a tired understanding he found unnerving.

"Dagen. It's been a while." He sat stiffly, crossing his arms.

"I'm sorry, Luik. I should have been there for you."

The apology took him off guard and Luik shifted in his seat.

Dagen sighed and put his book down.

"It took every minute I had to get everything ready to get her out, and I couldn't leave her there." His voice turned soft as he whispered the next words reverently. "My wife."

Luik frowned. He had believed this past year that Micahle'thia was really running the kingdom in some mastermind move to prove she was the Heir of the Prophecies. Of course Syra and Belick would take her side. But seeing her today tore that schema apart.

"What happened to her?" Luik turned to Dagen, watching his face darken and jaw clench.

"From what we have pieced together, Jyres have been masking themselves as Anarathan high royalty and somehow created a device that would siphon the magic from her royal blood and use it to create a new version of the *jinti* drug. Reports from Enith say the royals in the kingdom are living outwardly like zombies but are experiencing hallucinations of a perfect life. We still don't fully understand it, but Michale was the key."

Dagen paused abruptly, bending over to stare at his open hands. Seconds ticked by and Luik glanced over at him.

Dagen's voice came out broken then, the shattered man showing beneath the strength.

"They locked her in a cage barely tall enough to stand in and left her there to be tortured day in and day out. I had to enter that cage to get her out, and the pain... it was like something ripping apart every part of you and shredding it over and over again. I can't..." He ground his teeth against hot tears gathering in his eyes.

"I don't know how she's alive, Lu. The pain was unlike anything I could imagine, and she lived it every moment for a year. I don't know if I could have done it for five minutes."

Luik sat beside his friend, watching tears flow freely down his face now as he sat back and shook his head in disbelief.

"I'm sorry. That sounds… awful." But even as he said the words his gut twisted. At least she could come back from it. Her muscle would return, her hair would shimmer again, and even if it took years *she would get back what she lost.* He would never. Because of her.

Luik stood quickly, hiding his fists behind his back.

"I am going to explore. I'll see you later, Dagen."

He could feel Dagen's eyes on his back as he retreated from the balcony, nearly running to get away. Where was the bloody door out of this building?

He eventually found a long staircase down and made his way out of the structure lining the walls of the cavern. If he was going to accomplish his end of the bargain, he would need to learn everything he could from these people. Specifically how to drug someone with magic.

The library was more like a city in itself, shelves of books looming above ladders with small shelves attached lining every row. He turned past the first row and found a map of the library showing symbols of the book groupings on different floors. He followed the map up toward the staircases up and only managed to whittle down the book options to about ten thousand.

A Loharan child in a brown robe noticed him and hurried over, carrying a notebook and pen alongside a basket of books.

"What do you search for?"

"I am looking for.. Um. Well, two things. I want something on herbal remedies and another on people who had the Ancient Magic in them."

The child looked at him in confusion, glancing around for help before turning back to respond slowly.

"Yes, but what are you searching for?" The child said the words carefully, as if Luik couldn't speak the language well enough to understand. It took two or three more responses to realize the vast amount of books made such a request akin to saying "I want food" when a bakery is prepared to take your order. He gave as much detail as he could, hoping the child didn't repeat this to his elders, and found himself in a corner with two stacks of books taller than himself.

He growled at the stack and rested his head on the table. How was he going to do this? Where was that bloody kauf when he needed it?

Hours of study only brought him one or two facts of use and at least three hundred he didn't need to know. He finally stood up to stretch his back, wondering how many days Michale'thia and Dagen would stay here. As he stood, dull curls caught his eye and he found Michale'thia sitting at a table, a stack of her own books waiting to be read… Except they looked much older than his.

He ducked to turn away and slip out the door, but thought better of it and turned around instead.

Luik strolled over to Michale's table and plunked himself down, watching her start in surprise. At least she still had her weird concentration thing. She never could see someone coming if she had her nose in a book.

"So, uh.. What's your latest project over here?"

Michale'thia blinked, looking around at her books and notes, as if remembering where she was.

"Oh, this. I am reading prophecies and histories Anaratha hasn't had access to." She pulled out a page of notes to hold up, setting it down with heated cheeks.

"Not that we would have interpreted it right anyway, I suppose."

Luik gave a tight-lipped smile in return, edging around that conversation.

"Ah, I see. And are you finding anything good?"

For a moment her eyes lit up before she ducked her head again, fumbling with her books.

"Yes, it would seem the prophecy we had was a single verse in what may have been a four part prophecy. Each part of the prophecy was recorded as being said by seven different people in *very* different parts of Elharren. The Loharans must have been collecting these meticulously to have so many original scripts saved and frozen in embalming gel. It is hard to understand how to rightfully interpret these now, since I have grown up thinking different words meant specific things the text doesn't necessarily define, but the Loharen's believe that the Perfect One actually refers to the Ancient Magic and Its own guidance to the utopia lost in Jyren's betrayal."

He could see her eyes glaze over and knew she was lost in her project again, but it lasted a slow minute, ending with her bringing a hand to her head and wincing. She glanced at him and her face reddened, a welcome color in her near colorless skin.

"So... that means you aren't the Heir of the Prophecies... and there is none?"

Her head bobbed up and down and she searched her notes until she found a specific piece.

"Yes, you see, the Loharans claim they have histories showing "the perfect one" to be a phrase used in the early years for the Ancient

Magic, so the prophecies then would be given through their own linguistic understanding. The Ancient Magic spoke through people, but kept their own personality and culture in tact."

Luik squinted his eyes, not following. She looked around the table and found a blank sheet of paper, quickly sketching the form of a human and a cloud beside it.

"If this is the Magic, and these the humans, what would you consider a human who was so completely overtaken by the Magic that they were no longer themselves?"

Luik thought for a moment, remembering tales from his childhood of people possessed with evil spirits and committing atrocious acts they would never remember.

"Creepy...no possessed. They would be possessed."

Michale nodded, pointing toward the page, "Yes, exactly. And do you think that is good or bad?"

Luik watched her face for any sign of where this was going, thankful when his response was what she was looking for. He took a seat across from her.

"Bad? Yes, bad. We want to keep ourselves, thank you very much." He shifted uncomfortably, feeling annoyingly like his ten year old self in front of angry tutors again.

"You're right, we don't look kindly on "possession" of our bodies. Something in us sees it as intrinsically bad. But what could happen if the Ancient Magic say, brought incredible wisdom to their minds and they had a sort of epiphany, but the exact epiphany the Magic placed there, and they spoke that knowledge out. They would do so with full control of themselves and proclaim it in their own natural tongue, using phrases and examples relating to their specific culture and time. It's brilliant!"

She sat back smiling, obviously getting *much* more out of this than he was.

"So what does that all mean?"

"It means the language cannot be understood today as we might understand the words. The culture at the time of every prophecy needs to be studied to fully understand. There is a "there and then" to understand *before* we interpret it for the "here and now". Which is something we were never taught in Anaratha, it's why we missed the real meaning."

She folded her hands in her lap as she finished, leaving Luik unsure of what to do next. Luik could feel a growing pit in his stomach, the echo of whatever was left alive inside his soul. What if there was still hope for something better?

Luik squeezed his eyes shut and pinched the bridge of his nose against the onslaught of images flooding through his mind. Face after face of those who would never know whatever hope was still out there in the world, because the woman before him slaughtered them. He launched himself up from his chair, catching it before it fell to the ground.

"Right, well that sounds like a lot of work. I'll let you continue on." He stood and left her there with slightly bent shoulders, too eager to say the things he didn't want to hear.

Two days passed, and Luik swore Michale'thia looked bright and fuller each time he saw her. Her hair was gaining more volume and her face filling out. Were they feeding her ten bloody meals a day?

But each day he spent in the library he became even more disheart-ened. With the Ancient Magic in someone's veins, there was no 'sur-prise drugging' a person. In fact, there was no attacking them at all without threatening to blow themselves up with magic. Was that his enemy now? The Ancient Magic? He could feel his own soul throbbing at the admission, not from grief but in a hot, angry agony. The Ancient Magic and these prophecies are what destroyed his people. He looked toward the library as a fleeting idea took hold in his mind. It was time this bloody prophecy stuff died once and for all.

Luik found himself watching Dagen watch Michale'thia, his insides warring within him again. He *hated* Michale'thia. But he loved Dagen. And he longed for Syra. Michale had them both spellbound and they continuously chose *her* over him.

He walked into their shared eating room after having spent the past hour in the fields, learning how they grew crops without sunlight. His people could have hidden underground if they had known what was coming. Michale *finally* began talking with Dagen without murdering him with her eyes, and they sat amiably now, cups of steaming tea half drunk and their own notes and books strewn about every surface of the room.

When he walked in the room, the pair looked up and Dagen waved him over.

"We may have found something." He nodded eagerly, rising to pour Luik a cup of tea.

Michale was on the edge of her seat and began speaking rapidly.

"I believe the prophecies were speaking about the Ancient Magic somehow physically leading people to a *new* land *It* had specifically cre-ated for us." She pushed herself up from the table, pacing about.

"And but this point in time, we have Elharren mapped out, there is no stone left unturned. But there is one place we've never been able to explore: the gray lands to the west."

Luik shot a glance over at Dagen, realizing he had no idea what Michale's goal in all of this was.

"Lu, it means the prophecies were wrong, but their end proclamation may have been correct. There is a perfect land out there somewhere waiting for us to find. An "other" that we can settle into and start over."

Luik stuttered. "Wait, you want to go *find it?* And then what? Who is the "we" that you want to resettle?"

Dagen and Michale looked at each other and shrugged as if they hadn't considered that.

She tightened the string on her hair as her brows knit together.

"Anyone who wants to. Dagen told me Anaratha has continued hunting mixbloods. There has to be a place we can all go. But I suppose I don't know who the prophecies refer to...that isn't entirely clear in any scholar's study that I can see. I don't know if "pure" refers to a bloodline, a lifestyle, or something else. I suppose we shoot for anyone who wants to come and figure out what to do if some can't."

"And you are going to base your entire lives now around this small possibility?"

Michale'thia lifted a corner of her mouth into something close to a smile and nodded. "If there is a place untainted and unbroken by humanity, that is still ready to welcome us in, then I think it is worth the journey."

Dagen looked thoughtful as he nodded and Luik felt his own panic rise. His friend smiled then and nudged Luik.

"Well, are you ready to journey somewhere we've never been?" Dagen smiled. "Two places actually. The Botani mountains to meet up with Belick and Syra and share the news, and then west. Where no living man has gone."

But Luik wasn't. He wasn't sure how many more journeys he could take with the growing weight in his chest. The more it grew, the more sure he was it would be his death.

CHAPTER 11

DAGEN

D agen could smell the smoke before he heard the screams. He sprung out of bed and sprinted down the steps toward the open air, eyes searching for flames. Loharans around him ran screaming, while others wept on their knees, crying out and clutching the grass.

His eyes found the flames easily. The center of the city, the Library, was engulfed in fire. Lines of Loharans were desperately pouring buckets of water onto the mass of angry red only accentuated by the glass around it. The building would survive, but the fire inside was consuming the work their entire lives were centered around.

Michale'thia came to a halt beside him, gasping as she brought her hands to her mouth in horror. Dagen didn't need to look at her to know she was crying, and without thinking gathered her into his arms as she wept. She tightened at first but didn't pull away.

They watched, unsure of what to do or how to help as the Loharans worked tirelessly until even they just sat and watched the flames devour everything they held dear. At least ten men and women who had tried to go into the building to save a few books were lost, and dozens of others were being hauled out by herbalists to treat severe burns covering their body.

The weeping continued from the Loharans, a mass mourning of wailing and anger. From the smokey rubble Dagen could see a larger form jogging away from the fire in their direction, eventually recognizing Luik's face beneath the black soot and burnt clothing. Luik's stark white eyes flicked toward them and Dagen *almost* thought he stumbled, but the Brend King squared his shoulders and came to meet with a face filled with hardened grief and anger.

He sat down on the other side of Dagen and hung his head.

"I tried to help. They are... broken down there."

Dagen felt a stab of pain as he imagined the rich culture and knowledge so dear to the Loharans, lost.

"Their lives were dedicated to this. Now it's all gone." Dagen looked down, feeling his own anger surface. Did *everything* everyone loved have to break? Was that their new reality?

"I don't know what they will do now." The warm hand that slid into his was so surprising he forgot to breathe. The small, delicate hand that held more strength than any human he knew, now lent it to him. He glanced over at her, but she kept stern eyes forward.

Springs, she was beautiful. She was beautiful when they met, and beautiful after the cage, and she was beautiful now. It was a beauty of change and survival, of having endured and come back. And he loved her. Somehow in this past year without her, he had realized how fiercely he wanted their lives to be done together, side by side. And the agony of not knowing if she would ever return to him, the nights of nightmares and wondering had nearly been the end of him. But seeing her eyes now, just like on their trip here, still full of strength she didn't even realize she still had but fully directed against him...it was a gift.

She *would* heal, no matter the years or lifetime it took. She was still alive inside and that was enough for now.

His eyes took the new color to her skin, showing her Anaratha roots below light freckles and cheekbones that could be described as high instead of caved in. Heltr waves were returning, pulled into a bun behind her head but straying around her face. It took every ounce of self control not to kiss her shoulder peeking out from her Loharan tunic shirt. To kiss his wife.

Dagen looked back at the smoking Library, reminding himself that it may never come to pass, and that was ok. She was his *wife*, and that meant they would honor each other to their last breath. If she needed a friend for a lifetime, he would fight this fight day after day. And maybe do his best to woo her along the way. He smiled at the thought.

Another hour passed before the flames were out, having eaten alive all the scrolls and books in the Library, and the three of them moved slowly to find something to eat and prepare for their journey.

As they made their way back to their cutout in the clay, Meili found them, tears streaking her full face and black stains covering her robes. She kept her eyes lowered, refusing to look them in the eyes.

"Excuse me, Dagen and Michale'thia, but the elders wish to speak with you."

Dagen glanced at Michale, whose face darkened even as she nodded and let Meili lead them away. She slowed Dagen and spoke in a low voice.

"They think we did this."

Surprise shot through his body and his mouth opened, only to shut. Of course they would think they did it. The Loharans loved their Library and had lived peaceably for a thousand years, only to take in a few refugees and then have it burn down. He ran a hand through his hair, suddenly wary of their surroundings. He would not let her be taken again.

"I don't know how we can prove to them we weren't there except to call for witnesses who may have seen us come out of our rooms. I think we are going to have to hear what they have to say and go from there."

She nodded, rubbing a hand over her free arm.

"They have lost so much today. I don't understand how they are even ready to talk."

Dagen processed that, realizing this may be a harder conversation than they thought it would be.

They reached a cutout at the northern point of the cavern and were led into a large room with a ceiling tall enough to hold at least two more floors. The elders sat on the floor, mats under each one and tears evident in every face. It was not hostility they were met with, only a deep, deep grief.

The lined eyes of the Loharan elders met Dagen and Michalethia's with sorrow as their hunched forms bespoke a loss too great to bear. They could each be well over a hundred years old, he noted. These were not naive and new leaders, they were seasoned in the ways of humanity through both knowledge and experience.

Two mats were open for them, with children in robes pouring tea for each person around the light-filled room. When everyone held a full cup, all eyes turned to a woman who seemed even older than the rest, her eyes barely seen through drooping skin, but her grip strong on her cup. She bowed her head for a moment, unperturbed by the silence, took a sip of her tea before setting the cup down and lifting her head.

"We knew this day would come." Her voice croaked in a high note, echoing throughout the room.

"Our prophecies spoke of a time when we no longer had a will to stay and must journey away to the fulfillment of the prophecy." Her gaze turned toward the Anarathans.

"Yes. We knew this day would come." She pinned them with a hard look. "But still, the grief is much more than we can bear." Her wrinkles seemed to droop further down as she sighed, rising from the table to half heartedly point to a map behind her.

"But we do not know the outside world like you do. Our knowledge is not enough to protect our people. You will go and find the path, we will prepare, and you will bring us out of this place and into a new land."

The room was silent again, and Dagen looked around for any more explanation, but none came.

"So you want us to tell you if we find what the prophecies alluded to?"

The woman's eyebrow skin moved upward in what may have been a raised brow, and she spoke more forcefully. "You *will* lead us there, child, not just tell us. We must have a guide."

Dagen shook his head and looked at Michale, whose compassion shone evidently in her eyes. She looked back toward the elders, and gave a small nod.

"We cannot ensure our own ability to come back, but we will provide a guide for you if we should find something."

The elders looked at each other and then to the eldest woman, seeming to take their cues from her. To Dagen's relief, the woman accepted the response with a few nods of her own.

"Good, good. We thank you."

Michale pushed her loose strands behind her ears. "How did it start? What happened?"

The elders murmured to each other quietly, her question bringing out their aggravation.

"We do not know for sure, child, and it is not wise to accuse without sure knowledge. What is done is done, and we move to the next age."

Dagen left the room in confusion. They knew who started the fire, and would not take action , but he couldn't help wonder if their failure to invite Luik to the meeting had anything to do with that.

Dagen packed his new cloths, thankful for the salves, herb, and variety of food the Loharans had gifted them for the road. He didn't understand them, but he was thankful. In the midst of their suffering they would care for their guests so well. It was foreign to him.

The new pack they had provided was lighter somehow, with pockets inside allowing for a multitude of items to be packed. Michale'thia came with a smaller pack of her own, her blankets tied to the top and her arms looking more ready for the task than they had days ago.

Luik silently joined, his old pack and clothing stubbornly in place. They said their goodbyes to the few Loharan's who would see them and turned toward the white trail up and out of the underground kingdom.

As they began to leave, Meili ran to meet them, towing a a rigul behind her loaded with water, extra blankets, and baskets heaping full of food. She came to a halt and gave them a sad smile, handing the reins to Michale'thia.

"We are in the middle of the desert," She explained. "You could make it out without this, but you would barely be alive. My rigul knows the way back to us and will take you to the southern edge of the desert."

Michale's eyes sparkled with fresh tears and the two new friends embraced, saying their final goodbyes. They rode the rigul out of the cavern and back into the scorching heat, well hidden when they were beneath the sand.

Dagen turned to Luik and Michale, running his hand over the rigul's leather skin and glancing back at the map the elders had given him.

"Well, we have about a day and a half if I am reading this right, and then we will be on foot for another week until we reach the Botani mountains. We should have quite the reunion when we get there." Michale and Luik mirrored a mix of excitement and fear, neither having seen their loved ones for too long.

They began their journey and rode in silence, lost in thought and too drained by the sun to engage in conversation anyway. Night came sooner than Dagen imagined, and they opted for taking shifts asleep as one person guided the rigul. At this pace, they could be back on green grass by morning.

Dagen took the first shift, allowing Michale and Luik to lie back between the rolled blankets to sleep for a sweet few hours. He could hear Michale'thia tossing and turning for what seemed like an eternity before feeling the blankets shift and hearing her rise up quietly to join him in front, a blanket wrapped around her shoulders and her hair loose down her back. He was suddenly more awake than he had been all night.

She stared at him as he scanned the horizon, busying his eyes with anything he could. When her stair became too pointed to ignore he glanced back at her, alarms raising in his mind as he could see a war within her own thoughts. Why did she fight him so much? He knew she was *trying* to keep him out, but he felt like an idiot wandering blindly about, trying different things to see what she needed and what she hated. He wasn't sure if it was pathetic or poetic of him.

"I can feel it still."

He turned to her fully then. "Feel what?"

"The Botani Mountains. I couldn't feel it before, but I feel it again. It's a longing so deep I am not sure what to do with it."

Dagen studied her a moment longer, wondering what their future would hold.

"I'm glad we are going. That you get to be there."

It seemed to be the correct response and she nodded quietly, resting her chin on her tucked knees.

"Can you tell me about it?" His voice was low and almost too afraid to ask.

She turned her head away, silent, and Dagen worried he had asked too much too soon. But after a few minutes her fragile voice began to speak.

"I had met with my father and his council and decided to tell them where my studies had taken me. All I remember after that are vague pictures until I woke underneath the castle, tied to a table. They kept me in the... cage... everyday, letting me out for water and a small piece of meat or bread to keep me alive. I would have five minutes to eat and drink all I could before going back in. I think they would leave water in the cage too, and I must have drank it, but I could never think clearly with so much pain. Sometimes I would count to ten over and over again to try to get me through the next minute, and then the next." Tears were flowing down her face now, but her expression remained blank.

"When people would come to look at me, at first I would try to beg them to help, but I couldn't form the words or stop screaming.

And no one stayed." She turned to look at him then, hurt painted clearly in her eyes. She hurried her face in her knees and choked back a sob, sucking in a shaky breath.

"Why did you never come? I wondered every day if I would see your face, and you never came."

Dagen felt his own breath catch, the aching in his heart overflowing as he watched the pain he caused reflect back to him. He shook his head, squeezing his eyes shut and running a hand over his eyes to wipe his own tears. How would he make her understand? What words could ever describe the breaking his own soul had endured at her pain?

"I was a coward. Weak." He looked away, blinking back tears to no avail.

"If I visited you, I knew nothing would stop me from murdering every guard and trying to save you right then, and it would have gotten me killed and ruined our chances of getting you out. The thought alone of you being... there, kept me awake night after night. I would see your face again and again..." Dagen's voice cracked and he brought a hand to his face as sobbs began to rack his shoulders.

"I couldn't see you and live with myself. I couldn't see the reality and not throw away every chance we had to get you out. It would have broken me, and I needed to be strong to save you." He wiped at his face and continued.

"I couldn't be wise *and* watch my beautiful, incredible wife be tortured. That's it. I would have ruined everything to save you, so I left you alone. Because I wasn't strong enough to be both there and here now." Saying the words aloud brought his failure closer than it had been that past year. He hung his head.

"I'm so sorry, Michale."

Without a word, with just sobs of her own, she leaned in and wrapped her arms around his waist, and together they mourned the life they were forced to live.

Morning came too quickly and Dagen woke to the sound of packs hitting the floor beneath them. His body was sore from sleeping in odd angles around their supplies, but the sight of lush green was enough to make him smile. They had made it to the southern edge of the desert.

Michale'thia was sitting up by now, her eyes bright at the sight of the mountains closer than before. They unloaded the rigul and sent him on his way, using the extra water to give the creature a drink for his journey back.

Luik pulled a pack onto his back and turned to them, pointing toward the west, away from the Jyre forest beside them.

"Belick told me once that there is a path this way. It should give us protection for the journey."

Dagen nodded, adding the last of his rolled blanket to his own pack.

"The delviors have been seen more frequently in the west, so we need to be careful. Keep our eyes peeled and ears open on this one. Lead the way, Luik."

Michale looked around as they began their next journey, probably having only just heard of the larger number of delviors that had been ravaging villages in the past year. He put a reassuring hand on her shoulder and smiled when she looked at him. He would protect her or die trying.

The days passed quickly with a new normal settling in. They would wake hours before dawn, Dagen would boil water to drink with the tea leaves the Loharans had left, Luik would hunt for either a nearby town, berries, or meat, and then they would eat, pack up and be ready to move by the time the sun rose. Dagen estimated there were putting in at least 20 marks a day, making great time on this western route. As they neared the mountain and left the Jyre forest behind, the towns were empty and too many had been burned to the ground, sometimes filled with bodies and other times obviously abandoned. Luik began to turn inward and Dagen could *feel* his bristling anger each time they found a new smoking house, but they didn't stop moving. Dagen could only hope Syra and Belick's past year warning villages had been a successful one.

They settled in for an early evening as the light began to fade, making their camp quickly around a fire and pulling out food to pass around. The mountains were bigger here than he had expected, looming tall and glorious in their indigo splendor, making him recognize his own small finitude.

"What do you think it will be like up there?" He sat back on his pack.

Luik shrugged and chewed a piece of stale bread. "I just want to know how we are going to get up in the first place. That trail died out days ago and there doesn't look like there is any other way up. What does Belick do, fly?"

Dagen grinned at him, wondering the same thing. These mountains didn't exactly show signs of friendly stairs or pathways for the outsider, but Belick had hinted at there being a way.

The confidence in Michale's voice startled him and he looked at her closely, seeing the longing there.

"There will be a way. Or we will make our own."

And unable to argue with that, they went to sleep.

CHAPTER 12

ENITH

E nith stumbled on the upward path, nearly invisible in the dark of night. He held in a groan, trying to keep the pain from showing. He was at the front of a much smaller group now, having nearly lost a fourth of their number to the Anarathan band of soldiers. They would have lost more too if the soldiers hadn't been set on bringing back the mix-bloods alive and able to work.

He took a careful step up a large rock, hoisting himself up and trying not to think of how far they had left to go. Enith had memorized the map. He had precisely timed their leave. They had trained their men valiantly for months. But in the end those men were cut down, leaving new widows carrying children alone, and grieving parents mourning the loss of their too young sons. Ilytha had lost a few, but their small number made the loss a deep wound.

He stopped walking, his old dark friend inside flaring at the day's events. The old twisting, dark bitterness he held since his own failed Test day seemed to only grow now, nearly cutting off his breath. He stopped what he was doing and ripped off his blue Anarathan jacket, throwing it off the cliff beside them in a fury. He had lost men, mourned them, but this was different. This was a hope shattered and broken, a helplessness to do anything but *keep moving forward*. He could feel Ilytha's eyes behind him and he pressed on.

They had been climbing this upward path for hours already, many wounded and all tired. The lack of light made it impossible to gauge when they would get there, and as far as he knew, the Botani people could live at the very top, miles and miles above. But they pressed on because there was no turning back.

Hours more passed and Enith noted the air *not* turning frigid as he was taught it would at this height, but too tired to ponder it, he sighed with relief when they came upon a meadow clearing in the middle of the dirt trail. A place to rest for the night with no fear of Anarathan soldiers coming. He barely even found the trail entrance *with* the map Belick snuck him.

He stood to the side and began spreading the word that they would make their camp here, hearing audible sighs of relief as heavy footsteps fumbled to roll out blankets on the soft grass. There couldn't be much left of the night, but they all welcomed sleep anyway. No one bothered to make a fire or set up an overhead shelter before bringing their children close to their tear-stained faces and dreaming their losses never happened.

Enith woke slowly, the sun already at its fourth mark in the sky. Sitting up was a painful process, but the wound seemed to have healed enough while he slept to keep the wound shut. He turned to find Ilytha sleeping next to him, curled gently under a blanket which fell just off her shoulder while her dark hair cascaded onto the grass. *This* was his wife. The wife he once, albeit unknowingly, fought for who now fought with him. The peace on her face was surreal, and Enith wondered if she would pull out her knife if he stole a kiss on her soft skin. He smiled at the thought of a tussle in the grass over his kiss, mentally accepting the challenge, and brushed his lips gently against her milky skin, moving a piece of hair off her shoulder as he filled his eyes with her. The woman was unlike any other he could ever know.

Her own eyes opened and confusion clouded them as Enith tensed, unsure if this "I am your wife" thing only applied to her making moves on him. Instead, she registered his face and a smile more brilliant than any sunrise he had seen broke through. It was a smile filled with joy and peace, a "rightness" to it that welcomed him in and for a moment he forgot his name and his pain and everything else in the world. She was his and he was hers. .

Her joy turned to shock as her eyes landed on something behind him, and Enith whirled around with his own knife out, freezing with his mouth agape when he took in the sight. They were not in a meadow in the middle of the trail to the Botani people. They were at the entrance of the kingdom.

Enith stood reverently and Ilytha joined him. There below, nestled in between mountains with land reaching all the way down to a beach, were what had to be hundreds of thousands of homes, with the center of the city clearly marked by large stone buildings and a palace that soared high, but was made with no doors at all. As he continued to stare, he could start to see separations of what must be villages with their own small market centers, fields lush with growth and tiered steps on the mountains. This wasn't the frozen kingdom they had been led to believe.

All around them flowers sprang up and bloomed near trees with ample shade and green leaves, with multiple streams flowing down around them, clear and bright with fresh water.

How had they never known about this?

Ilytha slipped her hand into his and he pulled her into a hug. This would be a new life. With a new people.

Around him he could hear others rousing and he pulled Ilytha away with a mischievous grin. They ran toward a towering tree with rope like branches too thick to see through dangling in the wind. He pulled her behind the swaying privacy, emboldened by the giggle escaping her lips.

He looked at her then, searching her face for any hesitancy and finding only his own longing staring back at him in her eyes. He pulled her tight against his body and kissed her deeply. What began as a gentle touch grew with passion, and when they finally moved apart it was Ilytha who spoke, her eyes shining and smile full.

"I have dreamed of the day our marriage became real." She tightened her embrace and laid her head on his chest.

Enith laughed and shook his head, enjoying the way she fit in his arms.

"I never thought it would happen. I thought you would find someone of your own choosing and marry, leaving me alone to pine for you the rest of my life."

Ilytha arched a brow at him. "I did find a man of my own choosing. I do not come to you because you were tricked in marrying me, I come to you because I could not think of any other man." She rolled her eyes and tilted her head. "Plus, it's convenient, you know? We are already married so..."

She shrugged in mock indifference and Enith threw his head back in a laugh, moving back to hold her hands and look in her eyes.

"Ilytha, I want to know you. This next journey, whatever it looks like, I want to properly... court you." He hurried on at her mocking brows raised in laughter.

"Look I just... bloody... I sound like an idiot." He took a breath.

"I want to know everything about you. Every memory, every mannerism, every passtime. All of it. You have been my mind's favorite thought and greatest regret this past year, but I have no reason for that other than seeing a small glimpse of who you are and being incredibly attracted to this beautiful, dark-haired woman who can hold such a fire in her. Then you come back as a warrior and leader in your own right, bringing women out of abuse and into confidence again. That is enough for me to love you. But I want to *know* you." He laughed at himself and ran a hand over his face.

"Springs, Ilytha, I want to know you for the rest of my life!"

Her long lashes blinked back tears and her full lips parted then shut. Her answer came as she wrapped her arms around his neck and held him tightly.

They left their hidden refuge and walked back to the meadow, spurred on by the excited whispers and hurried packing. He smiled at Ilytha. They all were mourning and hope filled, not beaten completely down as long as there was a home in the distance. Somehow, they would be free and whole.

"I think it would be wise for us two, or a small party at least, to enter in first and make our plea." He whispered over to Ilytha.

She nodded turning toward her warriors and spoke to them for a moment, bringing three back with her while the others spread out along the perimeter of their people.

They strode toward the city below, following the trail to an entrance made of intricate stone work, white and shimmering in an archway with two guards standing by. Enith approached, ready to convince the guards they were harmless refugees, but the guards spoke first, staring ahead impassively as one gave clipped orders.

"Go, bring your people." The guard on the left pointed his spear past Enith's shoulder, causing Ilytha to tense and grasp her own. His shirtless frame was well defined, and his dark skin rippled with muscle from years of hard training his weapon.

Enith backed away and whispered to his small entourage. "I don't think they are prepared for a conversation."

One of Ilytha's warriors, the one with her dark hair tied tightly back behind her head, looked back and cocked her head, much like a bird would do.

"They did not seem threatening. That is a good sign, I think."

Enith nodded and they went to make the announcement, his command to follow making its way back toward the last thousand people slowly. Then as a large and slow number, they began to move toward the entrance.

The guards stood aside this time and Enith passed freely, eyes wide at the clear beauty around them.

Their people made their way down further toward the large city, but as they drew near, a large group of Botanis waited for them in turn.

Enith jogged ahead to reach them, leaving Ilytha to stop the group from proceeding until he gave the signal. He bowed his head as he came to a stop before the grouping of older, strong men and women.

A short man with a gold spear stood beside a tall woman with high cheekbones and tight curls gathered into a tie on top of her head, a firm but welcome expression on her face. The man spoke first.

"You must be Prince Enith, Royal of Anaratha. The one our Belick has sent word of."

Enith nodded, following Belick's instruction and lowering himself to his knees and bringing a fist to his heart.

"I am Enith, Prince of Anaratha no longer. I lay down my royalty and kingdom and seek to trade it for simple citizenship in yours."

He could hear soft gasps and whispers, the tones implicating respect and delight in his countenance.

"And do your people feel the same?" The woman's strong voice questioned.

Enith looked at the group then, going off script.

"The people I lead are outcasts and slaves of my own kin, who now seeks to murder all who have mixed bloodlines. The warrior women with me are those my wife has found outcast from her own society or abused until they could barely live. We all seek refuge here as new citizens, ready to learn and live a new life."

The man looked at him from beneath bushy eyebrows, his voice rumbling deeply.

"And you, Enith? You have nothing to lose from staying with your people. Why leave a position of honor to live with no position at all?"

Enith bowed his head then, fighting the flurry of emotions inside.

"The position of honor I have in my kingdom is only a truer dishonor to my soul and to the Ancient Magic. I believe my ancestor, Aleth, created beauty i na diversity of cultures, but that has been overshadowed by greed and power. He would delight in the changing and melding of food and tradition, and blood. So I deny my kingdom's claim and seek a better life here, where if you will have me, I can build a small hut and grow food with my wife and have a child or two or three that have both freckles and beautiful raven-black hair."

The smiles and laughs that broke out were those of men and women who knew love and saw it in the eyes of the young before them. And Enith knew then that they were welcome.

The tall woman clapped her hands warmly and laughed then, looking at those around here and receiving nods in return.

"You are all welcome here. Come, we have prepared food for your people." Enith's eyes widened at the prospect and he thought his chest would burst. They had made it. They were home.

He doubted they could feed a group of people his own size, and began calculating how he could spread the food they were given out among them all. They lead them through wide streets with a marbled stone buildings shining with flecks of pink and gray. When he walked through the city's center to the large field, he was overwhelmed. There were small fires scattered throughout, surrounded by baskets upon baskets of fish, fruit, and bread, all set beside large barrels of cool water. They had seen them coming.

Enith's eyes widened in wonder at the sight, watching his own people pour onto the field in mournful glee as they partook in food many of them had never seen the likes of. To most mixbloods who lived Anaratha, this was a feast. Fruit full and ripe with sweetness and bread soft and void of the normal stale mildew often afforded to them.

Groupings began to form around the fires, and he could hear the occasional laughing as children gained their energy and began to chase each other on the field, joined quickly by Botani children who brought round balls to kick and seemed well versed in the art of kindly making new friends.

Enith followed Ilytha down to a fire with a few less people, and they gathered around, smiling through their pain because the future was worth the joy. Eventually Ilytha's own closer friends joined their fire, and they all sat on the soft grass, enjoying the variety of bread and lack of soldiers needed in the safety of the mountain.

"So, royal prince," Jassah leered amiably, "what are you going to do without your grand palace comforts?"

Enith's eyes widened and he dropped his bread.

"Wait, you mean... I have to live without my *silk sheets?!*"

Jassah knew she was bested and rolled her eyes, laughing with the others at his dramatics.

He chuckled and tore a piece of his bread off, "You realize I've been living as a soldier for the most part of my later years, right? Cold floors, wet rainy nights. I like a simple life."

Ilytha arched a brow, "Well that simple life had better be able to afford *me* a comfortable bed. I will sleep where I must when I must, but I will always choose a bed if I can."

Enith nodded slowly, "Yes, I suppose we would need that, and a big one if all four of our children are going to snuggle in with us."

He waited for the rolled eyes and thrown bread that never came. Instead she just grunted in agreement and continued eating, lifting a slender hand to her mouth to eat a small blue fruit he had never seen before.

"No, I will not let them sleep in our bed. That is for us. You must build them a room of their own."

Enith's brows shot up and he glanced around to see if it was a joke. Instead he received nods as if it were the wisest comment in the world.

The picture then became crystal clear: waking up to Ilytha beside him, her hair strewn about in glory, and tiny feet with tinier giggles creaking the door to their room before spilling in and jumping onto their bed.

He found himself smiling ear to ear as he pictured a little girl with dark hair braided back, her light freckles peeking out above hazel eyes, and a little boy with a fake sword and puffed out chest below his angular chin, ready to try his hand against his dad again. Enith sighed, what a life that lay before them.

"Lovesick, fool." Jassah tossed bread at his head, but Ilytha was smiling contentedly herself, enjoying what she saw.

"Careful, Jassah, that is my husband. If you threaten him I will have to challenge you." Her smooth voice held a playful but dangerous challenge.

Jassah's own smile grew and she leapt to her feet. "Challenge me, commander! I will win this time!"

And in a flash every woman was up on their feet in a circle, grins covering faces as they cheered for both parties. Enith scrambled out of their way, wanting to stop the fight but certain that would only turn both of their short swords against him.

They danced back and forth playfully, sparring with easy smiles and he could see they were only warming up to the real fight.

Just as Jassah made the first thrust, the commanding woman from the Botani elder group approached, her own spear in hand and a knowing smile on her face. They faltered, stopping as if they might be in trouble.

The woman held up two strong hands around her spear, "Do not stop on my account. I believe you may be recruited into our own ranks if we see enough talent. We do need to speak with you though, Enith. There is much to discuss as we seek to get your people situated."

A pang of disappointment shot through him at the missed opportunity to see Ilytha train, but he rose and followed the woman, giving Ilytha a wink before he left.

He jogged to catch up to her retreating form, wincing as he remembered his own wound in his side.

"What may I call you? Are you an elder?"

She smiled and nodded as she kept her eyes forward, her regal steps more royal than anything he had seen growing up.

"My name is Hai'saray, but most of my friends and family call me Saray. You may do the same if you would like."

Enith smiled. There was something warm about her, and dangerous. He had no doubt she could lay him flat with that spear at his throat before he could blink, yet she seemed more apt to welcome people into her inner circle, like family. He had much to learn from the Botani people.

They walked a mile down toward the center of the city into the palace walls, which arched high over them with shining stone speckled with silver. They walked through the open archways up stairs and into a room overlooking the city. A large patio held an equally large table, big enough to fit the entire group of 14 comfortably. She took her seat around the table, which seemed to give no preference to a leader, and motioned to an open seat for him at the head of the table, making him stammer silently before obeying.

A light, refreshing wine was brought and passed around the table from elder to elder, each pouring a drink for the person to their right before passing it on. Enith's drink was poured by a lea man with lighter skin than most in the group, his own eyes showing his mixed blood as green stared back at him. Enith thanked the man and poured the cup to his own right, wondering again how Anaratha had missed learning about such a rich culture with so much to give.

He was prepared to begin discussing whatever the matter at hand was, but instead found the group raising their glasses and drinking, then turning to those around them to talk. Enith could hear questions about a cousin's health and a child's prayer answered, astounded at the intimacy this group seemed to have with one another. This was not a facade of friendship, hiding deep plots for power. It was a community. He was asked questions of his own, sharing their journey and his own new, or not, marriage to the sorrow and joy of those listening.

After a short time a man spoke up, calling the discussion to begin, and voices began to settle into silence.

"As you all know, the last of our refugees have made it safely to our land. We welcome them and share what we have. However, while there is much to celebrate, a problem has arisen we can no longer ignore." His sad eyes met Enith's then.

"Our land is dying, and we cannot stay here any longer."

CHAPTER 13

BELICK

Belick lay on his makeshift bed beside the river, flashes replaying in his mind of Syra's hand hitting the water and her body being engulfed in the white power of the Ancient Magic. It was too similar to his own fallen day when he and his brothers stole the Ancient Magic's Spring. He had been too far to stop her and his heart had nearly failed him, convinced she would either no longer have life in her veins or would know the same distance he had from the Ancient one. In the end, neither happened.

There was something different here. Different from their own journey to find more power from the Spring. In their time, so long ago, they had not sought out the Ancient Magic's wisdom or tried to think back on what It had taught. They had believed they knew wisdom and acted.

Syra did something entirely different. She didn't reach toward the Spring for more power. She reached out to connect with It, to pursue the Ancient Magic. To *ask* It what she should do. And in return, It poured power into her, and not just Its power, but as she explained it, a knowledge of what It declared good.

Belick looked up at the stars, fighting back jealousy and frustration. He used to have that. A closeness with the Magic that he called father. But he ruined it and now he held only a glimmer of that same communion.

They had been working the past day to build a boat light enough and deep enough to survive the rapids of the river, taking cues from Brendar and his *obsessive* knowledge about the water. Belick felt sick just thinking about being off land. He felt sick just being down from his mountain!

Sleep came hard and fitful, leaving him sore in the morning and more irritable than he would have liked. To Brendar's benefit though, he brought them food he had made using an abandoned bakery, which made everything seem brighter.

The grass around them was still wet with dew and the sky barely light. Syra looked over the fire toward the river, sweeping half of her hair back in a loose bun and adjusting her tunic.

"Does it look a little fuller to you?"

Belick turned around to study it, grimacing as he agreed. This could only mean the Spring was emptying at a more rapid pace daily. Which meant his own land would soon stop feeling the benefits of Its power. He tensed as his longing to be with his people returned, met with another fierce protectiveness of this small woman in front of him with stark white hair and large green eyes. He would stand beside her in this Unmade land. Then he would return to his people and find a way to live.

Brendar folded his arms and stood, squinting at the water and scratching his chin.

"Ai, it is getting fuller. I'm glad we made some high sides on this boat, but I think we may need to make something flatter now. That water level could fill us up and leave us out on our own."

Belick glared, not looking forward to another day of cutting and binding ahead of them.

"Brother, we will use what we have! Do not worry! I will just take the sides off and change the bottom a small amount. It will be done in half a day."

Brendar began his work, Syra kneeling alongside him to help pry off boards and pound in new shapes. The clanging of hammer against board went on for hours, and Belick eventually decided that creating a map of the Unmade in correlation to the River's direction would be more helpful than fighting the urge to rip the boat apart altogether.

He grabbed his pack and hiked further down the road, remembering a large rock structure he had seen a mile out that he swore was formed just like the Botani mountain range.

When he eventually reached the boulders, he quickly scaled his way up until he sat on the top. It was only twenty feet up in the air, but feeling suddenly lighter than before.

No more ringing of the hammer. No more insistent talking by his brother. Just outside to compliment his warring inside.

He breathed for a moment, his hands relaxing against the gray stone beneath him and his eyes taking in the sun to his right, already rising up out of the eastern sky. Belick opened his pack and pulled out a notebook, using his vantage point to see further into the Unmade land and sketching the likeness as well as he could. There was nothing for as far as he could see.

What was Syra and Brendar expecting? The brothers had *never* created there, and at the very most they would see the land crumble beneath them. He continued sketching, letting his mind wander back toward his own people and the problem they would soon begin to experience.

A pang tore through his stomach as he realized they would have to leave the mountain. His mountain. His refuge. It could never sustain a kingdom of its size without the Magic bringing about crops at such a fast and plentiful rate. *He* would have to leave his mountains.

His people would have to live down below, bringing the refugee mix-bloods back into a land surrounded by people who wanted them dead. The Botanis would soon enter war.

Belick shuddered and found himself suddenly unable to breathe, memories of blood-soaked bodies strewn about under a dark sky, limbs detached and eyes staring back accusingly as his blade dripped with their life. Then his own sweet Nira... and her own neck angled too wrong, too far.

He tripped over himself as he scrambled back from the boulder's edge, bile rising and his body preparing to retch. He dragged in a ragged breath, growling at his body as he fought against its revolt.

They would *not* become monsters again. He learned through broken memories and lost kin that the monster in man was not permitted to take life without consequence.

No, he would create again. Even if it was just with his bare hands. He would lead his people somewhere safe.

His eyes narrowed as he spun around and glared at the Unmade land, willing the mist to part and show *something* other than the nothingness he dreaded. No one but his brothers could understand that dread. The feeling of *nothing* that threatened to swallow one whole. How Brendar managed to ignore was a mystery to him.

Ancient Magic, please give us life where you are moving. Don't leave us behind.

Belick sat back down, his insides a little less twisted and mind a little less desperate. Syra was right. There was only one hope now.

A small form miles away caught Belick's eye, and he could just make out what seemed to be a large group on horseback, galloping their way. A hundred, maybe more, and heading directly toward Syra.

Belick jumped off the boulder, Magic pulsing in his veins to strengthen him for the fall, and began to sprint with every drop of energy he had. His backpack flew behind him and his feet were a blur, leaving trees and rocks behind. He had to get to Syra and warn her.

He arrived back at their site within five minutes and skidded to a halt before the raft, working to slow his breathing as quickly as possible.

Syra and Brendar started at his arrival, dropping their tools in and straightening a they searched the hills behind him.

"We have about a hundred heading our way."

Syra's brows lowered and Brendar whistled as he twirled his hammer. "That is a lot for the three of us."

Belick clenched his jaw. Brendar was right. They would never outrun the soldiers as long as they had horses, and there was nowhere to hide near enough. His mind raced, searching for a way out of this.

Syra just stared, turning back to look at the river as her eyes moved back and forth in thought. Belick could feel what she was thinking and nodded.

"Brendar, can it be ridden now?"

Brendar grimaced and wrinkled his nose nonchalantly, about to make a joke but taking a step back back instead when he saw Belick's own hardened face. They had minutes.

"It will be rough, but it will survive. I can nail on a few extra boards and take the hammer and rope with us if we need repairs."

"Do it, now."

Syra began throwing her extra hammer in her pack alongside the food and blankets, stuffing it tight and tying it off. She threw it on her back and jogged toward Brendar, who had already hammered a few extra boards in and was ready to push it to the edge.

Brendar looked at Belick with a serious glare now.

"Brother, you know we cannot avoid this any longer."

Belick nodded and Syra frowned, looking back and forth between them.

"Come, let us see if the Ancient Magic will permit us to come near."

The brothers moved swiftly toward the river, each tense and unsure, then looking at each other's eyes, thrust their fingers into the white power.

Brendar yelped and Belick cried out, both bringing bloodied hands back, searing with the pain of a burn.

Brendar shook his hand and Belick opened and closed his, trying to think quickly. It began to heal, but the message was clear. They were not welcome in the Spring.

He took Syra by the shoulders, looking her in the eyes with a hard stare.

"You must go alone. And *you must* come back. You are who was called, and you are who will be protected by the Spring."

Syra opened her mouth to argue, but the thundering of hooves began to ring out and Belick and Brendar shot one look to each other before pushing Syra on the raft boat, and pushing it off.

"Wait, no! Belick, you have to come!" The rapids began to take her and she clutched the main mast to stay upright. Guilt assaulted him at the betrayal in her eyes, but he starred back at her, determined to save her life even if it meant giving up their own. She was the only hope left.

And he saw it then, her panic soften into understanding and a nod to him. She would find what was out there and return. She must.

"I will stay, my sister." He whispered, before turning toward the horses skidding to a stop in front of him.

Instead of the Alethian soldiers he was expecting, there stood an army of Jyres, young, old, male and female. All prepared to take him.

Belick unsheathed his sword and Brendar picked up his heaviest hammer, standing their ground. Belick would not enjoy a battle, but he would fight to his end.

The blood pumping in his ears and the adrenaline rushing through his veins blinded him to the confused and scared faces staring back at him or Brendar lowering his hammer in surprise. The crowd parted and instead of a white-haired leader, he found tan skin, auburn-tousled hair, and freckles staring back at him.

Aleth's face broke into a smile and he opened his arms.

"Brothers!"

The world slowed back down and Belick blinked in confusion. What was happening?

He spoke carefully, keeping his eyes glued to the Jyres surrounding him, unsure whether Aleth was imprisoned or imprisoning.

"Aleth... this is an... Interesting surprise."

Brendar, on the other hand, rushed past him with a whoop and pulled Aleth from his horse, embracing him with glee.

"You don't look different at all! I see I am still the brother with the best hair." His dimpled cheeks and strong arms held Aleth at arms length.

Aleth grinned and winked at Belik, "I don't know, Brend, I think I see a bald spot." Brendar yelped and began feeling his own hair, glaring at Aleth as he did.

Belick felt his own anxiety melt and laughter rumble as their old tricks worked again. He glanced back at the Jyre people warily, catching Aleth's eye with a hidden question. He gave him a small smile.

"These are all that would leave Jyren and his ways. One hundred and twenty, counting children." He motioned to a woman with long hair flowing down her back, sitting stiffly beside a tall man whose face looked like it was etched from a painting.

"This is Raishara and her brother Nikoron. They have had a long journey but are part of the reason Dagen and Michale made it through the forest. Now they want a new life, and we are going to welcome them in."

Aleth looked at him squarely, and Belick could see the kingly stance he bore, unyielding in this proclamation. Aleth, the creator of peoples and culture. Lover of all. He should have been the sole king.

Belick nodded stiffly. Syra was different. They could be too.

He looked at the group and spoke softly. "Welcome. We have much to discuss. You are welcome to sit for a moment as we make a new plan."

Aleth frowned. "A new plan?"

"Let us talk in private, and we can share after. Please, there is much changing."

Belick and Brendar walked to the river, hearing the sharp intake of breath as Aleth took a step back, feeling the power pulse from each wave.

He turned sharply to Belick, bristling.

"This should be *hidden*."

Brendar stuffed hands in his pockets, chewing a blade of grass.

"But Brother-" Aleth's glare quieted his latest joke, and Brendar held his hands up and backed away slowly. Whispering a "good luck" to Belick.

Belick folded his arms and looked Aleth squarely in the face. It was time to admit what he should have shared long ago. The memories that rang in his ears every moment of the day.

It was all too clear, his time asleep not dulling the memory. To others, the wars were a thousand years ago. But to the Brothers, they were only a half-life in their past. What they did back then-who they were, it was war. And survival. And betrayal and loss and grief.

Belick closed his eyes against the ache in his heart. To betray a brother was a different kind of pain.

Dark clouds rumbled their threats but Broyane barely felt the downpour of rain assaulting his bloodied limbs. Everywhere he looked was death, with the ringing clang of swords and desperate pleas for mercy just moments before life was cut off, murdering something inside the killer just as much as the soul they took.

There was too much noise. Too many sounds and colors berating him from all sides and the world began to shrink. He picked up his sword, his fury growing as his own helplessness ripped his insides apart.

She was gone. With the daughter they made together in her womb. His people were mere hundreds now, too many slain, and he had become a monster, craving the blood of any he could blame for ruining their paradise.

He slashed another Jyre, the extra power from the Spring bringing him strength while raging against his use of it. He hacked and roared in anger, his cry lost in the angry battle surrounding him. Broyane screamed as he fought, slashing the last Jyre within ten feet of him. He paused, heaving in air and looked around at the never ending battle.

Then it was as if the Magic within him won the battle over his own mind and he saw it: something was wrong here.

Everything was wrong here. He dropped his snake of sword and looked at his bloodied hands as if for the first time, their background a pile of bodies young and old. How had he come to this? This beast?

Every justification he had given to suppress the guilt raced through his mind, each an inch toward this man he had become. He looked around helplessly, suddenly choking on the stench of slain bodies.

The crashes and screams of war around him grew louder in his ears and Broyane spun about, eyes wide as he begged the Ancient One to make it all untrue. But it was reality, and he had helped create it.

He dropped his sword then, the clang resounding in his ears louder than any noise. He could not be this monster this war made out of men.

No, not the war, their own selfishness and hunger for power. Their rejection of the Ancient One and rebellion against Its own law had caused the very breaking of the land.

The war hadn't turned men to monsters, it had began by men who were monsters.

And he ran.

He didn't think, or plan, or wonder at the consequences of his next few hours, he just ran until he found himself at his own mountains. The mountains he made to be a refuge from the world, and he climbed. The longing for peace and an end to broken humanity was so strong he could barely think of anything else but climbing the next frozen ledge. Purple fingers and a half-beating heart pulled Broyane onto the last ledge and it was with the heaviest of footsteps that he walked the mountain's summit.

His tears flowed freely in the quiet and he fell to his knees there, somehow feeling a new beginning settle in as he vowed to live anew. Without power and without fame. Without a sword. Simple and alone. Or so he thought.

Days later he found himself looking into the eyes of his own people, the people he had left on the battlefield, abandoned in his own remorse. And what he saw in their eyes broke him almost as much as the war did: brokenness. A deep, dark, mangling of who they were meant to be. Men, women, and children with sunken eyes and bloodied hands somehow made their way up and over the cliff's edge to stand before him and demand he lead them.

So day by day, they began to rebuild a land of peace. One the Ancient Magic had once spoken of. And little by little he watched as the white powerful trickle of a river began to flow through the crevice between the mountains, becoming a raging pit of roaring Magic that would fuel their new kingdom.

He would do his best every single day to forget he abandoned Aleth, his brother and ally, on the battlefield.

Belick finished his story to a storm brewing on Aleth's face. His hands clenched, eyes blazing as they bore into Belick.

"You left me to die." He ground out.

"I left you to fight as you will."

No longer diplomatic, Aleth's voice grew louder with every word.

"Your people *abandoned us*, Broyane, because *you* abandoned me! I watched nearly everyone I loved *slaughtered* that day! And all that time- you *knew* my love for the Ancient Magic, our *father*, and you kept me from it-"

"I'M SORRY!" Belick's voice roared, "I did it wrong, but I can't go back! If I could..." Tears were streaming freely now as he held his head, words failing.

Aleth's breath shook and his own tears poured out as he struggled for composure.

"If we could go back, we would never have stolen from the Ancient Magic and betrayed our father."

Belick felt something inside him break then, and he sank down to his knees as sobs racked his body.

"I see every life I took...Aleth, how did we take so many... I can't forget them. And my baby.. My wife..."

Aleth crumpled to the ground beside him, an arm on his rocking back as his silent tears attested to the truth of Belick's admissions.

Belick breathed deeply, wiping his face and looking up at Aleth with a scrunched nose in agony.

"I am sorry. So sorry, my friend."

Aleth grabbed his head from behind and pulled their foreheads together.

"We broke the world, Belick. And now we have to fix it. All of it. This time, we walk into the light."

Belick blinked back tears at their old childhood saying from when they were still naive and full of honor. The saying that reminded them of wisdom and truth in all they did.

"Into the light."

They rose and clasped arms, then turned to the Jyres who watched them with curiosity and confusion, some looking as if they might bolt.

Belick stepped forward.

"We have a long journey ahead. Eventually, we will follow this river out to the Unmade in *hope that* Syra returns with news of a place we can live. But until then, we ride to my mountains. It's time we joined forces with my family and start building what we need to get there."

Brendar smiled around his blade of grass, "Brothers, I have a few ideas for this."

CHAPTER 14

SYRA

There wasn't any time to process the goodbye she was just forced into as the waves rocked her raft dangerously, crashing over her head and sending her senses into a flurry. She grabbed a hold of the mast and gasped, unable to form a coherent thought as the wood floor was nearly ripped out from under her.

They pushed her out...

Another river wave hit her head on, sending the raft spiraling. She heaved for air, coughing and spitting out river water... or Magic.

They sent me alone.

The next hour was a blur, rapid after rapid assaulting her little raft-like boat, the sail only making her fly faster down the dangerous torrent.

She eventually found a rhythm, and managed to steer the boat slightly by leaning to one side or another and pulling the sail this way or that. A wave would crash and she would hold her breath, eyes searching and watchful for the next turn or boulder to avoid. After an hour, Syra finally began to feel like she was somewhat in control.

In what seemed like a blink of an eye, the river slowed to a gentle rush, moving her raft gently along its waters. Her sail was catching a breeze and she moved at a slow, steady pace, following the Magic where it would lead.

Syra sighed and sat down, her soaked shirt sticking to her skin and her long hair a tangled mess at her back. She skimmed the water with a hand, taking her gray surroundings for the first time.

"Where are you taking me, Ancient One?"

The warm sun began to dry her clothes and she knelt there, one hand on the mast and one firmly on the floor as she continued studying the Unmade land. There wasn't *nothing*, but what *did exist* looked like it would falter at any moment. The gray, dull clumps that lined the river weren't reassuring at all. Her hands itched to bring up life from that dull clay, but something in her always stopped with a confidence that this was not the place to create. There was a purpose to this Unmade, and she would respect that.

The gentle lull of the river continued, and Syra realized the river bed was actually wider here, much wider. If it stayed this way, she could have an easy journey... to wherever it ended.

A panic began to rise to the surface as she realized the vast amount of unknowns before her. Would she be on this river for days or for months? And would it end somewhere empty, like this?

The sun was now directly above her and her clothes were dry again. She rummaged through her bag for food, laying out items to dry and dividing what she had into portions for three days. Hopefully she would be somewhere sustainable by then, or she wouldn't last long. She cut a portion of an apple and a few bites of meat for her meal and ate quickly, still afraid the rapids would return as quickly as they left. She wiped her hands and began to work through her mess of hair, tying it high on her head and finding nothing else to do, so she sat and waited. Her thoughts roamed freely as she leaned against the mast, facing the direction her raft was being carried. Before long, her eyes fluttered shut, and she slept.

Syra woke to the sun low in the sky and for a moment forgot where she was. She looked around and gave a small gasp as she scrambled to grab hold of the mast again and take in her surroundings. The land had changed. Subtle, but surely.

The Unmade was now a formed dirt, with patches of grass sprouting up ever so often and the smell of fresh soil evident. Her eyes widened and she stood up on her toes to see as far as she could. She swore she could make out mountains in the distance. Or buildings. *Something* else had been created, and she was drawing nearer to it. The sun was dropping lower into the sky, obscuring the sight more and more.

Within a few hours she would have her answers.

Sliding the pack on her back, she sat and watched, waiting to arrive at what could now be a land waiting to be inhabited. Could the Ancient Magic have made this for them?

Night night settled in and she continued to float slowly down the river, unnerved by the noises of the world around her.

Rustling turned to rhythmic padding, and blurry shapes in the night could be seen beyond the river bank. More than one thing was following her, and they were not trying to hide.

She gripped the hilt of her knife nervously, eyes twitching back and forth between the bank sides, unsure if an attack was to come sooner or later. As she moved swiftly through the dark night, a faint rumbling began to grow, strong and steady. It was a sound she couldn't place, but the power of it was enough to make her nervous.

What could be out there in this new land?

Whatever was following her grew fainter as the roaring grew near deafening, and something in Syra jumped in fear, the Magic within her urging her to do something. The urge grew into a panic. She didn't know what was in any direction but knew she couldn't stay on the safety of her raft any longer.

In one quick decision, she jumped into the water, finding it just above her waist but too powerful to walk through without being swept away. She swam toward the bank, grasping at the slippery dirt but unable to pull herself up. The creatures following grew close and she strained her eyes, choking on water and struggling to see straight.

Then, in one swooping move, strong hands pulled her out of the water and dragged her onto land.

She was heaved onto her back and she fumbled for her knife, wildly coughing up water and kicking whatever it was away from her. What she now saw to be a human form disarmed her with lightning speed and placed a firm knee on her chest.

"Steady, we are not here to harm you." The deep voice had a lilt she couldn't place, and it sang of regal posture, but she frantically fought anyway.

"Give her space, Coran. Where she comes from, men are not as honorable."

Her head snapped to the womanly voice behind and nearly cried with relief. There had been compassion in her words.

The man moved away swiftly with a smooth apology. Syra stopped and began to slow her breathing, calming her racing mind and rushing adrenalin. They were not a threat, or so they claimed, and she was surrounded. A knife wouldn't do more than the Ancient Magic inside of her could. She stood slowly to face the pair.

"Who are you?"

To Syra's surprise a young voice answered back with rushed excitement.

"We are guardians! And we protect all who make this journey! Well, I'm not a guardian yet, but I'm learning fast." The little girl a few feet away thumped something, pride emanating from her every word.

The man chuckled a deep rumble of a laugh.

"Thank you Ky. Yes, we are called Guardians in our kingdom. We are tasked with patrolling these areas as our people wait for the arrival of those in Elharren. We are here to aid any in their arrival."

"Father, don't forget, Deadlanders don't see in the night! We need to light our flame."

Her young voice was so precious and full of knowledge newly learned, Syra couldn't help but smile, quickly realizing there were more than a few things she was missing. Deadlanders? *They* see in this dark?

"Ahh, you are right. You may do the honors, but remember to thank the Magic."

It was silent for a moment before a small flame burst into existence, and Syra's eyes widened as she found its source. A pale skinned girl with dark hair and twinkling eyes held a flame in her hand, grinning from ear to ear as she looked at her parents with pride.

Her mother laughed, a woman of white hair and dark skin like Belick's. "Well done, Ky. Your practice is paying off."

Syra looked over at the man now, taking in his own auburn hair and brown skin, her mind confused and sputtering. How did these two have this child??

"I am Coran, and this is Lalise, my wife, and Ky our daughter. What can we call you?"

Syra shook her head, wondering if this was a dream. "Uh.. My name is Syra. And… I'm sorry, I am so confused."

Lalise's gentle hand found Syra's shoulder causing her to jump for a moment, until she realized how comforting the touch was in this dark place.

"You must have so many questions, and we have much to share. Come, the kingdom borders are not far from here. We will make a few cups of my famous Kriln and stay up as long as you need. Would you be comfortable riding with Ky?"

Syra realized they must have horses of some kind, and nodded, giving a thankful smile. They moved as a group toward what were *definitely not horses*, and Syra swallowed down a lump of fear. The creatures looked like oversized cats, but with sharp teeth and striking white fur. Ky climbed on and gave her a hand up. Syra could feel her suddenly start as if remembering something.

"Ancient Magic, thank you for the light."

And with that they were off, traveling at a speed twice as fast as any horse. Syra could see nothing but the child in front of her and held on tightly to Ky's giggling form, who didn't even hold onto any reins.

They stopped along what Syra could guess was a cliff's edge, the roaring now deafening. They made their way down rocks and small cliffs with agility and far more speed than she was comfortable with. As they descended, the view took Syra's breath away. Below them was a kingdom, lit with golden lights stretching far and wide, showing houses on the cliff side as well as below on the firm ground.

"This is your kingdom? There must be millions." Syra breathed. She could hear Ky shake her small head.

"No, our people live in groupings all along the kingdom, but we keep the lights on for the day when the Deadlanders, like you, finally come." They didn't descend far into the kingdom, but stopped at a well-lit group of houses, each white and etched with intricate gold designs on the outside, glowing with the warm lanterns set out all along the roads.

"What do you call this place?"

Ky stopped them and paused, reverence entering her voice.

"What better name than the City of the Sun."

Syra sat in her new, dry clothing and looked around the house in awe. Plants hung all around, and the table was surrounded by vast space, easily sitting up to twenty people. Then in an adjoining room were overstuffed cushions on wooden benches lining the walls, allowing people to sit around each other and talk for hours. The entire house seemed built to bring others together for long periods of gathering. Tears sprang to her eyes as she imagined them all. Michale, Dagen, Belick, Aleth, Rienah, Enith... Luik.

Lalise and Coran finished heating something over a wood stove and brought it to the table, laying out folded towels as Ky brought mugs painted with deep hues of red and blue, gold designs tracing designs through them.

They poured drinks, starting with Syra, while Ky embraced her parents before and explained she had training early in the morning to attend. Syra watched with amazement as the girl of no more than eight years held more freedom, joy, and maturity than most adults she knew. And her eyes! In the light she could see it in all of them. Their eyes were different colors than she had ever seen. A mixing of blue and purple in Ky's, a honey yellow with brown flecks in Lalise's, and something of a brown and blue mixed together in Coran's.

She did not study medicine, but she understood physical features and their tendency to pass through parents to a child. Even the parents seemed to have impossible lineage!

Syra turned her attention back toward her drink, peering at the soft white cream-like substance on top of it. Below was a warm liquid with a red and brown tint, smelling of both chocolate and berries. She drank carefully, allowing the sweet warmth to pour down her throat. It wasn't like candy as she first thought, but the cream on top gave a hint of sweetness to a slightly bitter, full taste of chocolate and raspberries.

She looked up to find Coran and Lalise covering laughs as they watched her.

Lalise gestured, "You spent quite a while studying that drink. I take it they do not have *Kriln* where you are from?"

"No, and I have never tasted anything quite like it!" Syra set the mug down and sighed, her insides warm. "This is wonderful, thank you."

Coran laughed, his trimmed beard moving with his head.

"I don't know how Lalise would survive without it."

Lalise wrapped her hand around her mug and laughed, "I would drink water. Or wine. And somehow continue on every day in mourning."

They all laughed again, settling in comfortably around the table. Allies reached out and brought a gentle hand to Syra's arm.

"Syra, you must have many questions. Let us first explain where you are and how it came to be. They, we will sit and help answer any question you think of."

Syra nodded and took a drink, eager to understand where they were.

"This will be hard to understand, Syra, but be patient with me." Coran's deep voice began to weave a story.

"Long ago, the Ancient Magic created our people, a people who would know intimately the Magic and use it for the sake of the Magic. We watched as the Magic bore Its sons and we grieved with it when they betrayed each other and the world. We saw the wars and the heartache and felt the pain as Elharren broke. The Ancient Magic gave us a choice: we could give up our ability to live only for our own service and be given a greater measure of both Magic and wisdom from the Ancient One and stay, or we could be let loose in Elharren with full freedom to experience all the joy and pain of power-wars. Those who would choose to join mankind in Elharren would not be welcomed back. About a third of our number left then and soon made a deal with the Jyren. From what we gathered, Jyren tricked them and forced into beast-like creatures you call *delviors*."

He shook his head then, and Syra thought she saw a moment of pain flaw through his eyes. Her own mind began to race, pieces moving into place from her own childhood.

She had believed delviors were dogs twisted and perverted by her father... but no. The twisting had begun hundreds of years before *into* doglike forms, and only morphed as her father's whim changed.

"The rest of us stayed and willingly gave up a fraction of our freedom, but oh the joy it brought. It was more akin to being free than anything we had ever known. We were given more of the Spring, and the Magic runs powerfully through our veins. With it, we have been commissioned to build a kingdom vast and far for those who would follow the Magic here. Those willing to give up all they own for a new life. So we have been building for the past thousand years. We do not grow past my own age in physical appearance and have the great gift of family and children. We are to be guides and rulers as we teach a new way, a way of peace and togetherness, with the Spring making our land plentiful, more so than any have seen. Someday, this kingdom will welcome foreigners with open arms, houses warm and ready for families to settle in. And you are the first to arrive."

Syra sat silently, trying to comprehend the new historical narrative but finding more questions than answers.

"How are the people in my land supposed to get here?"

"That is a journey they must decide to make."

Syra frowned, setting her cup down. "But when I go back, I am going to need to give an answer to that question... Making a raft for everyone would take years!"

This time Coran and Lalise frowned, and Lalise gently spoke up. "Syra, you cannot go back. There is no way."

Syra's breath caught and she stared at them, realizing they had not planned this part out.

"There has to be a way back. Through the Unmade, I will walk if need be."

Coran shook his head, his eyes sad. "The Unmade is there to purposefully keep others out. It will crumble beneath you."

Her head spun as the thought sunk in. It didn't make sense... She was *sure* the Ancient Magic brought her here to lead others as well.

Lalise took her hand then, her voice soft. "You can ask it. The Ancient Magic may have a different plan for you than for the people to come."

Syra nodded and held to that hope, wondering if it would be so easy.

"I think I need to sleep, and then maybe in the morning I can explore a little?"

They smiled and nodded, showing her to a large room the size of Michale's old room in the palace. It held a desk, bed, cushions, and a walled off area for washing. She sank into the bed determined to turn her mind off and get the sleep she needed. Tomorrow would bring enough worries.

The sun rose early, and Syra stepped lightly from her bed onto the cool ground, thankful for the thoughtful touches Lalise had put in her room. She brushed her hair and tucked it behind her ears, looking out the window one more time before tiptoeing out eagerly to go see the city.

To her surprise, Coran and Lalise were up, with Ky rushing every bite as she prepared to leave. Fresh sweet rolls were on the table along with fruit and cooked eggs, and a sleepy Lalise sat while Coran brought her a cup of *kriln* and a wry kiss on the cheek.

"Good morning Syra. Help yourself to whatever looks good. There are cups over by the *kriln* if you want some."

Ky finished her plate and gave Syra a quick smile before kissing her parents and grabbing a cloth pack, rushing to put her shoes on.

"Ky, do not forget to bring home some of Feash's squashes. I need at least two of them for dinner."

"I'll get them Mom! I should be back a little early today, so I will see you at lunch. Love you, bye!"

And all they saw of her was the tips of her long black hair as she sped out the door. Syra smiled, enjoying the girl's eagerness.

She sat and filled her plate with breads and fruit, adding an egg and filling a mug before sitting down to eat. Her eyes wandered to the windows as she chewed as quickly as possible.

"You are as bad as Ky!" Lalise laughed around her mug. "Go on, get out there and explore. Just take note of where our house is. If you get lost just let them know you are staying with us, and don't let anyone snatch you away! You are our guest!"

Syra grinned and got up from the table, slipping her shoes on and opening the door.

"Wait, take this in case you want to spend lunch out and about, though I doubt many will accept payment." Lalise put a few gold coins in her hand and Coran smiled, admiring his wife before looking at Syra with raised browes.

"Well, off with you!"

CHAPTER 15

SYRA

S yra stood on the edge of the mountain tier only a block away from the house she had slept in that night. The kingdom stretched before her high and far, giving way to smaller epicenters along the coast and distant hills which looked ripe for farming. To the very left was a forest unlike she had ever seen, rich with too many shades of green to count and sunlight glittering through leaves. The large expanse of trees opened to a small governing center of its own surrounding a impossibly large palace in a tree, made of woven and carved wood playing with lines and angles to create a dazzling structure.

Mountains rose high in the distance along the edge of the sea, covered with snow and gleaming in the sunlight. She could just make out a speck that looked like a building on its ledge. To south, close enough to swim from the beach was an island with a kingdom of its own, rising high above waves and made of a pink grainy coral. In between every kingdom were hills and rivers, unknown forest groupings and trails just ready for exploration.

She let out a breath she didn't realize she had been holding, bringing her hands to her cheeks in awe. It was like Elharren, but fuller, more robust and vibrant in every way. Every kingdom had clear lines almost inviting others to join with large, smooth roads for easy travel.

Well, travel she would.

Her mouth twisted into a grin and she sped off down her own path, making her way down the tier and toward the ocean. The house grouping she came from was built into the mountain's edge, tiered downward toward the level ground. As she jogged through the streets, smiling at shocked and delighted citizens as she passed, she looked over and could see the Spring at its end. A dangerously large waterfall that dropped into a swirling hole bigger than twenty houses. She changed directions and made her way to what may have been a small lake, watching the roaring Magic as it chased Itself within Its new home. This is where the river ended. This was the Ancient Spring.

The excitement she felt moments before vanished as her mind fell back toward her friends and the refugees yet to come. She reached out her hand for a moment, then let it drop, afraid to hear the wrong answer.

"Will you take me back?"

She expected something, a voice or a nudge or a pull or *something*, but the sound of roaring water was all she received.

Swallowing disappointment, Syra nodded in respect to the Magic and continued her journey downward to the sea.

Houses lined wide, open streets along the way and the smell of freshly baked rolls emanated from the city square. It took miles of jogging to break onto the beach, but when she did, the sight was worth it. Tall trees with fat leaves sat in clusters, providing shade and weighed down by some kind of red spheres on top. Benches made of stone were built all along the beach itself, cut with distinct accuracy attesting to tools Syra had never seen. She walked slowly to the water's edge and kicked off her shoes, rolling up her pants and letting it flow against her bare skin. *Luik.*

Syra squeezed her eyes shut, suddenly overwhelmed with the desire to see him again. In the ocean, like the first time. When his eyes were less hard and his shoulders less angry. She could imagine him throwing his own shirt off and running into the waves, laughing and joking as he invited her into those strong arms. The pain was like a severing of her own heart, watching him darken. She wanted to slap him awake and pull him from the dark hold he clung to, but nothing helped. He loved her, but not the life she was walking toward. Not the light.

The forest before her was as different from her childhood home as the day from night. Trees rose with grandeur, bolstering spirals of brown in their trunks speckled with gold flecks and bursts of color. Their leaves danced in the wind, gentle films for the sun to peek through for its own creative pictures of light on the forest floor. It was breathtaking.

Hushed memories of dark, mangled branches reaching out in desperation flashed across her mind and she froze, wondering if this place too could be evil inside. But then, was it the forest that was evil, or the one with the power over it? Had her *been created* to be this same warm, adventurous kingdom of browns and greens?

For a moment she felt something of the shame the Ancient Brothers described. The shame of a human race who had twisted what was meant to be. She stepped into the covering of the trees, brushing a hand against a tree trunk and gasping in delight as the gold speckles moved from their place on the tree and began to fill the air around her, eventually flying off toward another tree before settling their wings back down.

Syra held her breath as she walked, feeling small in comparison to the majesty around her. Somehow this felt *right*. This gathering of trees was like a warm home with unlocked doors, prepared for the lost and lonely to belong.

She passed a few new sprouts with lighter brown stems and bright fanciful leaves. She touched one gently, feeling a strange kinship to it. As her fingers brushed its smooth wood, the magic in her veins pulsed, as if jumping for joy, and she could feel it. Its present, its future, and even its death, many, many years from now.

This tree would grow in strength and height, withstanding strong winds and changing colors before winter. It would warm in the sun again and again and be a safe home for a multitude of creatures, giving back to the land what it took. Little children would come find the secret sweet juice it produced, and the strong tree would freely give it away, rejoicing in their laughter and smiles. They would make it their special place and many would find love under its branches. Then, after a thousand years, it would fall, having given the land thousands of its own children to spring up and take its place.

Syra's mind flashed back to her own body and she panted, tears streaking down her cheeks. She *knew* the tree. As surely as she knew herself she intimately *knew* this glorious creation. She brushed her knuckles against its leaves, smiling widely as she whispered.

"You have a beautiful life ahead."

Moving to another, she touched it. When nothing happened she frowned, touching another and another before folding her arms and sighing in frustration. Why just this one? What if she forgot it? Yet even as she questioned, she knew. She would always know where this tree was. Somehow it was *her* tree.

Syra continued her walk toward where she had seen the forest castle, eventually wandering into what was an entire village of people. Homes were set up between trees, moss climbing up the sides of strong wooden beams surrounding overly large windows. Some of the houses had entire walls made of windows. The inside of the houses were different from Lalise's too, with burnt oranges and dark blue pots strewn about with everything from tools to water inside. The houses were smaller, just big enough for people to have beds in, yet outside they gathered jovially around campfires, laughing as they weaved, cooked, and built.

Banging stopped and laughter quieted as each face turned her way and surprised eyes stared back at her from shades of dark brown to almost translucent white. A young man no older than thirty rose from his place around the fire and dusted off his hands. Jet black curled hair framed a strong jaw with a dimple in the chin and warm blue eyes studying her before he moved forward to meet her.

"I, uh.. I'm sorry we are all staring." He laughed nervously, a rich, smooth sound, as he turned around to acknowledge those behind him.

"We had not received word that our people had finally come." He wiped his hands on his pants again and reached out a hand. "I am Julin."

Syra stared at him for a moment longer, forcing her eyes away from his broad shoulders.

"I am Syra, the first of my people to come." She shook his hand, her pulse race as he held it a moment longer than necessary, then blinking as if realizing what he was doing and dropping it.

He cleared his throat and took a respectful step back. "Your people are not with you?"

She shook her head, guilt assaulting her that she could forget their plight so easily.

"No, I came to see if there was anything here at all... Or I should say, the Ancient Magic called me. Now I must find a way to go back and bring my people here." She stumbled over her words, berating herself for giving so much away.

Julin whistled in surprise, folding his arms. "That's quite the task. We all believed there was no way back. The Ancient Magic seemed to make this a one way road." His brows knit together as he thought for a moment, turning around and surveying tools around him.

When he turned back his face was lit with a wry grin.

"The Ancient Magic never said you couldn't go back, and if It called you hear before your people, there must be a reason." He turned fully toward his own people now. "I say, if the Ancient Magic allows our hammers to ring, we find her a way back."

To Syra's surprise the people shouted in agreement and moved into action. Groups began to form groups around tables and fires, some sitting with paper and pencils, measuring and gesturing to each other, while others began carving down wood into piles sorted by similar height and width.

Julin laughed and looked back at Syra, his eyes twinkling.

"This is going to be fun. Want to join?"

She nodded shyly, unsure what exactly she was joining but thankful to be brought in.

"First," He pointed over to the different groups in camp, "you can decide where you best fit. Anyone can join a group, but the goal is to be a part of a group where you are either learning to be helpful in the future, or are currently helpful now. So we have writers. They get excited about creating new ideas and drawing them into reality." Syra's smiled as she thought of Michale'thia sitting in this group and furiously arguing points with them.

"Then we have a group that puts plans into action. You can see them hanging around and starting to listen to the ideas of the writers early. The sneaks. They usually have a prototype built by the time the writers have it on paper. And then there are groups who prepare wood and basic resources, those who go gather wood from dead trees, those who go out to find stone, and so on. Groups who prepare food and drinks for everybody, and a few more groups. We all fit in somewhere, and we all love what we do." He turned to her again.

"What about you? What would you enjoy doing?"

The question startled her and she realized she had never even thought about it. Her life had been too full of surviving to ever choose.

"I haven't ever thought of it. Where I grew up there hasn't been much time to think on what I want." She scanned the village, smiling as children attempted to form their own groups mimicking their parents.

Julin smiled at her gently, his own voice soft.

"Well, you will have plenty of time to figure that out here. It's ok to just take it all in. You are welcome to join and meet people, but you are also welcome to just breathe."

His understanding brought tears to her eyes and she looked away quickly, pointing to a group around a fire weaving tree vines together.

"Can I learn what they are doing?"

His brows rose in challenge and he smiled, walking backwards toward the group.

"You can, but you see, this is quite the elite group. They are only preparing for what we *really* do. And if you are going to join, you're going to need to have a bit of adventure in your soul."

She rolled her eyes at his theatrics and laughed, following him to the fire where a few seats were left open.

Her jaw dropped when she realized he was right: this was not a weaving group at all. They were making harnesses in preparation for a climb to the top of the trees, where they gathered specific nuts that could be crushed into a paste and used to almost permanently bind things together.

They spent the next hour weaving large and small pieces of vine and tree limbs together, creating remarkably sturdy devices for themselves that would not only hold their weight if they fell, but would allow them to lower themselves down quickly in an emergency. Syra held her harness up, staring at it doubtfully.

Julin walked up beside her, giving her a friendly thump on the back as he laughed.

"Don't look so fearful, it will hold. Believe me, you'll be safe as can be."

She looked at him with fake indignancy, her eyes locking on his for a second too long. His dark curls fell on his forehead and the dimple in his strong chin only further defined his jawline. Her heart was racing, but it had nothing to do with their upcoming climb.

Suddenly, Luik's face flashed before her eyes and she stepped back, eyes wide with surprise. How could she so quickly forget him? Guilt crept intoher stomach and she turned away as tears brimmed her eyes.

Julin was light. Easy. *Here.* And Luik clung to a darkness growing inside of him... yet he was *home.* She walked away without explanation, following the other women toward the woods.

The hours flew by, and Syra found herself exhilarated by the climb. They didn't just climb trees, they made jumps from sturdy branch to sturdy branch, gathering what they needed from the top and moving

to new trees. The work was simple and filled with comfortable conversation and lighthearted joking, but the views were breathtaking.
One hundred feet up in the air with only the majesty of the rising
mountains and crashing seas. She *needed* to find a way to bring the rest
of the people here.

By the time they were back at camp the sun was setting and Syra had
to say her goodbyes. She caught sight of a wooden object being built.
It was the size of a human but with strings attached and boards sticking
out at odd angles. She couldn't make sense of it and decided to let the
building crew worry about it.

Julin insisted on walking her to Lalise's house, though she doubted
anyone was ever worried about robbers here. He was the cause of too
much turmoil inside of her and she felt helplessly swept away in it all.
In just a day she had come to enjoy his compassionate eyes and ready
tease more than she ever thought she could, and she didn't know what
that meant.

They walked in silence, just clearing the forest and enjoying the
radiant purples and oranges in the sky when Julin spoke openly.

"Syra, I need to be honest with you."

She held her breath, panic settling in at the conversation to come.

"I set my people to work on this device to bring you back to the
Deadlands, but if the Ancient Magic is set against it, all our efforts will
be useless." He turned to look at her then, compassion edging his eyes.

"And that isn't a bad thing. It would just mean the Ancient Magic
will make a way of Its own."

Syra swallowed down an angry retort, his gentle look breaking down her anger and making her want to sob.

She shook her head, wisps of hair coming out of the bun she had tied high on her head before their climb.

"I don't know why I feel this responsibility. I know you're right. I feel it. The Ancient Magic will not allow the people who want to join to be kept away... but at the same time it's like this insistent pull to find a way to bring them here. This place is beautiful," she looked around, the crisp air making everything even more clear.

"And every minute I enjoy it is a minute everyone else spends in a land dying and filled with blood."

Julin nodded, his eyes glossing over as he stared out in the distance.

"I'll never fully understand, Syra. I know that. But I do understand to an extent. We have the Magic in our veins here, and with that comes an echo of the Magic's own emotions. We *feel* a deep longing for a people we don't know." He shrugged and sighed, shaking his head. "We may even love them."

Syra frowned, taken back by the thought. They had always viewed Ancient Magic as an essence.. But emotions like these brought an uncomfortable personhood to It she didn't know what to do with.

They climbed the steps to Lalise's house and Julin knocked, a smile breaking out when Ky opened the door.

"JULIN!" A squeal of delight was the only warning before Ky threw her arms around his neck, nearly knocking him down the steps.

Lalise came to the door next, her own joy evident at the sight of their guest.

"Julin! Come- Ky, settle down, dear one. Julin, please say you will stay for dinner. It has been weeks! How are Gulrin and Ren? Is your sweet sister well too?"

Syra watched as they ushered him inside, Coran's booming voice calling Julin from the sitting room before his large frame scooped Julin up in a hug.

They settled into cushions around the room as Coran and Lalise poured drinks.

"Julin is the son of our dear friends," Lalise explained, "and we have watched him grow since he was just a small baby."

"Yeah, and when *I* was younger, he would take me on adventures to the forest!"

Julin smiled and ruffled Ky's hair, earning a glare from her and a swat of his hand. Coran leaned forward.

"Tell us Julin, how are our kin in the forest? Any new inventions we should know about? It would be well worth the walk if you created a device that can make high-pitched squeals more palatable for poor fathers like myself." He gave a pointed look to Ky, his beard shaking as he rumbled with laughter.

Julin chuckled, setting his drink down on the floor next to him. "No, the only invention for that is a patient mind. We have made headway on wind-life, and that is proving to be extremely helpful. From what we understand, the wind forms some kind of unseen force we may be able to use if we could just figure out how. We'll get there. I'm convinced we will find more wonders of this land in our lifetime."

Coran nodded thoughtfully, his own mind working. Lalise leaned toward them with her knees tucked under her long rose colored robe, her eyes eager as she asked more about the wind-life Julin spoke of. Syra leaned back against the cream colored wall and closed her eyes, listening to the lull of the conversation but finding her own mind wandering.

She replayed the images of the journey from Elharren, searching for anything that could allow her to go back.

Sitting up suddenly, Syra looked around with wide eyes, "I know how to get back." She turned to Julin then. "I'm going to bring my people home."

CHAPTER 16

MICHALE'THIA

The air was frigid as the sun dissolved into the smoky sky. Michale lifted a shaking arm to the next hold and heaved herself up over the ledge, gasping as she inched her body forward on the hard cold cliff's edge.

Dagen came next with a little more ease, rolling on his back a few feet away to catch his own breath. His lips were beginning to turn blue, much like her own, and she knew they were entering a dangerous time of night. They needed a fire to survive, but Michale couldn't move. Every muscle was locked in cold exhaustion and she lay there on her side, staring at Dagen as Luik pushed his own body over the side, moaning with pain. He had shed his pack hours ago, now only wearing his heavy jacket. They lay still as the minutes passed to silent hopes dying. It had been an eternity of climbing. They spent an entire day searching for whatever trial Belick had once spoken of, but found nothing.

The first hour of the climb was steep and exhausting, the easiest of their journey, they would find. From there it was an upward climb rock by rock upward, each small break large enough to rest on only reminded them there was no way down. It was upward or die. As they continued their climb the air had turned frigid, their limbs locking in spasms from fatigue and fighting movement from the freezing cold around them. Only a half day into the journey and Michale was sure they would die, but somehow they had found a way each time to continue on. Until now. Their bodies were too tired, cold, and weak to do anything other than die. Michale closed her eyes, begging her body to stop shaking with murderous cold.

Shuffling beside Michale coaxed her eyelids open, and she couldn't find the energy to do anything but stare as Dagen painfully lifted his body from the ground and took a step past her. Slow steps and grunts continued as he managed to find branches and roots to stack between them all.

Dagen knelt slowly, every movement labored, and struck something again and again, cursing in between and falling over from the exertion. A final strike and he began blowing a flame into existence. The flame grew into a warm shield against the cold that burned more than it helped, but at least they would live. A vague memory of Belick disgruntled at how fast wood burned in Anaratha flashed across her mind and Michale wondered if they might actually live past the night.

Michale could slowly begin to feel her limbs thawing and her face heating as the fire's warmth worked its way into her bones, and slowly, she gave into the dark sleep beckoning her away.

Hands touched the bars and a lever was pulled. The pain ceased and Michale collapsed forward onto her face, only to be dragged out by guards. Her sour stomach lurched and she tried to eat, desperate to avoid what would happen if she didn't. Footsteps began to sound all around her and faces towered over her, a ferocious hunger in their eyes as they closed in. She tried to scream but couldn't breathe, and the mob grabbed her limbs and hair, pulling in every direction as their frenzy ensued. She screamed in agony as they tore her limbs apart, her torture fueling their bliss-

Michale woke with a start, tears wet against her face and her throat sore from what must have been screams. Dagen and Luik were still asleep, huddled against the almost dead fire. She rose unsteadily, looking toward where Dagen had gone to get kindling.

She slowly heaved herself up and walked to the face of the cliff, forcing herself to ignore the cold. Michale began pulling sticks and anything else she could find in hopes of creating a backup pile for when their fire dulled. She couldn't let what Dagen made die.

A root stuck stubbornly out from the mountain and she struggled against it, finally wiping her hands, unable to wrestle it from its crooked home.

She looked up at their journey ahead. The mountain rose for what seemed like an eternity. The pull she once felt was lessening, and the path ahead was nearly unbearable. But the path behind? Now impossible.

It suddenly felt like the mountain itself was crushing her as her dream fluttered before her eyes. She wanted her father. And her mother even. She wanted to have been more important than her parent's utopia, to be more important than their power.

Sobs wracked her body and Michale felt herself suddenly drowning in anguish she hadn't known was there. She grabbed ahold of a crevice on the side of the mountain and blindly lifted her body up. She found another hold and lifted herself again and again, running from her own emotions just as much as their situation at hand. When she reached another ledge and pulled herself over, her tears had dissolved into hard determination again. She could not let them win.

Michale stood, waiting for the bitter cold to cover her again now that she was standing still and far from the warm coals of the dying fire, but it never came. She moved forward, her eyes attuned to the dark but still unable to make sense of what she was seeing.

The air felt like it had gotten *warmer* somehow. She looked around and began to make sense of objects strewn about, too large and oddly shaped to be rocks or plants. She stepped up to the first vague object strewn across the ground and nudged it with her foot before bending to open the flap. It was a pack! She reached inside to pull out the contents, gaping as rope, dried meat, shawl and what looked like small wooden carvings. She stood, puzzled. Moving a few feet away, she found a small doll with woven hair and a simple wooden body. But how could a *child* have made it up this fare? Unless…

Michale froze, taking in the ground beneath her feet and nearly hovering with joy as her eyes were just able to register the trail carved into the mountain. They had found it. They would survive.

Unable to get down the ledge, Michale fell asleep wrapped in a discarded shawl and a few shirts. When she heard Dagen's panicked cry, she rushed to the ledge and peered down at the men, the twenty foot difference suddenly looking *much* greater than it had in the dark.

Dagen spun in a circle when he heard her, and her heart nearly broke. Sheer panic was painted there, along with deep-seated devastation and terror, only leaving when he saw her face, gulping in deep breaths of air to calm himself.

She spoke softly, guilt-ridden over causing him to feel such a way.

"I'm sorry Dagen, I couldn't sleep and I made my way up."

Dagen just paced in a circle for a moment struggling to calm himself. She hadn't been there, and Michale was sure she would never understand what he felt. To stand helpless for a year as someone you vowed to care for was taken and abused. To wonder if it would happen again. She swallowed and parted her cracked lips.

"But here, I found some rope. You need to see this."

She tied a knot into the end of the rope and jammed it into a crevice, allowing them to test it before using it to climb up quickly.

Dagen hoisted himself over and looked out at the path before laughing with relief and swooping Michale into his arms as he spun around. His joy was infectious and her own laughter bubbled to the surface. She wrapped her arms around his neck, smiling genuinely for the first time in ages.

He slowed them to a stop and she allowed herself to sit in the moment. *He* was safe. Strength. Home. He smelled of warmth and his eyes never ceased to look at her as if she was inherently valuable rather than in need of proving her worth. He stared right back at her, searching her face, and she felt panic sink in again, his arms suddenly becoming a cage and his lips too near her own. But he gently set her down and kissed her forehead before whispering to her.

"It's ok."

It was then she allowed herself to think it: she loved him. And it terrified her.

"Well this will make the trek easier. We should get going and cover as much ground as we can before sundown again." Luik kicked at the dirt path and traced the horizon behind them with his eyes.

The path was easier than climbing, but Michale's muscles quickly reminded her how weak they were, despite the Loharans' help. They walked silently as the hours passed, breaking the silence with occasional grunts and murmurs of wonder.

The sun had begun to fall when they reached the clearing, an archway leading into the grandest kingdom she had ever seen lay before them.

They had made it, and all she wanted was a hot bath. Her first in over a year.

The next hour was a blur as Michale was ushered before a group of elders, questioned, and given rooms. She could see the city, but it felt like a faraway dream. Like she was back in the cage with horrors awaiting her when she woke the clanging of doors. It was her only warning before the lever would be turned and-

"Michale?"

The voice washed over Michale'thia, easing her out of her own dark mind and back to a reality she never thought would come. She whirled around to face him, her throat closing with tears.

Enith crossed the distance and wrapped his arms around her, holding her silently. She grasped him back, desperately hoping it wasn't all a dream. When she felt his body begin to shake with sobs, her own flood of emotion came rushing forth and they clung to each other in her dimly lit room.

He pulled back and held her at arm's length, shaking his head as he spoke.

"They wouldn't let me get to you, they just took you, and then I couldn't get you out until we were sure we didn't waste our chance- I'm so sorry, little sister." His breath was ragged and he stood with his shoulders squared, lips trembling. A soldier waiting to receive his due punishment.

Michale threw her arms around his neck again, not knowing what to say but not wanting him to ever leave.

Words finally came, and they were the healing both siblings needed.

"It wasn't your fault, and it wasn't mine, Enith."

They sat, leaning back against her bed and talking around the meats and breads brought in by Ilytha. Michale'thia was surprised by how thankful she was to see the fiery beauty. She was thankful to see anyone she loved from *before*.

Eventually Dagen found his way in, and they sat in a circle, exchanging stories.

Michale nearly choked on her bread when Dagen finished sharing his own year after Enith and Ilytha had. She couldn't believe or even understand all that had happened, much less all that had been sacrificed *to save her*.

"So… Enith, you stayed in Anaratha to build trust from the inside, but my blood was somehow used to create a hallucinatory drug the Jyres have every royal in the kingdom on." She looked at him with a flat stair, annoyed she somehow mattered so much in the Jyre's scheme.

"And in the meantime, Ilytha you were training with Rienah and formed *a band of warrior women??*"

Ilytha flashed Michale a proud smile, giving her a wink, and Enith shook his head in affirmation.

"They began to trust that I was drugged, but they still would never let me see you. It was insanity. Everyone lived the live they were given as if it were their dream. Inmy drugged state, they had my 'dream life' as me being married to *Gianne*."

Michale did choke then, grimacing at the cruel girl's name and laughing as Enith shivered remembering.

Ilytha's eyes darkened and she flicked her knife out.

"I'll kill her."

They laughed, not quite sure if she was serious.

"And Dagen," She kept her eyes lowered, unable to meet his own.

"You spent the entire year digging the tunnel, making trips through the Jyre forest, and preparing teams to rescue me?"

He picked up her hand and kissed it gently, bending his head to catch her eye.

"Michale, I'm pretty amazing. Get used to it."

Her jaw dropped at the timing of his humor and she smacked him on the arm, a full smile giving her away in the process.

Their laughter died down and she sighed, closing her eyes.

"So, what's next? We build houses near each other and finally live in peace?"

No answer came and Michale's eyes snapped open to pin her brother with a stare. He shifted for a moment, looking down until Ilytha nudged him forcefully.

"Man, up. Tell her. She can handle the truth, husband."

Enith frowned at Ilytha and swatted her hand away, folding his arms.

"It would seem, the Botanis were hiding a secret here. The Ancient Spring is here, or was. Well, it still is, but it's moving now, away from here. That means the land will no longer hold its warmth or produce crops so easily. It won't be livable here anymore, and we haven't figured out what we are going to do yet."

Michale's eyes widened as her mind woke up, moving at lightning speed.

"How is it moving? What do you mean moving? Is it just disappearing?"

The prince looked around, bewildered, "No, they said something of a river has formed, and through the river it's carving a way through the land."

She stood then, her breath caught and her hands frozen as she looked back and forth around the room, finding her pack and dashing to rummage through it.

She opened a few folded pages and searched for a writing utensil, shaking as an epiphany began to unfold.

Michale pointed a pencil at Enith as she pulled more pages out of her bag, desperate to find a specific set of notes. "Go find some Kauf!"

"What? It's too late-"

"Enith! Bring some Kauf! We may have just figured out what the prophecy means!"

Enith muttered and shook his head as he walked out. Dagen slipped a notebook in front of Michale, which she took gratefully without looking at him.

Ilytha rose gracefully and walked out of the room, returning with four more large candles to spread out and a few more cushions for the floors and chairs. Enith arrived shortly after with a tray, setting it on the floor when he took note of the table covered in notes and texts.

Dagen gave him a wry smile and poured them all cups, adding sweet cream to Michale's before giving Enith a half-hearted salute and wink, permission to leave. Enith chuckled knowingly and left with Ilytha. This was not their gifting, and it would be a long night for the scholars in the room.

Dagen took a seat at the table and scooted a few pages aside after handing Michale a cup and taking a drink of his own. Michale looked up briefly, not really seeing anything but the theories flying through her mind.

She laid out the prophecy, jotting notes down as she verbalized her newest finding.

"The Loharans may have been right. The "Perfect One" must have been referring to the Ancient Magic Itself, but in river form. And look, here, the "pure" according to the Loharan was the term *kidu*, which was a fruit that was considered to be a "gift plant", since part of its fruit was poisonous and the other part was sweet and nourishing. The only way to tell the difference was the poisonous fruit would not separate easily from the stem. You would almost have to cut it off. The "pure" fruit nearly fell off in your hand. They called it the "gift plant" because they considered it a gift from the Ancient One to so easily know which to take and which to leave. So "pure" here may be referring less to an outward moral state of being, and instead an inward inclination to move toward something, or leave what they once knew." She tucked her hair behind her ear and tapped her pencil against the table. "A willingness to go."

Dagen lifted his own text and pointed to something. "You know how it says the "Perfect One" will "lead the pure into the sun"? Could that be a literal direction? The sun rises in the east and sets in the west. Is the river going in either of those directions…?"

Michale gasped, locking eyes with Dagen.

"'Children wait for the perfect one, who will lead the pure into the sun'. This whole time we have been trying to force one of ourselves into this role, but the Ancient Magic was actually saying to wait until *It* moved Itself literally toward the sun!" She sat back, dazed by the simplicity of it all.

"This whole time, all we had to do was wait and follow… who came up with the Jyre Forest Test Day??" Michale shook her head, realizing the Jyres must have been feeding them twisted interpretations of the text for longer than she had first thought.

"Do we know which direction the river is going?" Dagen leaned forward, checking the clock in disappointment at the hour. "We can't see or ask anyone at this time."

Michale shook her head absently.

"It is going west." Belick's deep voice startled Michale'thia and Dagen both, but was quickly met with smiles of delight and a rush of embraces.

Michale looked around, her heart pounding in her chest at the thought of seeing her other half. But Syra was nowhere to be seen.

She looked at Belick with pleading eyes, but he shook his head.

"She is not here. Sit. It would seem you have come to the knowledge I have just experienced."

They stacked their pages and poured a cup for Belik, eager to hear what he meant.

"The Ancient Magic moves west, to the Unmade Lands. And Syra has gone to see where it leads."

Her mouth hung open, in part because they *knew* where to go, and in part because Belick let Syra go alone.

"You sent her *by herself-*"

"I DID NOT HAVE A CHOICE." Belick's fist thumped on the table as he met Michale's burning gaze with one of his own. Dagen set a comforting hand on his shoulder. Knowing the anger was only a hardened wall hiding pain.

Belick relaxed his hands and bowed his head in shame. "I could not enter. The Ancient One does not see me fit. We thought we were being attacked and the only way to save her was to send her on the raft down the river. She is in the Ancient Magic's hands now."

"I'm sorry, Belick. I should have asked. I just... I miss her more than I can say."

He nodded, the deep browns of his skin nearly shimmering in the candlelight.

"Now, we trust. Even when the one we love is too far to see."

They sat in silence for a moment before Dagen spoke, bringing them back to the conversation at hand.

"So, the river is moving west, and we need to follow it."

Belick nodded, rubbing his face in exhaustion.

"Yes. We do not know how, but my brother, Brendar is working on ways to make that happen."

Michale rolled her eyes, "Of course your brothers are awake too. What else did I miss?"

Dagen shrugged, "I didn't know that either."

"It does not matter, the point is, we have to find a way to move what may be close to 150,000 people down the river safely, with an army of Anarathans and Jyres trying to kill us."

"So we wait? Is that all we can do?" Michale felt like she was about to break, her own mind desperately searching for an answer to the problem.

"No, there is no time to wait. We don't know how far the river will go or what lies ahead. We need to prepare food, somehow water-proof our packs, and prepare our people for battle along the way. And all that just in the slim chance that we are correct this time."

"And if we are not?" Dagen dared to ask.

Belick's eyes glazed over as he looked toward the west.

"Then we all fade away into nothingness. Our fate is owned by the Ancient Magic."

CHAPTER 17

ENITH

E nith woke to the sun reaching between the mountains and through the small crack between the curtains and the wall, landing directly on his face. He scrubbed at his eyes for a moment and sat up, careful to keep the covers on his wife's peaceful body.

His *wife*. Springs, he was a lucky man.

He shrugged on a shirt before tiptoeing out of the room and out the door. He paced himself on his jog, knowing the upward climb ahead, and turned his thoughts toward the land before him and their problem at hand.

To mobilize an army of 10,000 would take months and there had to be at least 100,000 people here, some injured, some mourning, and many either refugees who had seen too much, or Botanis who had seen too little.

He reached the base of the large mountainous hill he had heard the elders call, *Methunitous,* meaning "deathlife", and mentally prepared himself for the arduous run ahead of him. He learned last time he ran

Methunitous that "deathlife" was exactly what this route ought to be called. You died going up it and were brought back to life by the view.

Enith arrived at the top with sweat pouring down his torso despite the pleasantly cool breeze and bent over nearly retching, proud when he didn't this time. That was progress.

Catching his breath he found a *Nup* tree and picked a ripe pink sphere off, enjoying the sweet and spicy drink inside.

He could see the entire northern land below him, every kingdom smaller than he ever thought possible. Up on the mountain even the grandest of kings could feel insignificant, and beautifully so. What would Anaratha be like without Michale fueling their hallucination of grandeur? And without their slaves to hold the weight of the kingdom on their backs? He shook his head, the old, simmering anger coming back.

He groaned. No matter how much good, or time, or space, the darkness inside still remained. It was a festering part of him and one he was becoming better and better at hiding. It scared him.

Enith threw the outside of the *Nup* down the mountain, wishing he could actually have hit the kingdom below. The shell fell out of view and Enith's eyes traced the landscape. When had the land become so ashen? Surrounding the Jyre forest for what looked like miles on end was a land that was completely black, as if a blazing fire had torn through. Was the Jyre forest gone? Did it burn to the ground?

His heart leapt at the idea, but his joy quickly turned to horror as he began to see the blackness moving ever so slightly. It was slow, nearly impossible to see, but it was clear this was no scorched land.

Enith stood on the edge of the mountain, straining his eyes to understand what was happening. His stomach dropped as he began to suspect the worst, measuring the width and length of the black mass in comparison to the forest beside it.

He stumbled back, falling down with wide eyes.

No. This can't be real.

He flew down the mountain, jumping over rocks with ease to cut through the land toward his own room. Enith burst through the door, barely taking in Ilytha's arched brow, and rummaged around his bag frantically, then sped off to a closer lookout. He would only be able to see a sliver, but it would be enough.

He knelt on one knee to see between the ridge and took out his looking glass, begging the Magic to not let his theory be true.

He steadied his hand and focused on the dark form in the north and dropped the looking glass.

It wasn't one large mass. It was an army. Of delviors.

The next Dark War was upon them.

"We must fight this time!" Saray stomped her spear against the ground, staring down those around the table.

An older man to her left closed his wrinkled eyes and sighed, "We cannot enter into this. We would only be slaughtered. There are too many."

Saray sat up straighter, her knuckles white. "It is better to die fighting than to never fight at all."

Belick spoke up then, his voice low but firm.

"Mother." He bowed his head in respect. "I have lived that saying, and it is furthest from the truth. It is better to die fighting for what is right, it is true, but it is better to never fight at all if there is nothing good in the battle."

She looked down then, her passion quelled as she thought through his words.

Enith glanced around and could see the elders all lost in thought, even Belick now in a different time of his own. He cleared his throat and spoke up.

"I am new, but I have fought these beasts and many armies in the north. Can I share?" His own cup sat untouched before him, his chest too tight to drink. Nods around the room gave him freedom to continue.

"One delvior alone can take up to five trained warriors to kill, and that is after a long battle and three men dead. They are faster, stronger, and can hear further than anything I have ever seen. I've done the calculations and for that much land to be taken up by them, there has to be *tens of thousands* down there. We cannot fight them." He met the eyes of the elders and waited as he wrestled with his next words.

"We had teams, one of which Belick himself was on, scour that area. As far as we know, anyone in danger is here now. There is no one else to protect except ourselves. But we will need it, and we will probably have to fight."

He took out a map and nodded in thanks when a blue-robed child rushed to help pin it to a wall behind them.

"If what Belik and Michale said is true, we are going to need to move our people here," he pointed to a place vaguely west.

"The Spring is moving west, and our only hope is following it. We don't have time to prepare. At most we can give everyone a log or a board or something to help them float, but we have to get there. We *will* encounter delviors and we *will* need to protect our people, but not in all out war. I propose we send word to every village here and begin preparations. Everyone will need to bring four days worth of food per person and whatever weapons they can hold. We can use any animals for transport, but they won't go with us past the river. When we get to the river, we hope we make it. Maybe some of us will live through Its rapids."

Belick shook his head, pointing toward the desert, "The Loharans are still there, and they were promised escort to safety."

Enith squeezed his eyes shut and gritted his teeth. There was no way they could get them out without slaughtering anyone who went to rescue them.

"Belick we don't-"

"We will get them out. Or die trying."

His low rumble filled the room as he locked eyes with Saray, who nodded in grim determination.

Enith's own frustration grew as tall as his helplessness and he glared at Belick.

"And how do you plan to do that? This is a suicide mission! I want to get them out, but there is no way you could get there unnoticed, Belick."

Belick turned to him with full calm then, only his blazing eyes giving away his own growing fury.

"Do not forget, princeling, that my brothers and I know this land better than any and still hold the Magic's power inside of us. We were tasked with caring for this world, and we *will* get them out."

Enith stared at him a moment longer before giving a nod. "You save the Loharans, and we will guard the people as they make their way to the river. You will need to leave soon to meet us there. Would you all agree to this plan?"

The elders nodded, concern creasing many brows as they rose to begin preparations.

Belick moved to leave behind them, and Enith nearly choked on his next words, knowing he could never live with himself if he didn't.

"Ilytha and Michale are seasoned leaders. They don't need me. You will need all the help you can get. I'm coming with you."

Belick paused his exit and waited, turning his head to the side but not fully looking at Enith.

"We leave in four hours."

The next hour was chaotic and Enith dreaded the conversation to come. Not just for Ilytha's sake, but for his own. He jogged back toward the tall building and settled against the mountain's face and made his way around back, knowing Ilytha would be training at this hour.

He found her dancing in practiced combat with Rish, a smaller woman with lighter brown hair than the rest, cut to her shoulders and often divided into small braids when practicing.

But Ilytha is who his eyes couldn't leave. Her movements could only be described as graceful, even if deadly. She flowed through the air with precision, her blade slicing with a ring against Rish's own, not wasting any time before pulling back and spinning for another opening.

The match was over within minutes, and Ilytha grabbed Rish's hand and pulled her close, hanging an arm around her neck as she spoke to her in a lowered voice, likely giving her tips on her form. Rish nodded and moved into a form, her arm pulled back with the blade ready to plunge and one leg stretched before her and one behind.

Ilytha nodded and gently moved the woman's foot closer to her body and nudged her elbow closer to her side. Smiling widely when she looked over the form and applauded.

"Rish, you have grown faster than I ever did. Too soon you will beat me."

Rish smiled back and relaxed her form, sliding her blade back and rolling her eyes.

"Somehow, I don't think you will ever allow yourself to stop growing, so I don't know how I'll ever catch up. But thank you."

Ilytha caught Enith's eye and sent the woman on a jog and a water break afterward, turning to walk toward him.

Enith's own smile faded as he remembered the conversation he was about to have. He took her hand as she neared and walked beside her silently until they were a short ways away, heading up the trail to *Methunitous.*

When they arrived, he see she knew something was coming, her own wary eyes confused. As he brought her to the cliffs edge with him.

She gasped softly and turned to him, questions evident enough in her eyes that no words were needed.

"It's an army of delviors. It would seem our timeline for moving the people out of here has moved, and we now have days to start moving down toward a river near the west."

"The one Michale and Belick say is the Ancient Magic moving?"

He nodded gravely.

"So we are following the Ancient Magic and just *hoping* it is going somewhere we can live?"

He nodded again, feeling increasingly naive as she spoke.

"Yes. Do you have a better plan?"

She shook her head and looked back at the land below, her brows lowered in concern.

"We may not live. You know this." It was a statement, not a question.

"I know. But right now, we have no other way. This land is dying, the land we came from is taken over. We have nowhere left but west."

Ilytha squeezed his hand, strands of her hair tucked behind her ears, only making her beautiful brown eyes even more pronounced.

"And there is something else..." His voice faded as his throat closed. How could he say goodbye when he had just found her?

"The Loharans asked for help getting out, and they were promised aid. I am leaving with a team to go get them."

Ilytha dropped his hand and backed away a step, anger clouding her face.

"That is suicide and you know it."

"It may not be. Belick knows the land and his brothers will be helping. They think they have a chance."

"This is foolish and you know it!"

She turned away, but not before he saw the tears welling in her eyes. He pulled her back and wrapped his arms around her, burying his head in her hair as he tried to memorize her smell for the days to come.

She held him back, her voice muffled against his shoulder.

"And yet I know it is right. But I hate it. And I hate that you want me to stay, or you wouldn't be saying this like a goodbye."

Enith pulled back and held her head gently in his hands, looking into her eyes. He *needed* her to know he would always rather have her at his side.

"There are too few people here with the knowledge of the land below. Michale is smart, but she has no skills as a soldier, and she is still weak. Dagen will be a help, but they need you. They need warriors who can lead this massive group."

She nodded, tears dropping onto the soft grass between them.

He held her close again, kissing the top of her head and marveling at how they could love each other in such little time. Springs, he had to come back this time. He had never cared before, but this time, he couldn't leave to die. He had to make it back.

They walked back down the hill toward their room and spent the next hours together, only parting in the last ten minutes for Enith to throw his few belongings into a bag and meet Belick outside with a small group.

Belick had a horse for him and sat beside Aleth and Rienah, who looked at Ilytha with a soft smile and nod before riding forward. Enith climbed on his tall, deep black horse and nudged it into a fast trot to catch up, the ache in his chest already threatening to burst through.

But love couldn't stop him from doing what was right, or what kind of love could he offer at all?

The horses walked down the steep trail with ease, and Enith found himself squeezing his legs and leaning back just to stay on. They made it down the mountain within hours, winding left and keeping close to the unmade land. They now couldn't see where the delvior army was and would have to be careful.

They had only moved a mile out when Belick and Aleth shared a look, stopping their small party and climbing off.

Aleth smiled broadly and Rienah grimaced.

"Now, for the fun part." He bent down and lifted dirt to his face before looking back up.

"The delviors can pick up scents from pretty far away, so we are going to cover ourselves head to toe with this first, and then with a *booroo* plant, which will give us a scent that *most* creatures stay far away from."

Rienah slid off her horse, "For good reason." She grumbled as she strode over and began picking up a sickly plant protruding from the ground with wilting leaves with yellow spots.

Aleth laughed and began spreading the mud onto his arms. "We only need one each, their smell is quite pungent. But this is how we used to play hide-and-seek as kids. Back then our magic was stronger and we could find each other too quickly, so one day Lohan covered himself in this gross muck, and we couldn't find him for days!" He shook his head. "Brilliant boy."

Enith joined the others reluctantly and began spreading the mud onto his face, then moving downward until he was completely covered, resembling a madman more than a soldier.

Rienah passed out the plants and Enith immediately understood why the delviors, or anyone else for that matter, would be deterred, his own eyes burning along with his nose.

After a half hour of covering themselves and gagging at their own stench, they mounted and began riding at a faster pace toward the Lo-haran desert, hoping to reach it within a day.

CHAPTER 18

SYRA

"See, every person in our forest came to be here because they bonded with one specific tree. It's the Ancient Magic's way of teaching us to not just be providers for the land, but to actually care for the forest around us and see past how it might benefit our own lives. We honor the Magic by caring for Creation."

Syra pushed against the board, holding it tightly as instructed.

"Would that mean then that I am supposed to be a part of the Forest Kingdom? Would any Jyre person transfer that way?"

Julin grunted as he pushed the board on the opposite side, nodding. "Well, maybe. I don't really know. And it isn't a command. You are still free to live in any kingdom, but most of us at this point have found the Ancient Magic gives these signs not to force us into a mold, but because It knows us and knows what we will love the most."

Their sand timer ended and they both stopped pushing, breathing heavily as they sat and inspected their work. The boards had been cemented into place by the paste and would now be a very small part of what was being called the "mid-water boat". The boat would be as thin as possible, allowing space for Syra's legs to enter in while her upper body navigated above, covered with a canvas which would wrap around her waist and keep water out. They calculated its size would allow it to cut upstream if she was rowing fast enough.

Other builders stood around their work, sweat glistening on many foreheads but pride marking puffed chests as they inspected every detail. Julin picked up the wooden length and brought it over to a group in the middle of camp who were carefully arranging each small piece into a larger whole based on their drawings.

"Anything else, guys?" Julin called toward the workers whose heads were huddled around the boat. One with orange hair and pale green eyes turned with a smile, his rudy cheeks bright with delight as he waved them off.

"No, we are good here. Go have fun or something and check in tomorrow. We should have it ready for testing!"

Julin raised his brows at Syra and smiled, holding out a hand to help her up from the tired place she had settled into. She gratefully took his hand and stood, dusting off her pants and wiping her forehead.

"Well, that's exciting." She smiled back at him and looked down, trying to find something other than his face to land on.

He began walking and she followed, which was the norm these days as he took it upon himself to show her around.

"It is. How do you feel about it?" He tipped his head slightly in her direction, oblivious to the way his eyes on her made her feel.

"Torn. Guilty. Terrified. Thankful." She laughed as he raised his brows again, looking mildly shocked.

"Oh, is that all?" She laughed and pulled her hair out of the braid she had brushed it into for work that day, absentmindedly scooping some of it back behind her head and letting the rest flow about her.

"I want to stay, and I don't want to struggle through going back. I want to just believe the Ancient Magic will save them all instead putting myself through so much to help, but I can't help but think maybe the Ancient Magic wants to save people through others. What if *I* am the means of the Ancient Magic's care for those in the Deadlands? I can't give up." She sighed and looked him back in the eye.

"But then, I just want to stay."

He didn't say anything as he continued walking, leading them into the town by the sea and onto a stone walkway.

"I'm sorry this is so hard. I wish the answer was obvious, but I think that's the problem. It's not, and we aren't sure what's right."

Julin smiled at the market vendor selling meat wrapped in thin bread with fruit and spices tossed inside. He handed her one and they sat on the edge of a stone wall overlooking the sea. The sun still had an hour to go before it was dark, and the view was calming.

Syra took a bite and gasped, startling Julin, who looked around frantically trying to figure out what was wrong.

"This ehs, uhmzing!"

He cocked a brow and stared, stupefied before realization set in and he threw his head back laughing. When he finally stopped, he held out a finger.

"First, I don't know if you've learned this in the Deadlands, but it's extremely hard to understand someone with their mouth full. Second, *are there no gesh in the Deadlands??*" When she shook her head no, he continued, a playful indignation painted across his face.

He placed a hand on his chest and continued, "I for one am *very* surprised you didn't come here sooner then."

Syra smirked and tossed a piece of food at his face, rolling her eyes when he caught it in his mouth and grinned at her cheekily.

They finished their food and sat there longer, lingering while the sun began to drop out of the sky. The sunsets were unlike anything she had seen. The colors were more vibrant, and the longer she studied them, the more she swore she could see that they were made up of real pictures. Tonight's picture was of a battle, with men on horses yelling as they held swords in the air and sat frozen in their surge onward.

"It's history. The sun setting reminds us of what has been or will be laid to rest."

"I thought they were just pictures." Syra gaped at the magic before her.

"This is amazing. I wish I could capture the beauty of it justly." She leaned her head to the side and studied it longer, enraptured by the exquisite forms before her.

"Are you an artist then?"

She laughed at that, even as memories assaulted her.

"I wanted to be. I used to hide away from my father when I was younger and try to recreate things I had seen that I thought were beautiful. A smile, or a small bug." She laughed at a particular memory involving a slimy creature crawling up her glass.

"But unfortunately, my father was not intent on finding beauty, he was intent on mangling it, and I quickly learned to never create anything he could touch." She shuddered at the thought of his dark form ripping the page from her hands and studying it with a cruel smile. She had been four years old and her drawing had been a horrible depiction of a puppy she had seen born recently. Her small hands had made it bone thin, with legs that didn't bend and no tale or ears, but she had tried. The next week her father had brought her the puppy. Starved to nearly to death with half its legs cut off so they couldn't bend and both its tail and ears removed. He had shown her then his power to twist was greater than her power to create.

Julin gently touched her cheek with the back of his hand, drawing her eyes to his.

"I don't know where you just went, but Syra, don't let anyone take the beauty inside you. If someone has tried to steal it, strengthen it tenfold. The world needs it."

She blinked away tears and looked up at him, suddenly caught in a world of dark eyes and dark lashes. When he slowly began moving his own lips toward hers, she didn't stop. She was pulled toward him with something stronger than any bond she had felt, and when their lips touched it was like tasting home.

The warmth from his lips was gone too soon and her own were left parted as she tried to understand what just happened.

Julin cupped her chin in his hand, his voice strong and gentle.

"Syra, I don't know what the next few days or years will bring, but come back. *Please.* Come back and explore what we could be together."

She didn't even realize she was nodding until she felt the movements, cursing her body for betraying her. But she did want this, and she didn't know what the future would bring. In a swift movement she brought a hand behind his head and pulled his lips back down to her own, cherishing their taste a moment longer before breaking it off. Her nose was red from the chill and her cheeks flushed as she looked at him this time.

"When I come back, we will figure this out."

And with that she walked away, needing sleep for the day to come.

Morning approached all too soon and Syra scarfed down her drink and meat, hurrying out the door in a very Ky fashion.

She skipped down the familiar stone steps and back toward the river, her own nerves beginning to build as she drew closer to the place she may soon depart from. The grass gave way to the wide river bed and she joined the crowd at the edge, all circled around the boat barely bigger than a human. Its smooth round edges and long thin frame made it look impossible to fit in, but she trusted the crews. They would have tested the size before bringing it.

Julin and one of the designers saw her approaching and strode to meet her. The girl in front, Briy, if she remembered correctly, reached a hand out to give her a warm hug, her speckled cheeks lifted in excitement below her own black hair.

"I think this is going to work, Syra!" Her excitement was contagious and Syra found herself grinning back.

"Well, it *could* work, but we didn't account for the river level being even higher." Julin looked at Briy with a frown, concern lining his forehead.

Syra peeked over at the river, noting the more violent rapids.

"Why do you think it's higher now?"

He brought his hand to his chin, his somber mood starting to worry her.

"I will never know the Ancient Magic's mind, but... the timing *is* odd. It's possible It does not want this to happen..."

Syra stared at the river then, trying to ignore the panic growing in her chest. If the Magic didn't want it to work, it wouldn't, no matter their greatest schemes. But why would it want to keep her from helping her people?

She turned on her heel with a huff and walked toward the boat, snatching the head protector from a poor soul and clipping it on while throwing a pointed look at Julin. It *would* work. It had to.

She listened intently while someone wrapped the waterproof cloth around her and the boat's opening, explaining the force she would have to row with when she first hit the water.

She sat in the boat, leaning back with a helmet securely on her head as she studied the river. The minute she was pushed in it would take everything she had to move forward instead of backward toward the waterfall. And if she did get swept toward the waterfall, she would have few precious moments to get out and back on land before being sent over the edge.

Syra readied herself for the task ahead and locked eyes with Julin. Some black curly waves fell across his forehead and she felt her resolve wane in the wake of his eyes. But she gave a small smile instead and tightened her grip on her oars.

They pushed her as a group, inching her way toward the water. With a countdown, she readied herself until with one grand heave, they shoved the boat as hard as they could upstream.

Ice sprayed onto her face and Syra paddled with as much speed and force as she could muster, blindly trying to force her way through the waves even as her lungs refused to breath from the cold.

She couldn't tell if she was making any headway and gasped as a larger rapid covered her boat completely, shocking her into a quick breath of water and coughing through blurry eyes as she pulled water through her paddle.

Her grip was firm against the wood and she screamed at the river, redoubling her efforts. Syra felt her boat move forward and felt her heart lurch with excitement. She *would* make it back.

But as she pulled her paddle back, a wave of white foam shot toward her, spiraling her boat out of control. She tipped upside down, her head crashing into a hidden boulder below, and she grasped for the knife tucked into her waist, cutting wildly at the cloth tying her to the boat. Her lungs burned and she continued hitting boulders at every turn. She cut herself free and pushed to the top of the river, getting one breath in before a wave crashed on top of her head again. Her ears were roaring with pain–

Except it wasn't pain. And before she could register what was happening, she was flung over the edge of the waterfall.

Syra woke in a room with Julin sitting beside her, his head in his hands. She sat up and brought a hand to her head, squinting her eyes against the pain. He sat up and closed his eyes in relief, sighing out what must have been a great load of worries. He started to speak but Syra held up a hand. She had been through the bedridden thing and she was done with it.

"No, I can't do this. Julin, I like you and I want to stay, but this can't be the end."

She ground her teeth against the pain and lifted herself out of the plush bed, pulling on her shoes harder than necessary and stomping out of the house to the calls of her host family.

Her anger was growing steadily and by the time she reached the large cavern of water beneath the waterfall, she was enraged.

If not this, what should she do?

With heated force, she thrust her hand into the water as if she could grab the Ancient Magic out Itself.

When her hand hit the water, her world went white and everything else faded away. The icy warmth flowing through her was familiar. Like the oldest friend welcoming her in.

Syra expected war with the Magic, to feel Its wrath and to fight against it while fighting to be near it. But it was as if instead It had folded her into Its arms and held her there. She couldn't see, but her spirit jumped and her tears began to flow. She was angry and helpless and wanted what was right but was *so* tired of not knowing. She needed help.

Pictures flashed through her mind and she heard a whisper vibrate through her entire being, reverberating against her very soul.

GO.

Her eyes opened and Syra saw the world of color again, her hands in front of her open, and deep, intricate white designs covering her arms completely now. She stood on shaky legs, her mind working silently through all she just saw.

Julin and Lalise jogged up to her, worry evident as Lalise took her hands in her own, freezing when she saw the markings.

She brought a hand to her mouth and gasped, turning Syra's hand over to follow the designs further.

"Syra…"

Syra nodded, understanding more than they did what this meant.

"I know."

Julin shook his head in disbelief, running a hand through his curls. "You- You've been given more power than any of us combined. This has to be equal to or even greater than the Ancient Brothers themselves!"

Syra's own eyes widened at that. Perhaps she didn't understand as much as she thought. She closed her hands around Lalise's and looked at them, her words gentle but determined.

"I will make a way for my people to come, and I will do it with the Magic's help."

Lalise nodded with tears brimming her eyes and Julin smiled, giving her a playful nudge.

"Go bring them home."

She smiled broadly at him and took off toward her room, tossing a few essentials into a pack and giving quick hugs before running out.

She jogged along the river, studying the warm green ground beneath her, knowing within miles it would soon fade into unmade, unstable dirt. Time passed quickly and the lush green fell away to gray. She stopped her jog and froze as her feet stood on the Unmade.

Syra was suddenly hit with a void inside. It wasn't painful, or sad, or anything. It was nothing. It wasn't just land that was unmade, nothing was made. Language, color, knowledge- for a moment Syra felt a void of everything she had known. She could barely form words here, as if the air was thick and secretly full of mud.

With only vague inclinations, Syra lifted a hand and brought forth solid, green land a foot in front of her. It didn't just stop at the small foot she was trying to create in, the green shot out in every direction, springing up new plants she may never see grow to maturity, and painting color into what was once dull.

Delight grew in her and she felt a pulse of joy from the Magic, bringing a breathless laugh from Syra. She took another step and brought out solid land again, her excitement and love for what she was creating only magnified as the Ancient Magic inside her leapt with joy.

"Alright, let's speed this up." She whispered, and then took off running, bringing into existence pieces of land moments before her feet hit them. All around the river's edge now were trees and bushes, vines with white flowers and small creatures scurrying. By the time night had fallen, she could see Elharren in the distance. A burst of energy surged through her and she sped on, mile after mile, creating and running on a high of joy. It wasn't like a drug, addicting her body to something foreign. It was like becoming what she *should* have been. Entering into what ought have been instead of what was.

Syra slowed to a walk and took out a piece of bread from her bag, tearing a piece off and wondering why she hadn't brought anything to drink. She stopped before crossing the line into Elharren, looking back before stepping forward. She had made it. Now to the Mountains.

"Syra."

His voice startled her, and Syra turned around to face the figure clothed in darkness before her.

He held out his hands, the dimples in his smile showing in the moonlight.

"Luik!" She threw her arms around his neck, hope growing even as guilt set in. She wasn't tied to him, but she couldn't give up on him either.

Luik pulled back to look at her and laughed, shaking his head. "You are still more beautiful than anyone I have ever known. Did you find anything?? Come on, I have a fire over here with some soup. Join me and let's catch up."

She followed him to his camp and they sat down, taking a bowl of soup as she explained the beauty to the west. His brows rose as she explained the ocean kingdom and island she had been able to visit with all its rich flowers and sweet fruit.

He listened intently, his eyes searching hers, and she continued to paint the reality she hoped would save him. As they laughed and swapped stories, exhaustion settled in and two visions of Luik appeared.

Every breath was labored, and her vision began to darken. It hit her, only as she began to fall to her knees, looking up at Luik as she went. Syra held a hand to her chest, her heart hammering and her throat now swollen.

Poison.

A deeper ache filled her inside as she stared at the man she once loved, betrayal and pain evident in her silent gaze. He looked her in the eye with a jaw clenched too tight and breath coming too fast for him to not care. Yet still, her vision darkened and she lost feeling in her limbs before falling over into the dirt.

CHAPTER 19

MICHALE'THIA

T he streets were clear as Michale'thia wandered down the path, not knowing if it would take her to the ocean but taking it anyway. She hadn't seen Dagen all morning and decided to take the opportunity to explore the vast kingdom.

She gazed around at the tall mountain peaks surrounding her, majestic in their blue hues and sprouts of colorful flowers. The yearning was gone, or moving, perhaps. Maybe it was the Ancient Magic after all, calling her spirit to come.

Her shoes moved softly against the dirt path, eventually crossing a hill overlooking small villages tucked away on the seafront. She stood there, observing the small figures playing in the water. A smile crept onto her face as she climbed down the hill toward them, eager to smell the salty air again.

It was a longer trek than she thought, and she reached it just slightly out of breath, stopping a short ways away. Michale held her arms, taking in a shaky breath as she watched the children huddle around wood planks and tools, unperturbed by the tide rolling in at their feet.

They were refugees. Some part Anarathan, others mixes of multiple different ethnicities. They still held the innocent glow, as if the world hadn't actually touched them yet. She took a step back, somehow feeling too out of place to join. Too dirty. Too broken.

She sat down on the sand, feeling her hair blowing out of the low bun she had forced it into, and wondered if life would ever feel normal again. How much ocean water would it take to make her feel clean?

Footsteps padded softly behind her and Michale turned just in time to find a tall, elegant woman sitting down beside her. Gentle features and a tall form marked her confidence and a thick auburn braid hung down her back. She looked like everything a queen should be. Unbroken, beautiful, secure.

She spoke with a wry smile. "You seem deep in thought for one so young." The woman settled her simple, faded green dress across her legs.

Michale stared back at the waves and brought her knees up to her chest, sighing.

"Much life can be lived in one so young."

The woman took the answer as truth and nodded, not giving up.

"My name is Cirren, and one of those little fellows is my son, Benji. What's your name?"

The princess turned toward Cirren then, attempting to smile as she shook her hand. What should she say? She didn't want to be Michale'thia anymore, with all her baggage, yet she was too sure she could never lose her either.

"Michale. It's nice to meet you, Cirren. Your son looks like he is having quite a bit of fun." She smiled genuinely that time, enjoying the spectacle the boy was making as he held the board up, sanding something into precision.

Cirren chuckled, a rich, honey-like sound.

"My son is always having fun when he is near the water. It's like he was born with it in his soul." She paused before continuing.

"What's troubling you? Do you have family here? I know you only just met me, but I see a look in your eyes much like I once had, and I wouldn't ever condemn myself to that pain and loneliness again."

Michale sighed again, this time a mixture of relief and frustration. How sweet it could be to just let it out to a stranger she may never see again, yet how awful.

"Not too long ago, something... something happened to me. Now, the things I used to love feel out of reach, or terrifying."

To Michale's surprise, Cirren nodded knowingly, her own eyes on the ocean now.

"It feels wrong, doesn't it? To make it through something with only the pure will to live as your guide, only to live and find life is nothing at all what it used to be."

Michale rested her chin on her knees and turned her face toward Cirren.

"What did you have to make it through?"

Her head fell for a moment, and Michale almost apologized for dredging up whatever memories made her eyes look like that, but she spoke before Michale could say anything else.

"When I was younger, I fell in love. Or I thought I had. The man was beautiful, more than any I could have dreamed up, and he was so kind and confident, painting pictures of riches and grandeur for me." She looked at Michale then and let out a breath.

"He was Jyre, see. And he was a king. By the time anyone from home realized what was happening, I was already too far gone, willing to give up everything for him. But when he kept pushing for more, a cruel side of him would show, and I became terrified, finding ways to avoid his touch and searching for anyone in the Jyre forest who would help me get away. I did find someone. She was brainwashed with the others her whole life, but she still questioned if what they were doing was right, and we became… friends, I guess. As much a friend as you can be with grown Jyre women." She chuckled at a reality only she truly understood.

"And then one night, he dragged me to his room and took from me what he wanted. I became pregnant, like he said I would, and he made sure I couldn't leave until having the baby. When I did have the baby, he took it and killed it. I only escaped with the help of that friend and her brother. They both told him they had killed me in the chase, but I ran and didn't stop until I got to the furthest village away from them. Looking back, he had commented on my strength, and beauty, and height as if he were looking at a horse, not a woman he loved. I should have seen that."

Michale couldn't breath, goosebumps covering her arms as she sat frozen in fear, putting pieces together in her mind.

Cirren continued, "The worst part about that all, is I think he didn't kill my child. I think he told me that to break me further. And I think I met her, and then I let her walk away without telling her who I was because I was afraid she would ask why I didn't ask for the body. She might ask why I didn't fight harder to get her back, and I would have to look into the eyes of my child who grew up without a mother."

Tears flowed unchecked down her cheeks just as they did Micahle'thia's. She swallowed and looked back at the ocean, confused by her own jealousy growing, evil and insipid as it longed for a mother like this. More tears flowed and Michale dug her nails into her arms.

She hated herself.

Cirren wiped her cheeks and gave a half-hearted smile.

"I think I will see her again. But you see, life after that was more different than I can ever express. A new town, with all new foods and traditions. New fears and new anger. It took a long time and I don't think I ever felt "normal" again, but that's because my understanding of normal was just "before", not "what should be". Before, I wanted power and riches and to be the most beautiful, and I was quite frankly childish in my thinking. After years of working through all that happened, I'm quicker to listen now, slower to act, and I find myself thankful for such small things. I did fall in love again, and to a burly man who never pushed me and is as kind as he is handsome. And now we have Benji, our greatest joy." She smiled again, watching him stand on the board and wave his arms at the other children.

"I don't know what you went through, but I promise, you will find a new life. It will be a new normal, and it will be good if you let it be."

Michale didn't realize how long she had been thinking through those last words until she looked over and found Cirren gone. She stood too, but instead of going back, she walked toward the group of boys and girls, now with thin, smooth boards the size of their body on the sand.

She approached the group and stopped just outside, recognizing Benji right away, seeing both Cirren's and Syra's kind eyes in him. For one so young, he spoke with easy leadership, describing to each young person around him the force of kicking that would need to happen as a wave approached. His eyes lit up above his faded freckles and tan skin, and she could see a light in him so pure and genuine that she forgot for a moment that there was anything bad in the world at all. He locked eyes with her, giving her a wave and saying something to the kids around him before breaking off and coming to meet her.

"Hi, I'm Benji. Are you here to try out the wave-riders?"

Michale had no such desire, but he caught her hesitation and rushed on eagerly.

"Don't say no. I know it's new, but I *promise*, it will be worth it! The ocean is beautiful and powerful, so we have to respect it, but it's also playful and fun. We can *actually* use the waves to go faster and higher! Come on, I'll show you the basics, and then we can go out together and I'll help you catch the first wave."

His eyes were so bright as his young hand found hers, and she found herself following the boy toward the boards and into a quick lesson, which only made her more afraid. But she decided this would be her new norm. Trying new things and shrugging off the old.

Michale'thia waved goodbye to her new young friend, drenched and filled with salt water, but happy. She hadn't been able to stand up like he did so easily, but she had gotten to her knees once and he was right. It was incredible.

She walked back toward her room, deciding a bath was in order. As she passed villages, she began to notice a frantic energy in the air. The normally peaceful, slow-paced Botani people now seemed rushed and anxious, packing baskets and packs. Michale quickened her pace, finding Dagen on the path to meet her.

"What's going on?" She pulled her hair off her shoulders, looking around.

Dagen breathed heavily as if he had run to find her and ran a hand through his own hair.

"The Jyres released another Dak Army, and it's huge. A decision has been made to move everyone in three days down toward the river in hopes of following it out toward the Unmade land."

"Has Syra returned then?" Michale didn't want to let herself hope, but could feel it rising within.

Dagen shook his head, "No, but Luik volunteered to go meet her with horses so they could get back to us with a plan if she returns in time."

Fear coursed through her, intertwined with guilt and anger and too many emotions to sort through. Dagen took her hand and lowered his head to catch her eyes.

"Are you worried about Luik too?"

Michale grimaced at her transparency, but nodded.

"I just… He has had everything taken from him, and I'm the cause of that, I know, but there is something else there, and I can't figure it out. He isn't just hurting, he is festering." She rubbed her arm, still wondering if she was justifying a double standard or not.

Dagen's brows knit together and he looked around. "I was thinking something similar. I thought we'd be able to keep an eye on him a while longer, but he left some time today. I only found out because the guards at the fate told me hours later. But he loves her, we know that. Of all people, she is the one we can trust him with."

Michale nodded, thankful for the small consolation.

Dagen continued, gesturing toward the people around them.

"For now, I think we may need to help get people organized into groups that will fit on the trail down. Few know what it's like to ride through the lower lands, and that will be a weakness we have to cover. We'll also have delviors all around, so we'll need to move quickly."

She stared at a family in the distance, the parents surrounded by young children and large bags. "Are there any wagons or anything that can help the younger children and older ones?"

"Yes, but a limited number. We'll need every able body helping as we go."

She pursed herself lips, not liking the lack of resources. "And what about when we get to the river? How will we get so many people down it?"

Dagen let out a groan, holding his arms with a grimace. "I don't know. No one does. The plan is pretty sparse. We show up and hope Syra figured out how to get us there."

Michale suddenly remembered their own journey and gasped, "Dagen! The Loharans! We promised! We have to get them out!"

He put gentle hands on her arms and smiled.

"A team has already left to find them. Enith and Belick are both on it with Aleth and Rianah. They'll get them out."

Michale deflated a little, feeling more lost without a role now. Dagen took her hand and pulled her away toward a building.

"Come on, there's something you should see."

Michale let him lead her reluctantly, coming upon Ilytha and her warriors sparring. Michale watched with fascination as Ilytha stopped women ever so often to correct their form or show them what the move was supposed to look like. When Ilytha saw them she sent a knowing smile Dagen's way and approached Michale.

"So, sister. Have you come to finally learn our ways?"

Michale spun toward Dagen who was already retreating with his hands up in surrender and gave him a furious glare.

Ilytha laughed and draped an arm around her neck. "Do not be mad. He loves you and he believes you are strong. And we will make you even stronger still." She motioned then to the women standing around her.

"You see, we all know what it is like to be hurt and how to make ourselves stronger afterwards. That doesn't mean we are no longer women, or soft, but it means we are women who can be soft and can also cut the hand off the next person who tries to harm us." She said the last phrase with a sly smile and Michale laughed at the picture it brought of Ilytha doing just that to her brother, the Chief of the Syllrics who had beaten her in front of them.

Michale smiled and nodded, warmed that she would be invited into the exclusive group. And warmed that she would be invited by women who understood pain. She cocked a brow, turning to Ilytha.

"Alright, *sister*, show me what to do. I need to know how to defend myself should you ever disapprove of me hugging my brother again."

To Michale's surprise, Ilytha's cheeks burned at the memory and she laughed, glancing at the other women.

"I uh… might have thought she was another woman interested in my new husband when we first met."

The hoots and laughter following were enough to make Michale feel bad, but the look on Ilytha's face showed none of it was taken to heart. They were family.

"Alright, enough," Ilytha's casual command only garnered more laughter, and she resorted to ignoring them all as she came up beside Michale.

"We have three rules. First, practice everything 100 times perfectly, then practice every move 50 times perfectly a day." Michale's eyes bulged but she said nothing.

"Second, practice both offense and defensive fighting. Sometimes we will fight in battles with swords, but other times we will not have weapons and will only have our wits and training to protect others and ourselves. Third, we do this for love. Not hate. We love even those we have not met, the helpless, and even our enemies. It is for love that we teach what is right and make sure it happens, not hate. If you fight out of hate, you kill your own soul."

Ilytha pierced her with a stair then. "If I teach you, would you be fighting for the hate of someone or something?"

Michale was taken back by the question she couldn't answer. She *did* hate. She hated everyone. Her parents, her kingdom, Kallaren, Jyren, herself. But how was she supposed to admit that?

"No, I don't hate-"

To Michale's surprise Ilytha used her staff to sweep her feet out from under her, landing hard on her bottom.

"You already lie. I see it in you. Do not hide it." Ilytha held out a hand to help her up. "Face your emotions, accept them, and search for a way to let the bad go."

A woman with a shaved head grunted in affirmation, gazing at Michale with understanding.

"You aren't the only one. Many women here have had to leave before they could return, but you fight differently when it's out of anger. You're ruled by that emotion and it grows into chaos killing you faster than you can kill others. Go find a place to think and figure out how to move on. Then come back because I kind of like you."

Michale clenched her fists, indignancy and hot anger pulsing in her. She wanted nothing more than to bite out that they were all wrong and send them all landing on their back sides, but she realized even as she thought it that she *was* angry. And it *was* affecting her.

She accepted Ilytha's hand up and stalked away, waiting to hear snickers or whispers but finding none, just the clashing of staffs resuming their sparring.

Michale finally found her room and collapsed onto her bed. She looked around the simple, spacious quarters nestled against the mountain's edge and sighed, looking out the window and blinking back memories of her time under the city.

How was she supposed to just *get past* this all?

Her mind wandered toward historic figures she had cherished reading about, remembering the hours she spent reading their journals and essays, all of which showed the deeper realities of life history textbooks rarely showed. She thought back toward the stories she used to tell Syra as they went to sleep at night as children, full of life and adventures. The stories always featured Syra, and it was Michale's way of trying to help Syra be okay.

With that thought in mind, Michale got up and took a bath, changing into a loose, large shirt of Dagen's and pulling her hair back into a bun. She found the new notebook Dagen had gifted her from a Botani merchant and sat against the wall her bed leaned against.

She paused, opening the beautiful notebook and tracing it's pages gently. Then, with a deep breath, she began to write, weaving the beginning of a fairytale story onto the page and finally letting every ounce of truth come out.

CHAPTER 20

LUIK

The large hooves beneath him seemed to stomp heavier than normal. Luik winced at the noise, glowering at the horse beside him holding Syra's limp body.

Bloody springs. What was he doing?

He lifted his chin defiantly, pulling his shoulders back again. He was paying the price for Anaratha's judgment. And maybe after, he would have peace.

The echo inside calling him a liar was quieted by the horse's hooves, and Luik trained his eyes ahead. One life *had* to be worth justice for an entire kingdom.

Luik winced as he suddenly felt uncomfortably similar to Anaratha. The pit in his stomach raged against every movement forward.

The bloody Ancient Magic could die for all he cared. It didn't protect or care for justice. It just sat, far off, gloating in Its creating abilities while not *actually* creating a way for his people to have lived. What bloody absurdity.

He gripped the reins tightly but barely noticed the horse's indignant retort.

And if the Ancient Magic did care, it could have stopped it but didn't, so that would make it bloody useless. Not powerful.

Luik's coat felt heavier and he shrugged his shoulders.

Either the Magic wasn't kind or it wasn't powerful. That was that. And it sure as bloody Jyren's grave wouldn't stop him now. He would make sure Anaratha understood the weight of their actions. They would feel what he felt and know the death of his people.

But what about after? What would he do?

The thought came swiftly, causing Luik to stop the horse in its tracks.

What *would* he do? Save Syra and live happily ever after? No.

He would build a ship and sail away. Let the bloody ocean have him.

No matter how hard he had tried, the brooding furry grew inside. Every time he saw Michale smile or any other Anarathan free, his mind went back to the day his own people suffered.

Luik kicked his horse back into motion, walking straight toward the forest, now only miles ahead. The sun was already gone from the sky and Luik decided to make camp, pulling a blanket down and laying it out before sliding Syra off the horse and gently setting her on top. He eventually had a fire going, forgoing dinner with a soured stomach.

The wind began to pick up and he grabbed another blanket down, tucking it around Syra before settling himself into his jacket and laying down. The stars weren't visible with the smoke so heavy. Too many burned villages.

He closed his eyes and tried to calm his racing mind, wondering if he could really bring the woman he loved to such a cruel man. Instead of answering the question, he opened a bottle of concentrated rum he had begun carrying with him and drank it down, falling into an easy stupor free from the caverns of his own mind.

Luik groaned as he rolled over, covering his eyes against the violently bright sun. His head pounded and he grasped around the dirt for his bag, fumbling until he found the small vile and took a sip. The pain lessened almost immediately and he sat up, angry the morning even existed. He spotted Syra, tucked just as he had left her and frowned, angry his plan was working. Angry that she was so beautiful through and through. Angry that bloody sunlight was a morning thing.

He grumbled as he gulped down water and began to pack up camp, dropping one small ounce of liquid down Syra's throat before laying her back on the horse.

The forest seemed to open up around him, movements from above already rippling through the leaves, likely already alerting Jyren to the fact that he was there. Luik looked around warily at the trees, which now looked more brittle than he remembered, and turned the horses north toward the heart of the forest. It didn't take long before four Jyre guards dropped from above, landing with cat-like ease and walking beside him as they cast glances at Syra.

Jyren definitely knew he was there.

Jyren's face held none of the charm it had last time, though Luik knew it was a charade. Now he stood with a ring of Jyre's around him, waiting with hands behind his back and a fervent glow in his eyes. His hands twitched as they approached, as if he wanted to stride and meet them but held himself back.

Luik kept his eyes on Jyren, holding the horses tensely and walking pointedly as far from the Jyres surrounding him as he could. Dark shadows flew about, hidden in the dark crevices of the forest about them. Luik could only guess what poor creatures they used to be. He stopped feet away from the tall, inhumanly beautiful form before him and waited silently, keeping his own arms from wrapping protectively around Syra.

Jyren only licked his lips and swallowed, glee bringing a bounce to every movement. He held out his arms and let his head fall to one side, a grossly lacking reaction.

"Luik! You held up your end of the bargain I see. My daughter, here." Jyren walked around them and lifted a piece of her hair from her face to check her pulse.

"And alive too!" He clapped his hands together, looking around at his people.

"Today, our princess came home to us. Today, we celebrate days to come!"

The roaring cheer was closer to a hiss and Luik winced, wondering if these were really people at all anymore. He folded his arms and looked at Jyren warily.

"And Anaratha? This is the price I would pay for you to bring justice to them?"

Jyren turned to him slowly, his head cocked sideways and a feral look in his eyes. He walked around Luik, looking him up and down as he made a show of contemplating something. Each step on the rocks… or bones, maybe, below their feet heightened Luik's own fear. He knew the position he was in.

"I will hold up my end of the deal. In fact, I already have. Even now all that is left of Anaratha lay sick and dying, no longer drugged into bliss but forced back into their sad reality."

He tsked with mock care, bringing hoots and laughter from those around him.

Luik's eyes narrowed and his voice began to raise, "That was not the deal. You said they would die like my people died. This kingdom has plagued the land for too long, Jyren, and you are the only–"

In a flash Luik was on his back, the air knocked out of his lungs and Jyren on top of him with long, deadly fingernails at his throat.

"I do not answer to you, boy. I will do as I please, and *you will not question me.*" Jyren squeeze Luik's neck, digging those talons nails into his skin as a sickly grin lay plastered on his face.

Luik should have known better; he belittled a king before his people. He closed his eyes, ready to die. Jyren stopped then, getting up slowly and dusting off his pants as if touching Luik was grimy.

"You may leave here and go live whatever sorry life you can. We are through."

With that, Jyren spun around, pulled Syra down from the horse and began dragging her limp body by the arm back into the darkness.

He picked himself up off the ground, keeping his eyes down, and walked away. Was one life worth the justice of a nation?

And did it matter that it was an unwilling life?

The thought echoed against the nothingness that was inside him. He was officially alone and irredeemable. It was time to go die.

Luik trudged along the northern tip of Elharren, drinking down his third bottle and doing all he could to avoid delviors. As far as he could tell, they avoided water, and he was content to jump in anytime. Images swam before him and the sound of Luik's shuffling boots rang in his ears.

He heard the deep, furious roar before he saw the owner of it, briefly wondering how he had been found before no longer caring. He deserved what was to come.

Luik sank to his knees, hung his head and waited.

The galloping skidded to a halt and he barely heard the footsteps before he was seized by his collar and lifted from the ground before a large, dark face.

"WHAT HAVE YOU DONE TO HER?!" Belick's rage was something to behold.

The crazed look in his fierce eyes bespoke of rational long abandon, and Luik realized then he had forgotten something in all his planning: Syra and Belick were bonded, and Belick felt everything she did.

The laughter came bubbling up without control, Belick's face still swimming now as tears rolled down his cheeks. He bloody loved this man. The man who would save Syra.

"I did what had to be done. Anaratha would have gotten away with *everything* if not!"

A fist landed squarely in his face, pain shooting down his jaw through his neck and ending his hysterics. Bloody Springs, he was going to die this way.

"Where is she?!" Belick spat as he grabbed Luik again and pushed him down a few feet away.

Luik didn't answer, knowing it would only be worse. He needed to be right. He *needed* what he did to have been the right thing even as he knew it to be wrong.

Bloody... his mother. What would his mother say if she saw him now?

The tears turned to sobs as her face floated in front of her eyes, tears streaming down her own cheeks and turning into Syra's own disappointed eyes, piercing his soul like they had always done. He drove a fist into the dirt and screamed.

"My people all died! They died, and NO ONE did anything! You all spent the bloody year planning to get the bloody princess out, but NO ONE made Anaratha pay!" Luik was screaming now, bent over in pain as Belick landed another blow to his gut.

He heard vague sounds of horses arriving but couldn't find the energy to look up. He swayed on his knees, blood running down his nose and cheeks and mixing in with the vomit he spewed to the side.

"Justice had to come, and it was the only way… all he wanted was Syra and it took everything I had to make the deal. They were the only army capable enough…" tears now mixed in with everything else and leaned back, raising his head to the sky as he waited for another deserving blow.

"I sat on my throne every day, looking at every home of every person lost in my kingdom because of *them,* and no one would have been avenged, so *I did* what had to be done, even if it cost me everything I had left."

Belick muttered something and brought his fist back, straddling Luik now as punch after punch came and his vision began to darken. He was right. He knew it. And he was wrong. He deserved this.

Belick was thrown off him and Luik could hear harsh words being spoken as firm hands grabbed his face and looked him over.

"…become what he is? We cannot go back to what we were, Belick!"

A growl was the only response as the large man took a step back toward Luik. The woman, Ree… or something, stood in his way, and

Luik could vaguely understand he was being protected. Bloody springs, he didn't deserve to be.

Aleth's face came into view, nothing kind to be seen in his eyes.

"What exactly did you do, Luik?"

Luik leaned back and began to cry again, sobs shaking his sore shoulders.

Aleth slapped his face gently, bringing his attention back forward.

"You can live in your regret later. Tell me what you did first."

"I drugged her and gave her to Jyren." More sobs came, loud, agonizing sobs he didn't know he was capable of.

"What was his plan for her?"

"I don't know.. I don't know... "

Aleth stood, locking eyes with Belick. "She is still alive, and knowing Jyren he would keep her that way to use her magic. We can still get her out."

Luik stood, hope filling his body in its drunken, beaten state.

"I can help! Let me come!"

Aleth turned back toward him and glared, grabbing his head between his hands and bringing Luik's eyes up to meet his own.

His voice was low and dangerously steady.

"Let me be very clear, Luik. I will not allow killing if I can help it. You will not die today by our hands. But if you *ever* come near my niece again, you will die."

He let go, and Luik fell back to the ground, his choking sobs echoing hours into the night.

CHAPTER 21

MICHALE'THIA

Michale'thia inspected the small jar before her.

The dark green mixture looked as disgusting as it smelled with the tiny flecks of slime clinging to the sides of the jar. She set it down gingerly and turned to the Botani scholars.

"How much do we have?"

A tall, lean man with hair braided behind his back checked his notebook before answering. "Enough to hold off an army of delviors for about ten minutes."

All hope left Michale's lungs. Ten minutes? She brought her hands to her temple in an attempt to think past the panic, searching for any other information she may have that would help. It surprised her that they had invited her into their research group in the first place, but considering she was the only one left who had seen a delvior, it made sense.

She paced, ignoring the looks the others were giving each other at her frenzied state. There had to be something they were missing. If they only had more… they didn't need much, just enough to slow the delviors down.

She paused and looked up.

"You said each arrow covered in this would put a delvior to sleep, but what would it do in a watered down state?"

Conversation immediately picked up and calculations began to be processed in notebooks as they searched for the answer to the question.

Michale'thia walked around the room, feeling useless without anything helpful to give. If she was right on this, it could make all the difference.

After another hour of inquiry, they finally stopped talking, coming to a conclusion. Michale waited anxiously.

A woman answered this time, her brown eyes concerned as she referenced her notes.

"It is possible it will slow their movements, but that is all."

Michale let out the breath she was holding. That was the answer she needed.

"And if we watered this down to a level that would cause that…?"

The woman already guessed where she was going and nodded.

"Yes, then we could have twice the archers and slow them down considerably, giving us possibly half of an hour we wouldn't have had." She nodded to those beside her and they broke off in a dash toward another room, presumably to start watering down the contents.

The woman and man from before waited until the rest were gone before allowing their shoulders to slump forward. The man looked up and wiped at his forehead, sighing deeply.

"There is only a small chance we will make it. With the number of people we have, a half hour will be nothing."

Michale nodded, her own thoughts wandering in a similar direction. She bit her lip before continuing, knowing her plan would be hard to get past.

"There is a way we might be able to gain some extra time." She took their silence as permission to continue.

"Our plan was to leave in two days to give people time to pack, but every extra day we spend here is a day we risk the delviors advancing closer. We could leave tonight, quietly, and with as little weighing us down as possible. If we have to, we can bring board and wood to float down the river with." She felt silly even saying it, but it was the better of two options. Either risk drowning in the river, or risk being torn apart by delviors. She would choose the former.

"There is a boy here who made these boards he calls wave-riders. We wouldn't have enough, but the concept is a good one. We could give everyone something to float on and have those with small children bring barrels. Then, we dive in and hope we make it."

They looked at each other, despair evident in their slow nods.

"It may be the only way. We will send word at once and be prepared to leave by sundown."

Michale shut the door to her room and began to pack her bag, wrapping her journal and paper belongings in a waterproof cloth before moving to sort through her clothing. Dresses would be impractical, and she would need lighter shoes.

A knock sounded and Dagen slipped in, his hair tousled and eyes bright.

"So it sounds like we have a new plan?"

She glanced at him as she packed and gave a sad smile.

"We do, though it's hardly a plan. More of a mad dash to safety and a hope that at least most of us live."

Michale dropped what she was doing and sat on her bed, pulling a stray hair behind her ear.

"Is this really what the prophecy was speaking of? Because if so we should have been trying to avoid it rather than force it into being."

Dagen sat on the bed facing her and smirked. "Yeah, this was definitely not in any of the scholar's prophecy notes."

Michale smiled back at that, picturing him pouring over his studies in his father's vast library. She winced thinking of his father, realizing she had yet to ask after him.

"Dagen, is your father here?"

He laughed at that, rolling his eyes and lying flat on the bed.

"He was one of the first to come! I've never seen him more eager, but he led his own manor and every other village along the way up the mountains. He's been recently promoted into village eldership on one of the higher summit villages."

Michale giggled at the picture of Lord Thorn and his tan, wrinkled skin sitting around a small table with the Botani elders. Somehow it was fitting.

She looked down at Dagen, picturing his past year and noting the tension in his shoulders. His head lay near her lap, and she brushed a piece of hair off his forehead, allowing her fingers to linger on his skin longer than normal. He closed his eyes at her touch, and she leaned in before she could think better of it, kissing him deeply. She needed him. She *wanted* him. Every grievance and look and hardship was her own too, and for the first time since being rid of her cage, she realized she wanted to share her everything with this man. Every moment.

He lifted himself up without breaking contact and brought a hand to her waist. Their sweet, gentle kissing turned quickly to passion and Michale'thia held tightly to her husband, giving each other every inch of their bodies.

Night came swiftly, and Michale stood with Dagen on one side and Ilytha on the other, taking in the massive collection of now-refugees before them. The elders and warrior groups were leading rightfully, not in need of Michale and her small group, but welcoming them all the same. They would bring up the rear, ensuring every last person made it safely while watching for delviors from on high. If any deliors were spotted in the night, they would send a flaming arrow into the sky as a warning. Two if they were only a mile out. Three if they were nearly upon them.

Her mind wandered to her own parents. What were they doing now? Would they have chosen to come if given the chance? She swallowed back a mixture of hate and yearning, confused by her own desire to both hold them close and watch them suffer as she had.

She tucked her hand into Dagen's and waited, watching as the people below began to slowly surge forward. It would take hours before the last of them were starting the journey down the mountain, so they settled into their lookout positions to wait and watch.

Hours passed before they began to see the trickling of their last group move. They waited a few moments more on the cliff's edge, straining their eyes to see any danger before jogging down to follow.

Michale was amazed at the speed the mass was moving down the mountain, hopeful that they would be able to make it in one piece. She didn't know what she would do if she lost people here. It would be her fault, again, and she couldn't live with that.

She begged Syra silently to be there waiting for them. Michale stumbled over a loose rock and grasping onto Ilytha's outstretched arm thankfully, suppressing a gasp. They were all instructed to keep silent since the delviors hearing was so powerful, but they couldn't do anything about the sound of them moving. It would have to do.

The night slipped away quickly and Michale'thia was thankful for the sunrise, bringing with it at least the ability to see what lay behind the darkness.

They had nearly made it down the mountain and stood at the last viewpoint as the blue twilight gave way to a clearer dawn. She rubbed her eyes, startled when Ilytha sucked in a breath and Dagen cursed under his own.

Below the mountain not ten miles off, the army was moving. Not just delviors, but what was likely Jyres with them. Panic swelled inside of her as she remembered how quickly the delvior had come upon them in the Northern Brends. Ten miles was nothing.

They raced down the hill, Ilytha signaling to the others to light their flamed arrows, and within minutes one unified cry arose from the refugees. Quick walking turned to frantic fleeing and they began to redouble their efforts, many carrying children on their backs and elderly in small, rolling bins.

Dagen yelled back at her a few words she couldn't understand and disappeared into the group ahead. Ilytha instinctively drew closer to Michale and tossed her a short knife.

"If they come, you must run! And if they catch you, stab them directly in the eye!"

She gave a curt nod and focused on running. Her body looked normal again outwardly, but she still didn't have the stamina of a normal human.

Howls began to sound in the distance, an inhuman, mangled screech sending people into a sprint as the earth shook with pounding.

As they ran forward more and more Botani warriors began to emerge, creating a barrier between the people and the coming onslaught. Green goo dripped from arrows, and trained stances were taken as their muscled skin pulled back arrows.

Michale looked about, helplessly wondering what she should do. As she looked down the line she saw every elder and every able-bodied warrior there, arrows, swords, spears, and knives at the ready, creating a wall of human protection for the less able. And she knew what to do.

She raced forward, dodging refugees and putting all she had into getting to the front of the frightened mass. No one had went through the training she had for her Testing Day. No one else knew what it was to stay calm in the midst of every nightmare coming to life before their eyes. She had to lead the people into the river.

Michale'thia pushed through to the front, throwing apologies over her shoulder as she scrambled under outstretched arms and between frightened relatives holding each other tightly.

She heard the river before seeing it, her own excitement growing as the prophecies became more real than they ever had been before. Somehow the river had come out of the eastern side of the mountain and wound through the Unmade, only touching this area of Elharren briefly before curving back west. It was more than chance. It had to be.

Her eyes strained to see, searching for familiar white hair and large green eyes set upon faded freckles. She had to be there. But her searching soon turned to despair. Syra was nowhere to be found. Instead, she caught sight of a long auburn braid and rushed to meet Cirren who held Benji close and looked around, calm eyes, searching. Michale made her way to Cirren's side, exchanging thankful hugs as they held each other by the arm.

"Did your husband go to help fight?" She nodded mutely, fear evident in her silence.

"Cirren, I need help. We knew there was little chance Syra would be here, but she isn't and now we have to figure out how to get all of these people to safety."

Cirren's grip tightened on her son, but she looked around, this time studying the landscape ahead. She shook her head, her long braid falling off her shoulder. Benji looked up at her, ever the old soul and leader he would one day show the land to be.

"Together, we were able to make boards with handholds that could each keep three people afloat. It was only a thousand, but it's something." He looked between them and back at the water, his eyes alive with a courage Michale couldn't comprehend. He smiled and took both their hands firmly in his own.

"We will make it. I know it."

Cirren squeezed his hand back and gave him a tight smile, not quite able to muster the strength he had. She sighed and looked at Michale'thia, tears welling in her eyes.

"We jump in and hope we live. That's the only way." Michale walked to the river's edge and groaned. The water was too high and the rapids too powerful. Even if everyone *could* swim, they would still easily drown in this. But there was no other way.

She siddled up closer to the raging water, and looked around, her throat closing up as she realized their plan had failed. They would die either way now.

Screams were heard as minutes dragged on and Michale frantically looked about, running along the side of the river and begging Syra to come. She heard a shout from Benji and spun around, terrified of what she would find.

She saw him a few feet away by the river, a few feet *in the Unmade land.* Michale screeched and grabbed his arm, pulling him back before the ground crumbled.

Her chest was heaving and he looked at her in wide surprise. She knelt down and looked him over.

"Benji, that land is not stable, it's a wild wasteland. It can crumble under your feet if you walk on it. You must be careful!"

She didn't know when she started caring so much for the young boy, but she did and she wasn't ashamed. Cirren though was staring at the place her son had just stood, and a small gasp escaped her as she brought a hand to her mouth.

Benji wriggled out of her arms and pointed urgently.

"No, look! There is a small path by the river and it's green! This isn't all Unmade land. There is enough for at least three people side by side to walk!" He ducked his head with a smile.

"I was going to try to see if I could ride my board on it, but found this instead. Which is probably for the better because that looks mighty powerful."

His sombered look at the end was enough to break Michale's thoughts, and she began to laugh. Joyously and unabashed, she laughed and yelled in victory. There was a way out.

Their praise didn't last long and Cirren and Michale'thia began organizing people into quick groups of three. The plan was to send them them running with linked arms so as not to fall in either in the rapids or in the Unmade on the other side of the grass. Michale looked at the terror of those in front, wishing she could go first but knowing she needed to organize this group.

As they readied the first group, quickly reminding them to keep a fast pace, she could hear Benji talking calmly with a frantic Cirren.

"Mother, someone has to go first, and we need the room, even if it's just for a single person. If anyone falls in, *I'll be there.*"

Cirren shook her head angrily, grasping his arm and kneeling down to look him in the eye.

"That water is too much, Benji. Wait to be grouped, we will go together."

Benji backed himself out of her reach and stared back at her, his stance speaking louder than his words.

"They are scared, mom. Look at them. They need someone to go first, and *I know this river water.* The Ancient Magic created me to ride these waves, and I've got to do it."

The last words were thrown over his shoulder as he grabbed his small board and sprinted toward the river. Cirren didn't scream or cry out as Michale had supposed a mother would, but instead watched with hands clenched in a frozen waiting. The entire front of the crowd quieted as each watched the young soul give them a brilliant smile before diving into the river.

He was only under a swift second before he shot up to the surface, somehow managing to rise on his board to a standing position within seconds and waving to them as he wound back and forth across the river bank, yelling in excitement as he disappeared down toward the unknown.

"To our home!"

His joy sparked something neither Michale nor Cirren could have anticipated in the refugees, and a spark of excitement roared where hopelessness had once been. Those at the very front shouted the same rallying cry and began to sprint toward the unmade, leading row after row of people behind them shouting the same.

The pattern quickly spread and even those too far to see what was happening organized themselves, ready to sprint for their lives and the lives of those behind. Those in front had to keep running as long as they could to make room for those behind to fit. It was still a gamble, but Springs, it was better than dying and the people had a renewed courage to try.

Michale motioned for more people to pass, again and again sending people through, knowing it was only a matter of time before the line slowed and those in front could no longer run. But to her surprise it didn't slow. If anything, it began to move faster than before and she was able to keep sending groups through, keeping a mental note in her head of how many they had in.

Right now, they were somewhere around halfway through, and at least a fourth of their people were on the lines fighting.

In the next moment, too many things happened at once to keep track of. An explosion of white shook the earth, rattling everyone to their bones with screams and a surge forward. Those in the back waiting to move forward began to surge ahead, knocking others over and pushing some into the river on accident.

Michale yelled, trying to be heard above the uproar and calm the people but it was no use. Order was gone and survival had kicked in.

In that same moment, Enith came at the head of an army of refugees of his own, running frantically with delviors at their heels. But the delviors were slower and smaller than normal and Michale soon recognized them to be an army of Loharans and shouted to try to stop them as they ran directly toward the river. She couldn't be heard above the chaos and watched helplessly as they clung to their *rishi,* nearly ten to twenty people on each beast. They rode them straight into the river without pause, snatching people out of the water who had fallen on their way.

When hundreds of rishi had stampeded into the river, what Michale could only describe as hordes of people with bowl-like armor on their chests followed, jumping in without hesitation. Michale's head spun at the suicide ensuing, but to her surprise each one bobbed back up to the surface, spewing water but floating alive and well.

She tipped her head back and laughed, nearly hysterical. It was wood. Of course! They suspected it would be a river and had stock piled wooden armor all these years!

Enith tried to stop them too without success and only stopped screaming for them to stop when he saw Michale. He rushed to her side, covering her in a hug before trying to understand all that was happening.

"What was the explosion?" He yelled now above the roar of war and screams of the frightened.

"I don't know! I thought you all did it!" She watched helplessly as those from the Botani mountains raced ahead onto the slim land by the river and Loharans continued throwing themselves into the water.

"I think I expected the reality of the prophecies to be more dignified!"

Enith tipped his head back and roared with laughter. But she continued, her face comically serious.

"You know. Either me glowing as I lead or at very least a glowing ship. *Something* glowing. This is just madness!"

Enith put his hands on his head in dismay as a small child, no more than three years old, ran toward the river and plopped himself in. No fear. His tiny head bobbed to the surface and he was quickly grabbed by a man nearby who was flying down the river himself.

"Ok, so both of our lines are almost done, the delviors are almost here, are the warriors going to pull back and join us?"

Michale ignored the question, not knowing the answer but having questions herself.

"What about Syra? Is she here? Or Belick and the others?"

Enith shook his head, his eyes darkening considerably. "She made it back, but I don't know the rest. They said not to wait for them, and knowing now how well they navigated the land unseen, I'd trust them."

Michale chewed on her lip, reluctant to leave without knowing everyone was safe. Another white explosion boomed in the distance, reverberating through the land. Suddenly it was silent.

Her feet shifted on the grass, crushing a leaf loudly. She looked at Enith with alarm. They stared at each other for another beat before they took off running toward the battle, now completely silent.

Michale's stomach clenched as she neared the scene, images of every possibility making her sick. But none of the images could have prepared her for the reality.

Their army of Botani warriors stood strong, bodies of wounded strewn about, but still alive. They stared, jaws open and startled expressions frozen on their faces as they watched the scene before them unfold.

What Michale could only assume were delviors, now stood on two legs, more their gazes dark but eerily cunning. The army of wild beasts now stood, human. Or close to humans, their gnarled faces lined with scars, and fur-like hair still covering their arms and legs.

It was surreal for Michale'thia. To never have learned the history or suspected the reality. Somehow, these evil, violent creatures were also broken and bruised humans once. Was this humanity left to their own pursuits? Where every war and sacrifice of a soul beneath a castle would lead? No matter. They still had Jyren's twisted fingerprints all over them.

Michale didn't allow herself to think before stepping out in front of the army. Ilytha grabbed at her arm but she yanked it back, taking step after step forward.

She wasn't greeted by sighs of relief or helpless looks. Some put their hand on a shoulder next to them and gave each other dark looks of understanding, but others just watched her, anger brewing underneath their gaze.

Her voice echoed then, though barely a croak. They were her. Or she was them. Mangled humans mangling humans.

"Do you understand language?"

The voice that answered was between a rasp and a snarl, barely holding back rage, yet lined with confusion.

"We understand, and always have, you filth."

Michale frowned at the irony, not fully understanding. "Who are you?"

This time the one speaking to her stepped forward, dangerously close and yet staying far away as if afraid. His eyes were fully black and it stood a full two heads taller than her with raised scars covering its face and arms. She kept her eyes on his face, refusing to acknowledge his nakedness.

"We are from before you ever were. We are the Free. Those who the Ancient Magic gave the right to roam the lands without chains to Its morality."

She frowned looking among the crowd to understand more.

"You were given the freedom by the Ancient Magic itself? I don't understand... How did you become Jyren's?" The hiss that followed caused Michale to step back, but the creature now leapt forward, his leathered face a mere inch from her own.

No one moved.

She didn't cower, she stood tall and looked it in the eye, *seeing* suddenly not just anger and rage, but *survival.* They were not full of fury, they were full of abuse and now shrank back from pain by jumping forward to cause it.

"We were *never* Jyren's, and he will pay! We made a deal and joined him only to be betrayed and twisted into *this.* Or what we were before." He shifted from foot to foot, using its hands as legs.

She continued to stare into the large black eyes, making another swift decision.

She spoke calmly, just above a whisper.

"I'm afraid of you. This close, I'm afraid you'll hurt me."

It snarled at her, its teeth pointed and gums a bright bloodred. Then it snapped its mouth shut and turned away. As it walked a few feet away, she could hear the faintest, "Me too."

Michale pressed on.

"How did you change?"

It walked in a circle now, pacing.

"The Ancient Magic, or someone made very powerful by the Ancient Magic, has restored us. Yes, we are mostly restored."

Michale's mind was spinning and she threw the question out there.

"I think I know who restored you. Would you give them aid in return?"

The creature was before here with lightning speed, still looking as if he barely held back a deathly blow.

He ground the words out harshly, "We owe nothing to anyone. We bow to no one."

Michale stared at him, her own eyes fierce as she raised her chin and held her ground. He staired back, searching her eyes as if warring within itself.

He snarled and spun to face his people for a long moment before turning back to her.

"We will help the Restorer."

CHAPTER 22

SYRA

The nightmare was the same as always. Her father stood above her as she was held tightly against a tree trunk, branches slowly growing through her flesh. The blurry vision of her father's face cleared and she pulled against her restraints, blinking rapidly. The smell was putrid and she could just make out burned patches of fur littered across open cages before gagging and snapping her eyes back shut. There were too many bodies bent at too odd of angles.

Hearing his voice yanked her back into the present and she felt the cold dirt beneath her as reality rather than a dream. The memories came in a flood of emotion: Luik's face filled with guilt, the cramping in her stomach and her vision fading to nothingness.

It wasn't a nightmare. The poison still coursed through her, and her body was limp with weakness.

Dread paralyzed her and she shuddered at what was to come.

"Daughter." Jyren's slimy voice slithered out of his mouth. His skin looked thinner, not transparent in beauty but thin and waning, as if he himself were beginning to age.

"You, my dear one, have been hard to track down. And my, you have grown!"

She ground her teeth against a retort, the burnt fur quieting most of her courage.

He clapped his hands in front of him and sighed. "Now. We do have some business to attend to. You see, I went through great lengths to breed you, and you have a power I need. You see," he walked back toward a trunk and opened it, showing a collection of vials.

"This here is what keeps my own power strong. I found a way to enhance the magic in me into something much, much greater. The life of another is *actually* quite sufficient for my needs. I'm more powerful than you are even now. But alas, it's a different power than I would like. I can't create *new* from nothing, I can only create using what already is. Your blood, however, holds the magic to create from nothing. Or, from the Magic's storehouse of somethings. I never could quite figure that out."

Syra frowned not understanding anything but the large needle in front of her.

"So what," She croaked, "You take my blood and put it in yourself?"

He snorted and took out a vial, his good humor falling away into something close to glee. A dark, cruel glee.

"No, dear girl, much worse I'm afraid." He tapped the vial in front of him.

"It is not just your blood, it is the very binding agent of your entire body. I will quite literally rip the magic from your bones and out of your blood. It is excruciating, I have heard. My poor pets often die in the process, but I always reward the living ones with a new body. My generous gift to them." He gestured at the hair around him, and Syra struggled against the tree with all her strength, pathetically moving a mere inch here and there.

He laughed and patted her head, enjoying the show.

"There, there. I will let you be my personal pet when I am through with you. *If* you live through it. Do live through, would you? You are after all, my only child." He laughed then at some unknown humor and patted her head.

Syra fought again, not prevailing but not able to do anything but fight. He began setting vials and needles on a table alongside devices she couldn't name but held pointed edges and crooked blades.

She closed her eyes and breathed. She had to focus. If there was one thing Michale'thia had taught her, it was to slow down and clear her mind in the fear. Think.

The poison made her weak physically, but she could feel something west. It was faint, but moving closer. It was a part of her and could *see* her without seeing her. She let out a pulse in her own magic, bringing Jyren's gaze shooting toward her. He walked over warily and knelt down.

With a quick motion he sank a three pronged knife into her side, a smile creeping onto his lips as he gloried in her pain. The device was connected to what looked like a string, or tube, trailing off into the trunk he had opened.

She readied herself for the pain, the apprehension bursting inside. Syra flinched at every movement, waiting. The tree tightened its branches around her again, and she squeezed her eyes shut, wishing for death.

Whatever it was came closer every minute-

The poison cleared just enough then and her eyes flashed open.

Belick. And he was only two miles out now, gaining fast.

Her strength began trickling back quickly as hope coursed through her, and with a forceful heave, she opened the dam of magic inside and sent it coursing through her body, healing the poisoned areas and waking her even more.

She studied Jyren quietly then, waiting for a reaction and finding none. He could feel when she sent magic out, but not when she used it inwardly. Which meant, he had no idea what was coming.

Slowly and without sound, she pulled the prong out, healing the fibers of her flesh in simultaneous motion with excruciating exit. She had heard stories of heroes pulling swords from themselves to continue fighting, and immediately stopped believing all of them. Each movement was agonizing, and she felt herself sway with pain, almost emptying her stomach because of it. Yet still, she pulled until the last prong was free and her side stitched back together.

Sweat gleamed across her forward for mere seconds before the weakness was completely gone. She smiled, thanking the Ancient Magic for It's gift. She could have never done this two days ago.

Syra reached out with her magic and gently prodded the tree, seeing death rather than life and fighting the joyful desire to bring back what was. There would be enough time for that. Now, she just needed it to yield without letting Jyren feel her magic flowing.

She tricked magic into the branch, unwinding a string of muddled wood inside. At every inch the wood had been cut. This was no branch, it was a holding place for pieces of the dead tree, with only a thin, sickly line inside uncut.

Her heart hurt for what she knew was a vast misuse of the Ancient One's Magic and she began to sift through each broken piece, welding back together life inch by inch. The tree branches shifted, reaching ever so slightly up toward where light should be, as trees were made to do.

Minutes ticked by and Jyren moved to turn toward Syra, upping her timeline in the blink of an eye.

Syra jumped to her feet, reaching inside and springing new life from the ground all around her father, sending vines slithering up his legs and branches shooting through his line of vision as she built a protective dome of green around them, away from his lurking lovers in the trees. She disappeared, maneuvering right, anticipating the knife that launched itself where she had stood.

The Magic within her reached out and *knew* the forest around her. And she felt it then. The screaming agony of all Jyren had twisted- the stealing of every potential being trees had and the bending of all that was good in them into something tormented. She clawed at her head, crying in pain as she felt creation's pain under her father's twisted hand.

He launched a blackened vine back at her and she crumpled, half dodging it half dying inside.

But anger replaced her grief and she grabbed the ashen branch in her fist, pouring power into it and sending spikes up its spine and toward her father. She infused spikes on the inside too, small pieces of magic that would spurn the touch of anything else attempting to change it. Her father roared in anger and she smiled at her first lesson for him: He could not twist creation any longer. With a hand on the ground she sent a rush of magic into every green thing, creating safeguards inside from any other malicious intent. Flowers burst to life in celebration and Syra snapped her fingers, sending petals swirling in the air so thick nothing else could be seen.

She backed up against her own vines and waited, listening to the soft steps of her father stalking her around their enclosed dome. He hesitated to her left, still four feet away, and then all sound of him vanished. Syra held her breath and froze, straining to hear any sound at all that would give away his location. In one breath she let the petals drop, just in time to see Jyren's hand flash out and grab her arm.

She felt it sooner than she saw it, the shock rendering her speechless. Every small piece making up her bone began to splinter, breaking apart at its smallest substance. She screamed and fell as the pain moved through her arm and toward her chest. He wasn't just breaking it all, it was reshaping around itself, her bone twisting in a vicious circle where it should have been straight. She couldn't think or breath, she could only scream until her voice turned into a deep roar nothing unlike anything she had cried.

But it *wasn't* her own.

Barely conscious, she dropped some branches from their shielding presence and Belick leapt through the opening, plunging a sword through Jyren's chest with a howl. Jyren shrieked and fought to twist around but the blade held him where he was.

His pause gave Syra the chance she needed and she ripped her maimed arm away, shaking violently. Jyren continued to shriek and fight to get her back, only stopping when Aleth brought his own blade down over his neck, both anger and sorrow evident in his gaze.

Syra fell back onto the tree brush and tried to make sense of everything taking place. Jyren was dead. Her father and torturer died and she didn't kill him.

Syra's mind raced and choking sobs began to escape, whether from the death of Jyren or the pain in her arm, she didn't yet know. His death was such a small event compared to the giant he had been in her mind. She imagined it would be grand somehow, but instead it was the death of a normal man in battle. Jyren was no god after all.

She forced her eyes shut, attempting to concentrate on healing her tangled wound. Bones now protruded throughout her arm and she began to lose sight of the world as she tried to fuse pieces back together with her magic. Every attempt only brought more pain and the darkness around her grew, blurring her vision. She couldn't think of anything but the pain pounding in her ears. Her arm was bent at odd angles, turning in on itself again and again, only showing a small part of the real damage inside.

Suddenly, Aleth was holding her, his own hand on her arm and his eyes closed. Belick came beside her and they spoke in low voices she couldn't quite make sense of. She tried again, this time sending magic into her arm in a quick burst, and blacking out completely with pain. She woke again, knowing she had only fixed an inch at most, and looked at the entirety of her arm with agony.

"There is nothing we could give her to stop pain that deep." She heard Aleth argue.

Belick's voice was tight and shaky, and she wondered what he felt through the bond.

"This isn't easy over here. Hurry up with whatever you are doing!" Syra registered Rienah's voice at the opening, her vision still dizzy from pain.

She gently sent magic to the bone again, trying to fix it but unable to do so without moving everything.

Her father knew not just how to corrupt things, he knew how to twist them into such a mess healing was more painful than the actual breaking. She gasped and screamed, the bone moving only slightly but running into other bone fragments in its wake. Belick fell to the ground, his hands on his head.

Syra heard shuffling and opened her eyes just enough to see Aleth drag Belick over to her. Belick nodded and together, they grabbed her arm.

In her half conscious state she expected them to heal her, to do what she couldn't and make every bone better. But instead, she felt *magic*, in its purest form, pour into her. She already had so much, why would she be given more? Her eyes shot open to find a drained Belick and Aleth staring at each other in horror. Their expressions turned grim and Belick shook his head, fear etched into his eyes.

Aleth's eyes were dark as he yanked his sword out of Jyren's body and approached Syra. She tried to back away, fear coursing through her, but the pain was too severe. Aleth stood over her and raised the sword. Syra squeezed her eyes shut again, wondering what horrible nightmare was just unleashed. Then she heard him bring it down with trained precision.

And the pain stopped.

Panting, she opened her eyes and looked at him, a surprised laugh trickling out of her until she saw the look on his face. Shame. She looked over to Belick's form sitting hunched over on the ground, refusing to look at her.

Syra followed Aleth's gaze to her arm and screamed, fumbling away from her own body but unable to do so. Her arm was gone, leaving a bleeding stump behind at her shoulder. Sounds around her began to fade into a ringing and she couldn't help the quick breaths that followed. She couldn't form a full thought or find the strength to move. Aleth and Belick were kneeling before her, holding something to the bleeding wound. Aleth was looking her in the eyes and speaking to her with urgency but she couldn't hear anything. Belick appeared then, grabbing her face and training her eyes on him. He stopped trying to talk and held her forehead to his own. The pulse through the bond he sent was enough to wake her from her stupor and the ringing stopped enough for her to hear.

... "Syra, SYRA! You have to do it now or you'll miss your window! Do it now!"

She looked around confused, not understanding what he wanted. Belick pulled her eyes back to his, imploring her in a low voice.

"Syra, listen to me. You have to restore your arm. Create a new one where the old once was."

She sputtered as he spoke, frantically searching their faces. "I, I c-can't. I don't- I've never..." She calmed her breathing, counting the seconds between exhales.

"You can, Syra. We gave you our magic, you *have* the power. But you don't have much time. You are losing too much blood, and you either have to create a flame to cauterize it or create a new arm, but either way, you have to do it *now*."

She closed her eyes, too many things happening in too short of a time to understand. She didn't know how to do what they asked and searched, sending magic toward her arm in spurts but not finding any way to do it. She choked in despair, sobs threatening to break loose and clutched her bloodied shoulder in grief.

When her fingers touched the space her arm should have been, she saw what could be. A thousand options of colors and build and a thousand uses- but none as wise as what she had. The Magic leapt inside and without her trying, raced through her fingertips and into the arm, taking over what she could never understand.

It was a sensation unlike any other- not sweet, and not comfortable, but passionate and somehow joyful even in the agony. Every inch of her arm began to be remade, and she *felt* every moment of it, her stomach lurching and her vision going wonderfully black again. It wasn't beautiful to watch or feel. And yet the joy accompanying it was severe. To *create*. To *restore*. To care for all that was placed around her. It was like stepping into a doorway of identity always made for humanity yet never fully realized. To be small images of grace and mercy to every-thing around them and in that be a mirror reflecting back the Magic's own joy and love for Its creation-

She gasped as it finished, tears streaking down her cheeks.

She was whole. But the land was not.

Syra stood, a rage filling her as she touched the ground and felt everything in Elharren. The broken pieces and twisted bones fighting in mass against her people. Jyren had no right. *No one* had a right.

Wailing, she hit the ground with open hands and a white burst from her body and passing through anyone she chose and landing on those she desired.

She listened and felt again, broken minds and shredded bones alike amassed in the East and West but decided to wait. First, she would deal with the forest. So every Jyre left standing could see what should have been.

Syra opened the dirt before her and grasped the roots below, feeling the thousands of deadened trees in the forest and quickly working her way through them in batches, healing as she couldn't do for herself but was now simple. Life bringing.

She could hear the hisses and screeches as her own kin ran for cover, but would find none. The trees began to stand tall again, unwinding themselves from each other and lifting their arms back toward the sun, covered by clouds but soon to shine through. There was water in the soil and she sped up a process of nourishment she had no name for, cycling through again and again until the trees were filled with green leaves.

She moved outward then, focusing her attention on the misshapen bones to the east she now knew as brothers of the Guardians she spent so much time with. She built up the Magic inside, this time a greater amount and slammed her palms into the ground, another explosion even greater than the last pushing through the air. Every soul hidden beneath the dark cage of Jyren's mind began to uncurl again, straightening back into something more than a dog at Jyren's feet. She could feel as minds woke back up and fingers opened and shut as they once had too long ago.

She couldn't restore the creatures beyond their own chosen brokenness, but she could restore them back to what Jyren stole.

She stood and faced east, knowing a people like never before. A people proud and cruel in their pursuit of the Ancient Magic, but a people blind, now sick from their own charade.

She couldn't fix them. They would have to choose to be healed further, but she could give them every chance possible. She calmed sick stomachs and raging temperatures and broke apart their need for the drug they had been on the past year. And then she gave them the choice. Each of them quietly in their rooms saw it: they could join the City of the Sun, and live simply, without positions or power and without the ability to hurt or maim again, or they could live in Elharren. The deadlands. Void of Magic and any authority over them. Free to try to gain power and lord over others their good fortune. She felt more than saw the decisions being made. Tragically, too few chose to go West, but those few breathed great sighs of rest few others could ever understand. Sighs of having carried the heaviest burden on their shoulders and finally being invited to shrug it off.

Others screamed in indignation, clenching their teeth and all but growling their resounding "no".

She felt the Syllric kingdom next, knowing minds more fully than they knew themselves and giving the same choice the others had been given, thankful for the larger number willing to start anew.

Syra quietly gathered up in a forceful wind those who had chosen to come and brought them west to the river's edge, unmaking the land beside the river as the last of the Botani refugees crossed. The Anarathans would ride the river down, and the Ancient Magic would do inside what she never could.

CHAPTER 23

BELICK

It was quiet.

Quiet.

Belick sat on his knees by Aleth, his eyes wide and mouth open but no sound coming out. It was quiet inside. An empty quiet. Not quite a hole, but not quite whole either. He was something altogether "other" now. No magic. No weight of creation brought and lost. Just … quiet.

A bird chirped somewhere above him. An odd sound here. His skin felt different. His whole body felt different. Fragile. Finite. He hadn't known he had felt strong and infinite before, but he did. And loud, he must have felt loud inside to feel so quiet now.

A branch broke under his foot, and he shifted his weight to stand. The dome of branches and vines were gone, replaced by a familiar forest around him, spread out and sun-filled. A memory flashed through of his brothers playing tag for the first time after they learned to use their legs rightly. It was full of whooping and laughter and rolled ankles.

He laughed, his voice hoarse. Why was his voice hoarse? He looked at Aleth and saw wet cheeks and tear-brimmed eyes, a shocked stare trained on his hands. They had been crying. Yes. He had been crying.

He was no longer an Ancient Brother, but a man. The Magic was no longer a comforting piece of home, it was gone. Cut off completely. And now he would watch as the last of those he loved entered into a land he was not permitted to join. A relationship with the Magic he was barred from, and for good reason.

Belick put his hand in Aleth's, watching his freckled face turn to his own grief-stricken one. They weren't empty, they were just Other now. Not whole.

Aleth stood and licked his lips, breathing hard and on the edge of a panic Belick hadn't seen since he was young, filled with a need for perfection which often rendered him useless.

"No. No, Aleth." He stood and clenched his fists.

"We are still here. Rienah is still here. The land is still here." Belick grabbed Aleth's shoulders and looked him in the eye before pulling him into a hug. They wiped their eyes and gave each other a nod, lending each other strength they couldn't give themselves to see the day through.

Rienah watched them a short distance away, speaking to Syra in hushed tones. Syra turned back to look at them, her head falling.

The women approached and Syra motioned to the woods around them.

"We don't have much time. The Jyres were scared off, but I can feel them rallying back, and there are many of them."

Belick nodded, grateful he still felt only love for his kin before him with the large green eyes, no longer haunted but bright with life.

"Let's move then."

She frowned then and turned northwest, hearing something none of them could. Syra began walking toward whatever she could sense, throwing over her shoulder more information.

"The Spring is nearly drained. The last of it heads toward the bend in the river as we speak. We must go at once. The way will not be opened again."

He looked at Aleth, his nose wrinkling slightly as he fought emotions surging through him. They would escort her and watch her leave. It was the least they could do. Aleth sighed shakily and they followed her.

She paused, turning her head slightly left, her mussed braid swinging against her shoulder.

"They are coming, the Jyres. And there is a large army. And they don't mean to join us."

Belick lifted his spear and they started their sprint west.

"Can't you do anything to speed this up with that much power?" Aleth huffed.

She grinned and shook her head. "I've done too much. I could only bring us a foot before collapsing."

Rienah ran beside her easily, sticking a lip out in surprise. "I don't remember the boys getting tired after a full day of creating?"

Syra nodded, "They didn't. It's a safeguard. If the Magic is abused this time, it will be slower and take years. It is something I chose."

Rienah looked at her with appreciation and they continued their dash. The rumbling from the distance could be heard on both sides, and Belick looked about, seeing the army of Jyres emerge from the forest, forces of rage and chaos. They knew their leader was dead, and they were out for blood.

A group of twenty neared them, faster somehow than a normal person. Or was he slower now?

And Belick turned to fight.

The Jyres leapt into the air with feral snarls and he prepared for the battle, begging the Magic to let their last stand be enough to get Syra through.

Something shot from his right straight into a Jyre, knocking her on her back with a growl. The creature was one he knew well but couldn't believe was here. The creatures were less human than they had been and scars covered their naked bodies, but he recognized them nonetheless. These were the rogue group that scoured the lands when they were just children, calling themselves the Free. They made fun of them at a distance, but mostly kept to themselves until they disappeared. Their movements gave the rest of the story away as they leapt with wolf-like grace. He locked eyes with one who gave a nod before tearing into the flesh of a beautiful Jyre before him.

A large one walked through the frenzy coming to stand before Syra, recognition in its eyes.

"You." It sputtered, lost for words.

Syra watched it for a moment, and Belick could see her trying to understand. Then she brought a hand to her throat and whispered a name Belick couldn't hear.

He wasn't sure, but he thought he saw a glint of something wet gather in the corner of its blackened pupil.

"You are the Restorer. We pay back what you have done."

She shook her head and strode to him, throwing arms around his neck even as he snarled and tried to pull away as if stung.

"You had no debt." She pulled back before kissing the creature on it's gnarled cheek.

"I didn't know you were more."

Belick was completely lost but understood her signal to leave, and they ran, letting the war behind them rage on.

They ran until they could barely hear the sounds behind them, and Belick marveled at the world around. The sky was bright again, smoke vanished from the air. It wasn't lush and green, but it was clear. Livable, but not beautiful like it could be.

He moved to Syra's side as they slowed to a walking pace.

"What was that back there?"

Aleth and Rienah watched quietly, curiosity evident in the group.

Syra was silent for a few paces, speaking softly.

"I used to go to the cages and give them food. I thought they were dogs my father had found and twisted, and I hurt for them. He would even breed them and they would have pups..." She trailed off, disgusted.

"I should have known. They could barely control themselves, but ever so often I would see a look break through. Something more intelligent than my father let on. One night, a particularly cruel episode, I lay sobbing, bruised and limp. I decided then to die, and I opened a cage. But instead of killing me, the delvior looked at me like it *saw* me, and it grabbed me by the shirt and dragged me for miles underneath it. All anyone from above would have seen on that night was a loose delvior dragging something. It spit me out at the forest's edge and ran back in. I got up and ran, terrified of monsters outside of the Forest, but willing to risk it all."

She looked at Belick and then back at the western horizon.

"That was him. The reason I escaped."

Aleth whistled in dismay and Belick shook his head. How many small acts of grace did it take to bring this girl to this point today? The number of small acts were nearly impossible, yet here she was. Born in the Dark Forest, compassionate and kind. The daughter of the Twister himself, yet the one who restored the land. He laughed, covering the heartache in his chest.

They reached the river too soon, the water higher and fiercer than before. Belick felt his chest shake and they gathered around it, dreading the next step.

Dropping his spear and turning to Syra, tears gathered afresh as he held her small form and wished with all he had that he could go back and do everything differently.

She pulled back with a frown and looked at each of them, finally understanding their embraces and giving Belck a flat stare.

"You're coming, Belick."

He shook his head, clenching his teeth so hard against the yearning he thought they would break. "We can't. We tried, and we are not allowed in. The Ancient One has given us what we deserve."

To Belick's dismay, she rolled her eyes and put her hands on her hips, pinning them both with a look while somehow leaving an uncharacteristically silent Rienah out of it.

"You have given up what you once took. Both of you have paid the price the Magic required, but even *still*, it would have let you in. Brendar is already there or at least close. The Magic is no longer permitted for him, or any of you for that matter, which I am sure Syllric is mourning right now since he refused to come, but you are not just welcomed, you are wanted." Her own eyes turned glassy and she laughed softly.

"If you only knew the depth of love the Magic has for you. For creation. You would know you were *always* welcome." She turned, tossing a last look over her shoulder and wriggling her brow.

"Now, you just have to jump."

And Syra spun on her heel and dove in. Aleth and Belick looked at each other with rounded eyes, peeling their shoes quickly and pulling their shirts over their heads, pausing for only a moment after Rienah jumped in to wonder if they were about to kill themselves, but with a running start, they jumped in anyway. The hope of the truth was enough.

Into the dangerous waters they sank, where ice cold tore through more than their limbs and soothed something inside their souls. It seemed to seep into every dark crevice and hollow place, filling them with something beautiful and wild again. Like when they were first created. Simple, and humble, eager to learn and grow. The blood was washed away, and they were made new, somehow created a second time over as sons still, this time adopted from the Elharren back to their father. Redeemed and restored into an eternity more grand than they could ever dream.

CHAPTER 24

+———•———+

MICHALE'THIA

From the ashes, from the ashes
One perfect will rule
Free the land from
Ancient curses
To the days before…

… who will lead the pure into the sun, children wait, children wait, children wait.

The river was gentle in its lull, now only waist deep, prodding people along toward a destination Michale knew nothing of. Was there even anything out there?

It was a miracle that they even survived, the river having slowed into a wide mouth only a mile from Elharren, allowing thousands to jump in and make room for more.

The sun was in the middle of the sky but shining with pinks and oranges as if a sunrise were present. It was clear and bright, warm where the water was cold and somehow filled with hope. The Unmade around them didn't seem threatening in itself, just unstable. She waded through the water, breathing deeply. Dagen walked beside her, scanning the river and bank periodically, making sure no one was left alone or helpless.

Michale turned around and searched the river, her chest tightening. She pushed away her anxious thoughts and tried to focus on what was ahead. But Syra was behind them somewhere, and the ache for her was becoming more than she could bear.

It had been over a year since she saw her friend. No, not her friend, her sister, or...

She chewed on her lip, trying to find the right word for what she was thinking. It was something deeper than sisterhood or friendship alone but she had no way to describe it other than moments when she thought her heart would break from the desire to be near Syra again.

"They will come, Michale." He gave her a tight smile, betraying his own worries.

"And we will be fine, Dagen." She gave him a pointed look, receiving a chuckle in return.

She looked at the river bank and walked over to its edge, studying the dirt before straightening with a conclusion.

"I think the water level is actually going down. This bed had at least a foot more water than it does now."

Enith dropped back from his place with a group of Loharans and held a wet hand over his eyes.

"Do you think we can drink this... uh.. Water? Spring?"

She paled and shook her head, not wanting history to repeat itself.

"I think we'd have a better chance waiting. I've heard enough of Belick's story by now to know that would be a mistake."

He sighed but nodded, "Yeah, I thought so too." Enith looked back and forth between the two, frowning with a twinkle in his eye.

"Michale, you really need to lighten up. We have an entire future ahead of us, and here you are, high-strung as always." He wagged his eyebrows at her, giving Dagen a wink.

Michale recognized the look on his face far too late, and shrieked as she moved to run but was scooped up and tossed into the river a few feet away. She broke the surface and glared at him, accepting the battle he had started.

She froze then, her old tutors' voices echoing in her ears and her mother's lessons digging into her like claws. Perfection meant elegance and gracefulness at every turn, never letting her anger or pain show.

Michale began to smile then, looking down at the Spring beneath her with awe. She didn't carry the weight of the kingdom any longer. Her mistakes and honesty would bring consequences but on her alone, not an entire nation.

That whole time she was working to be and do what only the Magic Itself could be and could do, not realizing she was quite possibly created to be a little undignified. She dunked her head back under the water, scooping a fistful of mud off the ground and lifting herself out again with hands hidden behind her back.

Enith and Dagen both looked at her with concern, and she put on her best impression of her old self, breathing slowly and erasing all emotion from her face. Then in a quick movement, she launched the dark mass, successfully covering Enith's face with slimy mud

There was a moment of silence. Botanis, Loharans, and everyone in between froze as they waited to see what would happen next.

Enith wiped mud from his face slowly and in a quick move, dove down, scooped some and sent it flying toward Michale, his white grin shining through the muck. She ducked down and it instead landed directly on Rish's chest to Enith's horror.

That was all it took, the mud fight that would someday become a national holiday celebrating their freedom broke loose as children tore their arms free of parents and joined in, eventually leaving their tired, anxious group a little less tired and a little less anxious and a little more dirty.

They walked in groups now, learning about each other's past and where they were from. And Michale rubbed some dried dirt from her shoulder wondering at the courage the people around her displayed. They had all left everything to find safety and then lost everything again to find a home. She shook her head, grief and joy too mixed together to be seperated in the moment.

The river was definitely lowering, she noted, wondering what it would mean for the rest of their trip, however long it may be. She heard a shout and spun around, her heart thundering in her chest. There was only one voice that deep and rich.

The owner of it swam easily toward them, a bright smile radiating even as he yelled.

"That is not fair! You are cheating with your tiny arms! They move through water easier than mine can!"

She squinted and rose on her tiptoes, seeing what looked like Aleth in the distance with Rienah, floating on their backs and leisurely kicking their way toward the back of the group. She searched and searched, taking in fact after fact about the scene.

Belick was never that happy.
Belick would not be that happy if something happened to Syra.
Belick was racing someone- not Aleth.

Conclusion: Syra must be-

From beneath the water far ahead of Belick and only ten feet away from Michale'thia, Syra sprang up from under the water, looking back at Belick with a laugh before turning back to run and meet whatever finish line they had agreed upon.

Her tan skin sparkled with sunlit beads of water, and her arms looked stronger than Michale remembered, lean muscle showing under a sleeveless cream tunic. Syra's eyes found her and she froze, her smile dropping away into a fearful, guilt-ridden swallow.

And Michale crossed the distance and threw her arms around her neck.

Syra clung to her and began to ramble through tears, "I wanted to come for you."

Michale gently shushed her, shaking her head and holding her tight.

"You are not to blame. Syra, I missed you so much."

They held each other for so long they had fallen to the back of the line, wiping each other's face and laughing as the last of their burdens slipped away. Enith and Ilytha joined the group now with Belick, Aleth, and Rienah alongside, and embraces were exchanged as the group moved slowly behind the rest of the refugees.

Enith sidled up next to her and leaned over, gesturing to someone a length in front of them.

"Does that look like…" His voice faded out and Michale stopped walking, her vision suddenly swimming before her.

"How did that conniving woman get here." She spoke loudly, an anger she didn't know she had resurfacing with greater force than expected. She felt naked there, vulnerable and suddenly terrified. She brought a hand to her throat, willing herself to calm down.

Dagen came up behind her and took her hand in his, giving it a squeeze and not letting go. But it was Syra who stepped in front of her, her eyes piercing deeper than Michale was comfortable with. She tried not to squirm, glaring at Syra right back.

"I know." Her green eyes bore into Michale's own. "But they were given the same chance as everyone else, and she chose to come. Michale, her cruelty was not much less than our own capabilities. The depth of her brokenness is just the same. The only difference is she actually believed what her generation taught her." Syra looked at Enith with even less compassion.

"*You* should know even better. The same thing that was festering in you after your Testing Day festered in her, but it grew. The Spring has taken it, and you *both* have a chance to live anew."

Michale hated it, but she couldn't deny the voice in the back of her mind begging her mother to be a mother. She saw it on Enith's face too and saw his eyes soften before looking down.

As if on cue her mother turned around. Her long, luxurious auburn hair had been cut to her shoulders, and her normally extensive makeup was gone. Beneath the facade was a tired woman, scared and prideful still, but wondering.

Michale turned away quickly, rubbing her arm to ward off the sudden chill.

Maybe someday she would speak to her again and not be afraid. But not today. Nor probably tomorrow. Michale lost herself in thought, watching the water visibly lower as they spoke and gasped.

Taking Syra's hand, she led her over through the crowd, searching for the small family of three she knew wouldn't want to waste anymore time. When she spotted Cirren, Michale glanced at Syra one more time before nudging her head over toward them. Syra just looked at her with her large eyes and went without asking questions.

Maybe she knew already or suspected. She wasn't sure what Syra could do with her new power, but she knew she deserved to have a family.

Michale watched for a few minutes, Cirren holding her arms around herself and her large husband keeping Benji from interrupting with a firm hand on his shoulder. Syra stepped back, shaking her head and looking at Cirren from under hooded eyes. Cirren covered her face with her hands, her shoulders shaking, then composed herself and spoke again, looking at Syra intently.

Michale'thia saw it then, the look Cirren gave her on the beach that day and the one she had when they fought to find a way for the people to get down the river. It was the same soul-knowing look Syra gave. Knowing, seeing deeper than whatever front one was putting up.

Syra's own shoulders began to shake and she rushed forward into Cirren's arms, eventually joined by both Benji, her... brother, and then by his big burly dad. Somehow, Michale'thia could tell he would be exactly what she needed. From the little she had witnessed, the man's blunt but kind personality was so opposite of what Syra described Jyren to be, that it may just be the perfect fit.

They fell into an easy stroll, hungry and thirsty but enjoying the new faces and stories around. Benji had found the group of Jyre's Aleth had brought, and some kind of reunion between Cirren and man and woman occurred, solemn and subdued but full of emotion beneath it. Michale smiled as she watched Benji walk ahead of the Jyre group with a young girl his own age, her blond hair pulled back in a bun and her the beginning of a smile forming as she followed his instruction and tried to lay on the board floating in the water.

Hours more passed and the sun began its descent, beautifully lighting the sky with a depth of colors she had never imagined could exist.

The river was barely a small stream beneath them then, leading directly into the dusk sky.

The perfect one who will lead the pure into the sun...

Michale laughed audibly, drawing the attention of those around, including the Anarathans in front of her.

She shook her head and smiled, pointing to it.

"We are being led into the sun."

Gasps and whispers of awe spread through those from their kingdom, the surreal understanding that they were living out the prophecy they had longed to see fulfilled for ages *right then*.

Yelling began to ripple through the large mass, heard vaguely from the front of their wide line and spurring others to climb the side of the banks and lift children on shoulders in hopes of seeing what was happening.

And then, they too began to yell.

But it wasn't a yell. It was a roaring cheer so loud they could hear nothing else and joined with it were trumpets and instruments by the thousands ringing out from somewhere far ahead.

Michale scrambled up the slippery bank, joining others as they craned their necks to see. Only Syra didn't join. She instead stood in the middle of the river smiling, tears in her eyes.

Michale's ears were filled with cheers and music, but she could never have been ready for the sight ahead.

It was a kingdom, with no gates and no war watchtower, but laden with gold and as vast as the eye could see. On every wall and every housetop stood tiny specks of people, crowds greater than their own number, and she could just see their arms waving and their horns blowing as *they too* roared a thunderous cheer.

Michale turned to Syra, questions brimming her eyes.

Syra wiped her eyes and drew close to Michale'thia, leaning in to whisper in her ear.

"They have been waiting for us to come home."

And Michale's own voice joined the chorus then.

They were home.

AFTERWORD

Thank you, dear friends, for going on this journey with me. You now know me better than most.

Maybe you hear this a lot, maybe not, but *you* are what makes this book amazing. I could write a thousand stories and without readers to share them with, they would be nothing! So thank you. For enduring the heartache and sticking with me as I attempted to mend back together what was broken. If you want to keep up with all things life and writing, follow me on Instagram at charity_brandsma. Reach out with a message, come to Washington and grab coffee with me, meet the man in my life who inspired Dagen. All of it. You are welcome here.

Again, thank you for your support, it means the world. Cheers to another year of writing stories I wish I could read.

ABOUT THE AUTHOR

Hi, I'm Charity Nichole Brandsma. Professional day dreamer, thinker, and lover of all things messy and hard. I currently live in Washington State with my husband, son, and coffee addiction, none of which I plan to get rid of. Ever.

I believe stories are huge ways cultures change, and I want to be a part of that change! In my books you'll find modern day issues woven through new worlds and new characters.

Lastly, I love meeting new people. Send messages, reach out- I would love to get to know you!

Photographer: Rebekah Balthis

You can connect with me on:

 https://www.charitybrandsma.com

 https://www.facebook.com/charitybrandsma

 https://www.instagram.com/charity_brandsma/?hl=en

Subscribe to my newsletter:

 https://www.charitybrandsma.com/youngadultfictionauthor

ALSO BY CHARITY NICHOLE BRANDSMA

Magic, Kingdoms, and Wars.

Remnant: Luik's Lament

A small but fun project that accompanied these books were songs written from the perspectives of the main characters. While Through the Dark the album was released with the last book, we waited to release Luik's song until this one was published! Written and produced by David Lee Jamison, this song captures Luik in every way... especially the end of Through the Dark!

Legends of the Ancient Spring: Through the Dark Four Kingdoms, One prophecy, and a race to save thousands of lives.

Divergent meets Lord of the Rings in this fantasy novel filled with magic.

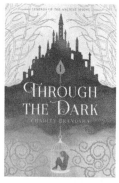

For hundreds of years, the Kingdom of Anaratha has waited for the Heir of the Prophecies, condemning their most promising royals to a Testing Day, where they journey through the sinister Jyre Forest. As Michale'thia prepares for her own test, everything begins to unravel: her maid begins to show signs of having the ancient magic in her veins, a legendary Botani warrior descends the mountain to appear at her Testing Day Ball, and the Northern Brends Kingdom makes a shocking declaration that may catapult the lands into war. Can Michale'thia ascend the throne as Queen and save the land of Elharren from utter destruction, or will she lose the race against time and condemn them all?

Made in the USA
Las Vegas, NV
10 April 2021

21171787R00164